Out of Breath

Terry White

red giant
books

Copyright © 2013 Terry White

Out of Breath

Cover Photo by Liz Maugans

Red Giant Books
ISBN: 978-0-9883430-4-7

10 9 8 7 6 5 4 3 2 1

Printed in the United States of America.

www.redgiantbooks.com

Table of Contents

for Judy

Acknowledgments

Besides the editors/publishers of Red Giant Press, Dave Megenhardt and Rob Jackson, who took the gamble that my fiction warranted the expense of their time and money, I would like to thank my colleague Roger Craik for bringing me to their attention. To David Fuqua of North Little Rock, good friend of many years: You know that life reveals to just a few a deeper place within the dark. I admire your courage and I thank you for your friendship.

Preface

Someone once told me about a writer who quit writing short stories because he said they were meant for youth. Maybe I read it somewhere or heard it in a classroom, but I've thought about it ever since. The primacy of the initiation story is hard to dispute and most stories do seem to have a reckoning or a yearning for equilibrium at the end. Yet I've always found it strange that anyone would assume youth matter so much and, by implication, ought to reign as the implied audience of the bulk of short fiction.

My own advancing age being a factor, no doubt, I find it easier to write about the middle-aged, especially those who have won or lost their battles—mostly lost, of course, because if there's one standard everyone seems to agree to it's that happy people don't populate storyworlds nearly as much as the discontented. My male characters do not much care any longer about the great themes of life and art, and no aging man in this collection has any desire to conquer new worlds. In fact, most are hard-pressed just to get by— like Macbride, the suicidal gypsy scholar of "Desideratum of the Adjunct Professor" and Shibley, the former professor-turned-book-thief who finds himself in thrall to a pair of Russian thugs. Maybe the most ambitious (in a worldly sense) character I have is the female sociopath who narrates "When Are You Ever Coming Home?" The title, I like to think, reflects the words of the absent husband she had abandoned for her road adventure.

There's one more thing, however, that appeals to me in my choice of older characters. It has everything to do with the theme of life's quirkiness in upsetting the applecart of one's life. As years pass, we get placid even as we get more reflective of the past and deceive ourselves into believing nature, human and otherwise, is no longer that interesting, much less that it can still be a real "threat" to our peace of mind. *We know ourselves*, we think. We can't be unduly surprised or disappointed as we were in youth when everything had more urgency. That's when things happen out of the blue. A man goes outside to cut his lawn and winds up in an embarrassing but life-threatening situation; another man is asleep in bed when home invaders jolt him into a nightmare he can't wake from. It may be that nature blunts self-awareness as we age, but nobody sent the Grim Reaper that memo. Violence can always jar us into new perceptions of reality. Nor does it have to be violence to the person; one's ego suffices as Jaroslav discovers in the title story, the first of my several discontented or violated academics.

Of the flash fiction, I can say that the reader will find a mix of the exotic, the mundane, and in a few instances, I have tried to create a *frisson* of horror that the story's compression will reveal at once. The reader alone will judge those efforts successes or failures as certainly will be true of every story. Fortunately, that remains the one constant in writing or reading all fiction.

Terry White
Ashtabula, Ohio

Out of Breath

He was used to the birds waking him up at five each morning despite the earplugs, but this time the hungry cries of the baby finches intruded into his dream. A hulking, shadowy figure adorned in the fiddle-back chasuble of a priest seemed furious with him for something he had done, but Jaroslav Grgat did not know what his transgression was. He shrank under the figure's scorn until he saw himself cowering in the sacristy, the fully realized altar boy of his youth. The priest's iron grip on his wrist was becoming unbearable and he flinched at the beet-red face of the angry priest. *He had dropped the cruet.*

The priest's foul breath washed over him until he snapped to, head perspiring in the chill dawn, and recognized the tuneless dissonance of the babies crying beneath the eaves. Soon the parents' shrill harmonics punctuated their shrillness and Jaroslav knew a regurgitated breakfast of chopped worms, grubs, and insects was just at that moment being delivered to the clamoring mouths. Jaroslav winced as an isolated image from surfing past *Animal Planet* flashed into consciousness; it showed baby pandas slurping away at the green drool of their mother's excrement. He recalled the smarmy voice of the narrator explaining that this was the only way the poisonous eucalyptus leaves could be assimilated into their bodies.

Grgat heard the mother or father scuttle across the gutter before flying off in search of more food for its hungry young. He was so used to the sound by now he knew to the second when the anticipated muffled flap announced their flight. The babies would continue their relentless squall until their tiny bellies were sated. He did not have the heart to remove the nest although he himself was a nocturnal animal who loathed the dawn. He had to argue every semester with the assistant dean who did the scheduling to avoid those ghastly seven-thirty classes in the auditorium. Grgat's accent and the man's sibilant Portuguese-English were two cagey boxers, each hoping to get in a first punch.

His dream was just another variation on the motif of his tenure woes. Last week he actually woke as Dr. Geltmen, his department chair, was choking the life out of him. Grgat came sputtering awake, pawing at the invisible hands locked around his windpipe.

Grgat, an American citizen of five years, wondered how any professor anointed to the estimable rank of university professor by the board of regents (not to mention blessed with a salary of almost a quarter million per year) would feel so compelled to harass a lowly probationary assistant professor making one-fifth that salary. It was the sheer lack of *kindness* that Jaroslav found so distressing. His uncle in Eastpointe, the man who guided him to his adopted country, had ascended the ranks of Wayne State with apparent ease until his retirement eight years ago.

Grgat's own European professors were characterized by sagacity and love for their discipline, which he rarely found in his American counterparts here or at the main campus. They all loved to float tiny boats of paper on the ocean of their aspirations. Politics and networking were everywhere, and the system forced everyone to abet the swindle of true education. Dr. Geltmen's latest email crisply informed him he was to find posthaste another name for his external reviewer list. This would be his eighth, with the previous two rejected for reasons that baffled him. One was his doctoral thesis director, a distinguished emerita of Prague. Both were former department chairs of universities that Geltmen would have been lucky to join as an adjunct.

He threw the covers off and eased himself from the bed. It was by now automatic to hold his right side as he did every morning, although the wire mesh he felt beneath his fingertips was the same every time he touched it. His surgeon last year had, however, assured him he could be as active as wanted and his leering wink suggested all the carnal bliss he could imagine. Jaroslav sat on the examination table and perspired his paper gown to tattered shreds and wondered if the man were mocking him. At that sorry point, the absolute nadir of everything that had gone wrong in his life since coming here, Jaroslav had not known a woman in three years; he was a pilgrim wandering across the Gobi of his own solitude he could not ever see ending. Until Christine, that is. She had saved him, freed him from his tightly wrapped cloak of celibacy and made him breathe again. He admired her—no, he *worshiped* her. He feared he over intellectualized everything, but she never complained.

He staggered into the shower and twisted the Hot valve all the way, but it produced the usual lukewarm trickle until he shivered with gooseflesh. He heard the phone while he was toweling off and slipped on the linoleum trying to answer it. His right big toe was already swollen, and the nail cracked down the middle, from a mishap last night with the corner of the iron bed frame. The stab of pain made him cry out and he hobbled toward the phone. If it were some telemarketer, most likely since Christine was away for a couple days, he was going to put his normal politeness on the shelf and make the intruder pay dearly.

It was his mother. *What now,* he wondered. She wanted to visit Uncle Otakar. Jaroslav did not want to go anywhere while his tenure decision was monopolizing all his time. His mother was very worried. Her brother was complaining of gastric pains when they spoke on the phone. Jaroslav's mother obstinately refused to understand his anxiety; there was no use explaining to her what tenure meant. Jaroslav had entered the academic profession late in life. Now that he had discovered a real passion for teaching after his first uncertain fledgling efforts, it had proved an elixir he could not give up. Besides, at his age, another job was out of the question. Giving up his government position in Prague was his Rubicon and there was no way back. One of the factors that had led to his decision to come to America was the knowledge that he was not applying at a major state university, where the competition was too keen, but at a small regional campus of a state university in northern Ohio, which he had to look up on the internet. He had imagined somewhere closer to Kansas. The glossy brochure he received in the mail happily blurbed about a picturesque campus "nestled in the hills of a small bluff overlooking one of the Great Lakes." Being seventy-five miles from the mother campus made no difference, he discovered, because the irascible Dr. Garrick Geltmen had a long reach. Every day now brought more another dismal tiding from his chair.

Jaroslav found himself increasingly isolated from his colleagues, and though the local campus decision was not much in doubt, he was by no means certain of that. His colleague across the hall kept telling him he was "a shoe-in," but Jaroslav did not believe him. For one thing, he had defied Dr. Geltmen by refusing to toll his last year. Geltmen thought it arrogant of him considering all that had transpired—namely, his hernia operation and its dire aftereffects, including blood in his stool, which he had never mentioned to a soul, not to Christine, especially not to his mother—during which his testicles had swollen like twin balloons from fluid retention. So painful was any movement that his eyes were wet with tears from the pain of his morning ablutions; first he had to dig his shriveled penis out of its pubic nest, an agonizing ordeal. For a month he kept a quilt on the bathroom floor and wrapped towels around the base of the toilet for when he would faint from pain and come to on the floor with bruises on his forehead or shin or elbow. Ever since, he was enmeshed in paperwork for the medical bills.

As bad as that was, the other was much worse and Jaroslav could not think of it without stifling sobs. His older brother had died of pancreatic cancer shortly after his fiftieth birthday. The news from his mother, while he was in recovery from the hernia operation, devastated him. Every writing project he had undertaken up to that point remained stillborn. Even now, Jaroslav felt a wave of nausea at returning to his writing tasks. A patina of dust covered the books and printouts spread across his dining room table; they lay exactly as he had left them months ago. Only his laptop remained active, and it was an exercise in masochism to open the emails and read what the latest thoughts on his diminishing tenure prospects were, or to be told that his failure to revise this article or that monologue resulted in yet another dropped publication.

The one bright spot in his life remained Christine. She'd taught occupational physical therapy at his college last semester, but the school did not rehire her back this fall. He wondered if the knowledge of their affair had anything to do with it. Once they had become lovers, Jaroslav insisted for her sake that they disguise their relationship as much as possible: no public displays of affection on campus, and every time they met by chance in the Commons he politely referred to her as Ms. Nielson. She thought his "European discretion," as she called it, was quaint but charming. They both knew several colleagues who "hooked up" with students; in fact, she was always up on the latest gossip whenever they did steal away for a discreet rendezvous or meet for lunch at a downtown restaurant. Jaroslav was often disconcerted by her calm whenever he brought up the subject; once they quarreled when he accused her of the kind of rumor-mongering he feared.

"For Christ sake," she snapped at him, "this is America, not that superstitious village in Hungary where you grew up." In fact, Jaroslav reminded her, it was Prague where he came of age until he was seventeen and then on to Bonn and from there to the Sorbonne. He spoke five languages. He apologized and felt guilty. He suspected she depended on the small income from the college as an adjunct instructor more than she said, even though her job at the clinic paid more than he made.

Still, he loved her exuberance. She was a happy, life-affirming, positive person and absolutely voracious. She exhausted him. She was always giddy after love-making and counted off her orgasms to him as if he were a disinterested observer who happened by the bedroom in time for her report. Jaroslav did not understand this side of her personality and he wished she weren't quite so vocal in the aftermath of their sex. He attributed it to the liberation of the American female and felt old-fashioned. It almost seemed to disturb the enormous satisfaction he felt while she nestled into his arm. He thought of a tranquil pool of limpid water rippled by long-legged insects going about the surface in crazy designs.

Christine forgot things constantly. He had her cell phone on his bureau and was worried she'd need it for work. It was especially troublesome because he had to leave for Michigan and she wouldn't have access to it until he got back for Monday's class. He remembered she had a key to his house, although she had never availed herself of it as far as he knew.

His mother's telephone call depressed him. His uncle was declining, although she didn't say what exactly what were the latest problems. Uncle Otakar sounded fine when they last spoke a week ago. They had talked for almost twenty minutes and he seemed in good spirits. They were talking about fishing in Upper Michigan and his uncle brought up something his mother had done as a little girl; then a few moments later, he returned to his fishing anecdote like a needle skipping grooves in one of his uncle's jazz collection of 88s.

Jaroslav didn't want to bring his mother along but she insisted he drive to Eastpointe first to get her. She had moved there five years ago from her old house in Hamtramck. That house in southwestern Detroit was long gone now; an Arab enclave and the ghetto had moved in and surrounded the few holdout neighborhoods of working-class whites. Uncle Otakar called it "the inky tide" and tried to get his sister to move farther north of Eight Mile because Eastpointe, after all, was still East Detroit except in name. Drugs, violence, gangs, crime, and poverty were the composites of the slurry of Uncle Otakar's inky tide. For a man devoted to cultural relativity, he did not like to experience it firsthand and refused to teach any night classes at Wayne State because of what he saw happening every day along the Cass Corridor.

Grgat strained in the driver's seat to see the remnants of the old Ford plant at the apex of the bridge spanning the River Rouge. *What history lay below*, he pondered. The violence, the strikes, the rise and fall of a great American Midwestern city, now a city America had forgotten. He imagined the caravansary of President Hoover driving through the city in the midst of the Great Depression while thousands of eyes glared at him in silent, a President who believed in serving eight-course dinners while people starved in their doorways.

Traffic on I-75 near the Henry Ford Expressway was a chaos of junk cars hurtling past, driven by blacks, young males mostly. Their beat-up cars gave him the sudden impression of a stretch of Mexico City or Havana magically transplanted to Detroit. Then it cleared, and the spokes of the founding fathers became more evident along with the highway signs and the predominance of late-model SUVs in the suburbs above Eight Mile.

Eastpointe was worse than he remembered. As the big city succumbed to the plagues of drugs and poverty, the city leaders renamed it to avoid the unsavory connotations of the metropolis they were handcuffed to. Grgat's mother had a cousin in upscale Roseville, far from the madding crowd, but his mother stubbornly refused to budge from her old neighborhood. Grgat told her he could not afford to assume the burden of moving her until his tenure was granted.

He was alarmed when he pulled into her driveway and saw her looking out through the picture window. Even in the glare of the late-afternoon sun, her broad face was lined with a new anxiety and he almost panicked, thinking his uncle had died while he drove and thought his own thoughts, mostly about Christine and her forgotten cell phone. He cursed himself for not dropping it off on his way out of town.

"What is it?" he asked as soon as she opened the door to greet him.

"What took you so long?" she demanded as she struggled into the front seat.

"Aren't you taking anything?" Jaroslav asked her. She had said on the phone that she intended to spend a few days with her brother.

"Oh, I forgot," she said. "I left my suitcase upstairs."

She made a fuss of getting out of the car, grunting, her rheumatoid arthritis flaring up again. He found her pain unbearable, and the sight of her bent back and swollen knees was pure torture. Sisyphus pushed his boulder up the hill faster than she climbed the three steps of her cracked porch.

Jaroslav flushed. *What was all this panic about then?* He had disrupted his life, thrown himself into turmoil with his lesson plans and class preparation, denied himself the pleasure of Christine's company, which pleasure definitely included an overdue romp, thanks to her flow during menses and concomitant discomfort this past week. Jaroslav watched his old mother fumble with the key and felt another pang of anguish.

The ride to his uncle's place occurred mostly in silence, with Jaroslav assuming a forced jollity and attempting to worm out of his mother exactly what was so wrong with Uncle Otakar that his life and hers had to be turned topsy-turvy—*was that the idiom?*

His mother's stern profile rebuffed any attempt at conversation, however. Apropos of nothing, as he was turning at an intersection, she said: "He's getting old, Jaro." Jaroslav did not reply.

His uncle's place looked the same until he helped his mother up the steps. Then the smell hit him like a wall falling on them.

"What—what is that?"

"Your uncle, he doesn't throw anything out anymore."

She grunted something, shook her arm free of his grasp and ambled to the glass door to ring the buzzer. They waited in silence, side by side, while nothing happened except that the foul aroma of raw sewage seemed to gain in strength. Jaroslav's mind tried to adjust to the olfactory assault: septic tank overflow, swamp gas, a dead raccoon under the porch but nothing added up; the sum was greater than the parts.

Jaroslav felt his knees weaken. It wasn't the smell that cloyed his nostrils; it was something deeper, something profound, and he was unaware of what it was—until his old uncle opened the door with a smile and tottered in front of them, smiling, leaning on his cane, and whispering a greeting in the Magyar idiom of his boyhood.

What he was unprepared for and immediately sickened by was that this man he loved was beaming at them between two walls of debris that extended from floor to ceiling. *He hoards*, Jaroslav realized. *He's unwell in his mind.*

As Jaroslav's eyes adjusted, he entered the old hoarder's house and felt like weeping in despair. Gewgaws, bric-à-brac, souvenirs from his travels—these words did not apply except on the rare occasion he noted some kind of pattern in the heaps of trash, like the figurines of Buddha that appeared out of nowhere in his vision. One three-foot-tall copper Buddha had spikes emanating from his head like a Roman Catholic halo. Junk, filth, rotted food, bags of garbage, and the stench of dead things made his nose tingle and he sneezed hard and then nearly gagged as the odor of the house redoubled.

His uncle led the way from the foyer, down a winding path where objects stacked in various arrangements and sizes like tiny buttes in a Western landscape touched if he didn't hold the center of the path. His mother, amazingly, threaded her bulk through the maze of things with indifferent ease right behind her brother. He had a vision of her slapping the side of his head once when his room wasn't tidy.

Jesus Christ, Jaroslav cursed. He wiped his eyes from the sting the collision of malodorous scents as they entered deeper into this domain of reeking smells.

Help me, Jaroslav thought. *My uncle, this distinguished scholar and author of ten books, this former president of the Midwestern chapter of anthropologists, this fine man who loves me, is insane . . .*

His uncle was saying something to him in Magyar and Jaroslav attempted vainly to reply but the words eluded him, skipped off the top of his brain like fish scattering in a pond, and he could not think straight. He resorted to English and gave his uncle a blunt, truncated version of his life the last few months.

"You have tenure yet?" Otakar asked, half-turning and peering at him behind a tower of professional journals near a tattered La-Z-Boy.

"Not yet," Jaroslav answered. "Soon, I hope."

"Come, come, brother," his mother interrupted. "We go to doctor's appointment now."

Jaroslav helped his uncle into the back seat and tried to suppress his gag reflex. Up close, the old man's skin possessed a leathery smell like dirt had been baked into the pores. His clothing showed no signs of wear, but he was stamped by the odor of his house.

His uncle gave him directions to the doctor's; however, Jaroslav could not follow them, nor did it help to have his mother countermanding her brother from the back seat. He finally pulled over and asked a man in a gas station how to get there.

He held both their elbows as he guided them into the doctor's office.

"I'll wait in the car," he told his mother while his uncle located a magazine he wanted. Her look of disappointment did not have an effect on his decision to get away, to clear his head for a moment. He could not yet take in the sudden collapse and he was bitter that his mother had not thought it necessary to inform him of his uncle's condition. He consoled himself with a cigarette and pulled the smoke into his lungs. For once, lighting up did not produce guilt.

Jaroslav took a last drag on the cigarette and flicked it out the window. He went back inside and saw his mother sitting alone.

"He's with the doctor?"

"Of course," she said.

"Why the hell didn't you tell me—"

"Be quiet!"

Uncle Otakar was just then being led out by the receptionist. Jaroslav tried to put a smile on his face but it withered and died.

His uncle gave them a friendly wave and then he grimaced. He heard his mother's shrill scream almost as an after-effect of the tableau that followed and froze in his mind: his uncle went down to the floor like a man in slow motion. Jaroslav was already halfway out of his seat, but not in time to prevent his uncle's face from hitting the carpet. The receptionist stepped back and stood a yard from him and fluttered her fingers as if she had been shocked with electricity.

Jaroslav cradled his uncle's head in his arms and hoisted him gently to his feet when his uncle's bowels evacuated in a noisy rush. His uncle looked at him and their eyes met for a long second. The air in the waiting room turned foul and Jaroslav's face burned with shame. A young doctor in his thirties with a stethoscope flopping against his chest demanded to know what had happened. He immediately did a U-turn on the carpet and left to call the hospital to have an ambulance sent.

"He needs gall-bladder surgery right away," the doctor said.

"No ambulance!" his mother screamed at the receptionist.

"We take him to hospital."

Jaroslav could have screamed at that moment, but he swallowed his rage against his mother and walked with his uncle's arm about his shoulder toward the door. With his mother pawing his back and then her brother's, the three of them shambled clumsily out the doorway into the parking lot like unhappy drunks leaving a saloon.

The drive to the hospital was agony. Every stop and turn produced a moan of pain from Uncle Otakar, who lay beside Jaroslav and from time to time dropped his head onto Jaroslav's shoulder so that he could not execute turns properly and just missed side-swiping parked cars. His mother kept up a litany of prayer and exclamation from the back seat in English and Magyar.

His heart raced as he saw the hospital. It was a massive, sooty red-brick structure from the nineteenth century. Its four-cornered turrets made it look more like a prison. Jaroslav wheeled into the emergency room driveway and nearly clipped the parked ambulance with its flashing lights.

"Stay here!" he yelled to his mother.

Inside, he managed to attract attention right away and indeed his uncle seemed to have recovered, although he wheezed with each step and groaned as the interns settled him onto the gurney. The pungent smell of defecation was politely ignored, and for that small mercy Jaroslav was grateful. He watched them wheel his uncle out of sight behind some plastic curtains where construction was going on in that side of the building.

After a futile argument with her, Grgat agreed to put his mother up in a motel near the hospital and that he would sleep at his uncle's. At first she demanded one within walking distance, but Grgat put his foot down. This area of downtown Eastpointe was crawling with street people, and he worried she would be mugged walking along the sidewalk with her purse. They compromised on a turquoise and cherry motel at the intersection of Duquesne and Iroquois; it was shabby and pockmarked from the outside and Jaroslav's heart sank, but she was adamant and he knew his mother's strength lay in her will. He watched her walk beneath the large vacancy sign that featured a neon parrot winking from the top of a palm tree. He could imagine what its beacon signaled to passersby at night. Christine called these places "hookup shacks."

Jaroslav tried to put his mother and uncle out of his mind on the drive back, but he kept replaying the day's events. Like an unsatisfied director watching dailies, he revisited the scene of his uncle's collapse at the doctor's office. Now and then a whiff of foul air would waft upward from the vents and he would feel his sadness and anger mount. How could his uncle allow himself to degenerate so fast? It was inconceivable to his civilized mind. The car behind Grgat honked when he sat too long at a light and the driver gave him the finger in passing.

He had no intention of sleeping inside the house, with its clutter and madness bellowing at him. He grabbed some blankets and a pillow from the couch and headed to the deck out back. His uncle had no neighbors within sight and the temperatures were mild. He had not slept outside since he was a boy; his mother had locked him out once when he arrived home at dawn after a night of wine drinking with friends from school.

He wanted desperately to call Christine. The books he brought were useless in this fading light. He went inside to see if his uncle kept any alcoholic beverages with which he could dull himself until his mind unwound enough to let him sleep. One expedition among the rubble proved useless and he managed to knock over a couple piles in his rooting. He'd begin the cleanup in the morning. He wondered how Uncle Otakar was doing at that moment, and he tried to imagine his mother resting in the motel.

He sat on the top step of the deck and wrapped an arm around the rail. His mind seemed to grow more agitated with every thought. It seemed that Dr. Geltmen, his mother, Uncle Otakar, and his dead brother's ghost approached in single file from the shadows like tin targets at a cheap sideshow. He thought of driving to a party store for a bottle of Black Velvet, but he was afraid his mother would call in the middle of the night with bad news, and he could not go to her drunk or smelling of booze, an unforgivable sin.

He laid out the blankets on the planking and cocooned himself until the odor made him so sick on his empty stomach that he rolled over and dry-heaved. His head and his heart were pounding. He got up and paced, but he could not relax. Dusk arrived, then nightfall, but his agitation increased. He thought of his birds back home, tucked away for the night in sleep. Grgat watched the stars, named the constellations aloud and waited for dawn.

His mother called his cell at six a.m. and jolted him out of his half-sleep. His arms and back itched from mosquitoes and his ankles were dotted red with chigger bites.

She was dressed and ready to go to the hospital. Nothing Jaroslav said could dissuade her. The posted visiting hours were three hours away and his stomach was a witches' cauldron. She told him to "get a donut on the way" and demanded he hurry up.

When he saw her standing in the lobby, he knew she had not slept much. She was no sooner in the car than she scolded him for leaving her "at that horrible place" where "bad people" kept her up all through the night. She awoke at four in the morning because someone was knocking on her door trying to get inside. She lapsed into dialect and continued her harangue all the way to the hospital. Grgat's blood pressure had dropped to such a point that he knew he had to eat something soon or he would develop a fierce headache.

In the parking lot, his mother got out quickly and went off toward the main doors while he pretended to be looking for something in the trunk. He was mortified that he had to steady himself against the fender, bent over from his stomach's revolt; he made loud retching sounds while the shift change happened all around him. Through his tears, he sensed a dozen people looking at him. Finally, a spume of yellow bile ejected from his mouth and he broke into a sweat. Dizzy but feeling better, he headed for the doors. He was thankful his mother was nowhere in sight.

His uncle's gall bladder surgery had gone well and he was in ICU but in recovery. The doctor said the prognosis was good for a man his uncle's age and he explained everything to Grgat, ignoring his mother's anxious face.

Grgat told her in the parking lot that he had to get back to Ohio if he were going to make his first class on time. She was appalled and immediately furious. She demanded he cancel his classes.

"Call them," she insisted.

"No, I can't, mother," he lamely said and wondered why he was resisting her like this.

It would have been no big deal to cancel; the first week was merely handing out syllabi and explaining class policies. Things settled after Labor Day. She called him a "mule" and a "stubborn boy" and berated him for all his past failures. Somehow Grgat knew that his older brother's death was involved in her ragged tirade too. He was too exhausted to fight back.

"I am going to clean your Uncle's house by myself," she said. It came out more like a rhetorical question than her normal assertion of fact. Grgat felt his heart lurch with sour tenderness. But he would not yield; something in him would not relent and give in to her. He felt like a sadist and every refusal twisted the knife worse.

Uncle Otakar was sitting up in bed when he returned to the hospital. A woman with gray hair in a disheveled bun lay in the next bed. Jaroslav thought she was asleep but she looked at him as he stepped into the room.

"How are you feeling, Uncle?"

"Look at my scar," his uncle said and immediately hoisted up his gown and twisted his body. "I look like a football."

Jaroslav peered round to see. His uncle insisted he admire the scar while exposing the lower half of his body. Jaroslav flushed with embarrassment at his uncle's brief exhibitionism thinking that perhaps the medication they gave him made him oblivious to his neighbor in the next bed.

They made small talk for a while and, as the excitement of his visit wore off, they both lapsed into silence. The woman in the next bed was propped on one elbow and seemed mesmerized by everything they said. Jaroslav looked for an escape. Finally, his uncle's responses declined into monosyllabic mutterings and he yawned several times as if the air were being sucked out of the room; then he looked at his nephew and said, "Stop talking shit."

Jaroslav, in mid-sentence, blinked, astounded, and fell back against his chair speechless, as if he had been kicked in the stomach.

His uncle's eyes went to half-mast and then closed. Soon a dribble of saliva appeared at one corner of his mouth and then he snorted once and was deeply asleep.

Jaroslav stood up, looked at his uncle and turned to go. At the door he realized he was walking out as if he had done something wrong, a schoolboy tip-toeing past a hall monitor, and turned to look at his uncle again, but Uncle Otakar's face almost glowed in exhausted slumber and nothing short of dynamite going off in the room would wake him. The old woman, however, was staring and Jaroslav could have sworn she winked as he turned to go.

He did not intend to stay long with his mother—just long enough to clean out one bedroom and widen the path to the kitchen. If she was so keen to stay in that rat's nest, so be it. Jaroslav felt a twinge of malicious joy at the thought of her bustling about in there without him. He drove to a Home Depot and bought a dozen boxes of lawn and leaf bags and fifteen plastic totes as well as a couple hundred dollars' worth of cleaning supplies.

He spent the next ten hours sorting through his uncle's belongings and packing up what he could according to a classification system that Linnaeus himself might have approved. He wrote the contents of each bag on an index card and duct-taped it to the center of the bag or on the side of the tote for easy reference. By eight o'clock that night, he had three rooms entirely cleaned; his uncle's small garage was packed to the gills. Jaroslav knew his uncle had stopped driving a couple years earlier so the car was essentially a yard decoration.

"Mother, I have to go," he said to her as they sat at the kitchen table and ate hamburgers from McDonald's. The smell in the room was citrusy with deodorizers and he had bought candles to burn off as much odor as possible to enable them to eat. Jaroslav's exhaustion competed with his nausea, but his hunger won out.

"Go," she said. "I don't need you."

He felt a knot in his stomach and almost snapped back at her.   "I must go now if I am to make the drive back to college in time for my class."

"Go," she repeated. "I'm not holding you back."

"You'll be fine?"

"Of course, when have I not been?"

Jaroslav could see her face was drained and her eyes rimmed with redness; she had worked too hard and he was concerned about leaving, yet he turned his heart to stone as the impulse to give in reared up.

"I heard you the first time," she said.

God damn it.

"I'll stay a few hours more," he said.

She grunted that he could "stay or go" as he pleased.

By ten o'clock, she was sound asleep on the divan in front of the television set. Jaroslav had found it beneath a mound of white kitchen bags stuffed with rotted food from the refrigerator. One bag held several hundred pickles of various sizes. There was a desiccated cat skeleton surrounded by a halo of its fur, looking as if it had been soldered to the floorboards. Jaroslav wanted to scream in despair.

"Good Lord," he muttered to himself. "Am I going to find a human corpse next?"

He covered his mother with a quilt that had been wrapped in a plastic bag in the downstairs closet; it smelled faintly of moth balls. He stroked her hair from her forehead and knew he loved her despite everything and knew they shared all those years when their lives were hard in the old country.

The ride home was harder than he anticipated. On the turnpike he had to pull over at the rest stops and close his itching eyes. There was little traffic except for the semis barreling past. The orange arc lights gave him the unsettling feeling he was passing through his own dream, and he thought of that Sufi poet Rumi who advised mystics not to leave the fire for the imagination's alluring shapes but to "stay at the flame's core."

He pulled into his driveway at dawn and the air smelled sweetly of autumn, as if he had left summer back in Michigan. In his bedroom the baby birds were chirping their hungry chorus of lamentation and, for once, the sound did not dismay him. He set his alarm and undressed.

He slept badly, dreamed of the last few days and could not

get his uncle's bizarre behavior at the hospital out of his mind. He continued to look at the clock after each short bout of sleep to assure himself he was not oversleeping.

The numbers on the clock face stared back at him for a long moment until enough cognition fired up to make him realize he was going to be late if he didn't hurry. Grgat showered and shaved, nicked himself badly under the chin and staunched the red flow as best he could with dabs of tissue. Desperate to get going, he tore and wadded a Kleenex into place and secured it with Scotch tape. His eyes burned and itched on the drive to school. His left ear throbbed. Last night, in an effort to stay awake, he'd kept the car window open even though he feared it might result in another ear infection, an old aggravation from his days of swimming in the Vltava.

Grgat made it into his first class in C-Wing only ten minutes late. Because he was brand new, his students were less likely to bolt on the first day. His class was filled to overflow, a few students standing in the back of the room. He told them the syllabus was not yet available but should be ready by their next class. He was unsettled by the snickering up front as he segued into his standard first-day overview, until the taped compress on his chin fell off and landed on his right loafer where he was unable to kick it off. Blood and sere had formed a kind of glue that kept it stuck fast. Someone in the back nickered and snorted like a horse pawing at his stall. A few laughs turned to guffaws.

Why he didn't turn this into a "teaching moment," he would ask himself after class—or at the very least join in on the fun, but it seemed the shade of Uncle Otakar was standing in the room with him, slightly out of focus, sternly admonishing any frivolity. That and his exhaustion dispelled the urge toward levity he would normally have felt. He bristled. His voice became stentorian. With no way out, he would go deeper in. He counterattacked with high seriousness and he would have gotten away with it if a slight onrush of vertigo hadn't sent him hard into the corner of his desk where he barked his shin painfully, bringing everything to a halt.

He looked down at the tissue still stuck to his foot like a cheerleader's pom-pom. This time the entire class joined in the revelry and he was, he knew, sunk for good. He tried to put the best possible face on the débàcle and promised them "a wonderful learning experience," but they were trooping out, talking excitedly to one another and pulling out cell phones. He heard the word *drunk* from one young whey-faced girl talking to a boy her age. Jaroslav's face burned crimson. He wanted to stop her but what could he say? He worried that the assistant dean might hear of this and summon him to the office for an explanation.

Cell phone . . . He remembered seeing Christine's at home on his night stand; he had slipped it into his jacket pocket and decided to drive over to her apartment with it, maybe redeem something of this bad start to the semester with a round of lovemaking in her pink-and-white bedroom amid the teddy bear collection. It boiled out of some abyss in his brain: the desire to have rough sex with her almost made him pass out. He imagined being behind her, pulling back her hair and demanding of her, *"Like that, huh? Want more, do you?"*

Grgat felt a pair eyes on him. The girl with the cell phone was in the doorway of the classroom staring at him in wonder. She had come back for something. He smiled at her but she didn't return the smile. She scowled, turned on her heel and left without a word. Grgat looked down to see that he had an erection and that his zipper was half undone. His body was in rebellion, all out of whack from the business with his uncle and sleep deprivation.

He was more determined than ever to see Christine and he left campus at once. When the assistant dean attempted to flag him down near the central office doors, he strode past clutching his briefcase to his chest, almost goose-stepping, like a man holding his severed hand to the stump of his wrist.

Out in the parking lot, he felt the tinny buzz of her cell phone purring against his leg. He flipped it open, curious. What came over the tiny display screen was a ludicrous mistake, he thought.

Do u wanna fuck me, baby?

At first, Grgat thought the sender had mistakenly sent an obscene message to him. Then it clicked. It was meant for Christine, of course. Grgat swallowed and stood rooted to concrete as he pondered the words on the plastic device in his hand. Each letter was an acid-drip on his skin, and he flushed. Like an obscene incubus, the sender buzzed another arrow into his heart. His reeling brain could barely assimilate what his eyes and neocortex were confronting. The words blipped across the screen in the infantile text-English of teenagers: *i cant wait to lick ur sweet pussy.*

Grgat almost dropped the phone; he felt sweat crawling down his back like a hundred baby spiders flowing forth from their mother's egg sac. Bile rose in his gorge and he came close to heaving against a fender. Feet passed by. He was almost blind from the exertion. Finally, he stood up, tottering and weaving like a drunk. A group of girls walked past, whispering and looking at him, but he couldn't really see them; he couldn't focus. A ragged vee of geese appeared overhead as if by magic and he stared upward in amazement that such things could be.

He stumbled toward his car, no longer sure where it was. A dozen thoughts and emotions tore at him and he felt bewildered by the betrayal.

Hope lifted a pennant up the mast of his spine and he thought: "It has to be a mistake." His heart began to beat again. He had an impulse to throw the wicked thing at the ground as hard as he could and then stomp the pieces into slivers. *It can't be true* . . . Grgat had a flashback to his long journey home under the hideous arc lights of the turnpike. He thought then he would ask Christine to marry him. God, he had even practiced asking her in the rearview mirror.

Another buzz from the tormenting demon in his hand: *Check this out, babe.* Jaroslav opened the jpeg attachment and saw a photo of a man's erect penis. It had a humpback bulge in the center right over the fat worm ticking below the stretched skin that fed the eel its blood supply. Jaroslav stared at the purple, spade-shaped glans in its ruff of foreskin; he heard giggling close by as a group of young males bumped him in passing. One of them looked over and muttered "fag" in a stage whisper as the others laughed and fist-bumped one another.

Another hum, another baleful message shaped itself into coherence before his burning eyes; this time, the liquid crystals left no doubt: *Meet u at ur dumbass boyfriend's house in one hour.*

Grgat's stomach seemed to expand with hot gas and then he felt his watery bowels loosen a stream of liquid filth down his pants. No one was there to see his shame. He thought of Uncle Otakar collapsing in his arms and the old man's hot breath on his neck as he lifted him to his feet. The shame, the horror of it came roaring back.

Jaroslav forced himself think calmly about where he had parked. It was in the south lot, he now remembered, because he had been late arriving for his class. He would have to walk several hundred yards through the haze of his own shit to get there. Climbing the steps of Cheops would have been easier for him, but he put one foot in front of the other like a toddler and headed in the direction of his car. The sun was higher and hotter now and the rancid effluvia he gave off with each step made him more aware of the noxious stench.

He gave a wide berth to any students he saw coming in his direction and hoped he would meet no colleagues on the long march. He thought sadly of his mother's fealty and of Uncle Otakar's demise, but he would assess his options later—first a shower. Perhaps he would park his car around the corner and see if the boyfriend showed. He entertained a grim image of slicing his rival's carotid as he entered his house; he would call it self-defense—a homeowner protecting himself from an intruder. He savored a morsel of what Christine would feel when she saw police cars and an ambulance parked on his lawn. He imagined her angelic face, uptilted to kiss him, the lovely slant of her cheekbones, her ice-blue eyes welling up with tears. *There, bitch.*

Jaroslav thought of her swollen labia opening to him like a pink orchid. It seemed like another lifetime when he had devoured her hungrily, rolling her up on her backside to lick his way up her ass crease all the way to the sacral dimples of her back. He knew he still loved her despite her treachery.

He kept walking, oblivious to everything but the sucking sound of his soiled pant leg sticking to the back of his thigh and then pulling itself free like the corduroy pants he wore as a child in Prague; it thrust him back to his childhood, an unbidden memory of walking with her and his little brother through Old Town, through Wenceslas Square, on their way to the Main Railway Station. He was on school vacation and they were going home to see his dying grandmother. He, his little brother, and his mother lived in a cramped, cold-water flat up two flights of stairs behind an alley on Hybernská Street. She cleaned apartments to support them and told everyone her husband died. The still powerful but lessening stink wafted like an evil halo all around him and he absently scratched the nick on his chin until it bled afresh. Apropos nothing (he despised that verbal tick left over from the quaint Constance Garnet translation of Dostoevski), he thought of his brother long dead in his cold grave, and without considering why *that*—or anything else—should occur to him now, in the wake of this disastrous beginning to the week, he hiccupped a single huge, chest-shuddering sob and then wept like a baby, the tears falling down his face like salty rain.

The Frotteur in the Dark

Herbert Pannecouke, recovering frotteur, missed the feeling of rubbing up against rumps in elevators. Before Loretta plucked him from Satan's grasp, as she put it that damp winter morning long ago, he used to get up before dawn to plan his detailed excursions downtown, commencing with the morning rush-hour traffic and the herd of office secretaries crossing the street to the municipal building. The thought of those days always mingled with the memory of his young wife, an earnest Jehova's Witness holding her little stack of *Watchtowers*, squeezing his hand after his sordid confession and then the two of them on their knees, in front of his couch. He remembered the warmth of her hand and how that made the blood flow south most inappropriately. Now almost three decades later, he sat rock still, his breath tight, and willed his fluttering fingers to cease.

Herb gripped the arms of the wicker chair as the deer, a young buck with horns, peered around the rusted fence separating his neighbor's backyard from his. Herb urged the animal to show itself, and as if summoned by the energy of his thoughts, the animal extended one leg, then the other, and moved stiff-legged into the open. The soft dawn light rippled over its back as it approached the bird feeder. The heady smell of iodine from last night's rain lingered. Herb felt himself long since freed from lust and able to think about Loretta without that bone-breaking ache in the center of his chest. He missed those warm puffs of breath she blew on his neck as they lay in bed. He always woke first, that old habit reminding him once again of her absence.

He admired the deer's spiky rack of antler and remembered how velvety it was just a few short weeks ago. Last night's storm over the lake had whipped the tops of the coal piles into gritty plumes. He saw the diamond sparkle of residue across his and his neighbors' yards. Herb testified at the last EPC hearing about how the coal storage piles were blackening their street like Dickens' London. He savored the literary morsel again. Torn remnants of webs fluttered against the panes like loose guy wires. Sunlight caught the tiny flakes of coal dust trapped in the webbing. Herb thought of those deep-sea creatures dangling luminescent tentacles to trap prey.

Something spooked the deer; it ceased chewing and froze. With an elegant turn, a dancer's tombé, the animal was suddenly gone. Herb got out of the chair, stretched, and moaned. He would have to cut the grass or risk some snide comments in the evening around the fire. The rain had come down in buckets all week long, a monsoon of gray sheets blowing off the lake which had prevented anyone from mowing. The humidity was already high. His flowerbeds of scarlet impatiens would be gorgeous red waves this time next month. Orange and yellow lantanas would spill over their brick enclosures. The sprig of larkspur purchased from Lowe's yesterday was almost at full height and the South African lavender was heavy enough to bow the shepherd's hook on the other side of the garage.

The last mouthful of coffee was cold and he made a face. To the garage, then, he told himself. No sense in waiting until the sun got higher. The fuzzy ochre and salmon streaks of daybreak were long gone. The lake was a silver sheen all the way out to the horizon where a jagged ridge of cloud was massing to the north. Herb imagined it upside down like a camera lens; it made him think of islands seen from a far-off ship, like the humps of pine-dotted mountains in Chinese landscapes.

He unfolded the arms of his lawn mower, tightened the knobs, and tilted it against a cement block to get at the muck behind the thick blade. With a putty knife, he scraped the soggy grass free, inhaling the swampy odor. He poured fresh gasoline into the tank and checked the oil level, air filter, and spark-plug connection. Routine was his nature.

He normally began mowing the side yard, worked to the back near the garage, and then did the front and back of the house. He always saved the hardest for last because of the backyard's steep slope. The ground out there petered away to a slick clay, and he had to step carefully. He decided to remove the grass catcher and laid it near the garage door.

Nearing the rise where his property line afforded the best view of sunsets, he looked over the bank into the clearing he and a neighbor had cut last summer for the deer.

Herb pushed the mower into a thick mass of Japanese knotweed, bumping the mower up and down to gain leverage over the rubbery stalks. He felt looseness in the upper extension of the handle bar and reached down to tighten the plastic handle knob.

Something greasy squirmed underfoot and Herb gave a startled jump, thinking he might have stepped on a snake. He flashed back to the many stares of anger and shock of the girls he had sidled up to with a newspaper prop in hand. Herb always knew exactly the right amount of pressure, a single paper's weight (he used to think), to gain the most satisfaction without incurring *that* look. He always had a calm apologetic manner to deflect the worst suspicions and most of the time he got away with it.

The mower stopped once he released the control bar. He'd have to lug the heavy thing up the slope to restart it on flat ground. Thinking he might save himself trouble, he used a nylon twist tie from his pocket to secure the bar to the mower's handle so that, once the engine caught, he'd just have to throw the drive-control lever. He leaned over the engine and pulled the starter handle. It almost caught but he needed more leverage for the pull. He tried it again. The engine double-coughed and died. A drop of sweat ran down his nose and itched. He was sweating hard and he had barely started. He tried it again—another chuffing sound—but the engine wouldn't catch. The awkward angle on the slope where gravity fought him made it hard to reach over to push the primer button.

Herb planted his feet a little lower on the hillside and gave it one mighty pull and heard the engine catch and hold. Flushed and a bit breathless, he shifted his weight around to push the drive control lever forward to move the wheels. That was when the ground gave way beneath his feet. It felt so odd—like the world tilting on a different axis. For a split-second that weightless feeling of being free from gravity astounded him. Then, with a *whoomph* of air leaving his lungs, he was on his back, one hand gripping the control bar and the other flailing helpless.

When his vision refocused, Herb saw the mower was canted away from his limbs, the blade chopping the air loudly but harmlessly. Herb tightened his grip to keep the machine from sliding in his direction.

Herb took his bearings. He couldn't move much in this position. His right foot and ankle had somehow become ensnared in the wild grapevines. His back hurt. When he tried to move to his right side, a spasm of pain shot through him from his sixth lumbar to an area below his spine. It was like being jabbed every few seconds between the knucklebones of his spinal cord with an ice-cold stiletto. Pinpricks of light scattered like fireflies around the edges of his vision and a rising mist of sweat fogged his glasses except for a thin crescent near the frames. He dared not release the throbbing handle to wipe them clear. Ripples of pain were shooting up his forearms.

Herb tried to gather his strength for one momentous effort to right himself. He uncoiled the tension in his back by easing his head farther down the slope. That proved a mistake: he slid a few inches downward and almost lost his grip on the bucking machine. He felt embarrassment along with the pain, lying splayed on his back in his own yard under a hot sun. Those few inches had been sufficient to tighten the vine's chokehold on his foot. It bit like a ligature on a murder victim's corpse.

How long does it take a mower to run out of gas? Herb guessed an hour. *Surely not longer?*

He began to sweat with the strain. Soon he was soaked through his clothes. He raised his head enough to see his hands and the deathgrip on the handlebar, his knuckles whitened to diamond points like a boxer's fists. His normal tinnitus became a symphony of dissonance. *Think,* he told himself. Years spent getting next to unwitting women had taught him how to work angles and focus.

Breathing in this spraddled position was beginning to aggravate his normal short-windedness. Herb could not predict with certainty that, given the combined forces of gravity and torque created by the whirring blade, the mower would miss him if he let go and the machine flipped. On the other hand, like a falling helicopter gone amok, that machete blade would slice through meat right down to bone. A grotesque image of his intestines churned up before his eyes made him tighten his grip despite the numbness in his hands. As a lonely boy, he had read in cowboy novels about Apaches staking out settlers, cutting holes in their abdomens and pulling the slick blue intestines out to drape them across the belly so that the smell would be sure to bring the coyotes. His young mind imagined the victim's eyes bugged out in shock and horror.

He forced pleasant thoughts into his head—women and girls he had nudged on buses and shopping malls, airports and grocery lines. A dizzying kaleidoscope of skirts and rumps, women bare-legged or be-nyloned, their perfume wafting through his brain. But danger always linked hands with anticipation, like one of those Middle Eastern martyrs strolling through a market in his bomb jacket with one thumb on the detonator, a microsecond from being blown to smithereens. Herb thought of the two angels hovering nearby, supposedly eager to discharge their duty to escort the martyr to Allah; then he remembered the seventy-seven *houris* deployed for the martyr's pleasure. He saw Loretta's sad, suffering face and banished that wondrous image.

Time—how much time? Herb guessed an hour had passed. The cramping in his forearms had spread to the tops of his shoulders and was working down his sides toward his ribs. The knife ache in his back had spread to all quadrants evenly and he was pinned to a red wall of pain. Insects had discovered him and were crawling inside his clothes. He felt sticky bites on his thighs and around his groin where his exposed legs gave free access. He couldn't remember whether black widows and brown recluses lived in the wild or were like rats and needed people to survive.

The engine sputtered, whined in a lower key, and then died. Herb gasped out a sob of joy, exhaustion, and relief. He felt like a prisoner in one of those old Foreign Legion films, languishing in his oubliette when a rope is miraculously dropped from above. His hands, which had been soldered to the handle, released and the mower dropped helplessly and rolled past him. Where it brushed against him on its way down, it scalded his ribs—one more out-of-tune instrument in the ragged symphony of pain being conducted inside him. The mower tumbled into the brush some distance behind him and came to a stop. Now that he was free from the awful night-mare of his imagined evisceration, every cramp and sprain redoubled in agony and called for his attention; every itch and insect bite announced itself at once. The strangled circulation in his right foot had numbed his entire leg.

Nothing he commanded his body to do worked. It was all physics now. He did not have the strength of muscle or the flexibility to get up. Thanks to Loretta's ministrations to his soul's welfare, he had expunged all naughty words from his vocabulary years ago. Somewhere in the abyss of his deepest mind, he found a seedbed of profanity so vile that it surprised him even as it came welling up from his parched throat.

By twisting his head slightly to the left, he was able to rub the arm of his glasses against a pointed twig, and by cocking his head a little, he could see a few anemic petals of a Rose-of-Sharon bush through the green mist of the jungle that surrounded him. He wondered how it had managed to poke through this thick canopy of tangled scrub. For several minutes he tried to catch the edge of his glasses on the twig, but it was too light and gave with the merest pressure. Herb thought if he could catch the twig just right, he could get these useless glasses off his face and see better, myopia notwithstanding. He worked at it, very careful not to upset the tug of gravity, and stopped for a while when the strap muscles of his neck burned from the exertion. This activity, pointless in the extreme, took his mind off his itching and the bug life seething around him. An oriole landed on a tree branch above and warbled a riff of lovely song. The notes seemed to pierce Herb lying directly below. He had a perfect view of its burnt orange chest and throat contracting like an old man's double chin.

Time expanded and collapsed like a balloon being slowly squeezed, although the light had not changed much except for a softening fuzz in the tree limbs. Herb wasn't sure time was following its normal routine from—when?—an hour ago? Five minutes?

Someone has to see me, he thought. *Not long now.*

There would be dozens of neighbors arriving next door if the cookout was anything like last year's. Herb winced—a fresh bite, sharper, between his shoulder blades. Where his pant legs exposed skin, black flies were alighting and devouring him. He felt each chunk of flesh torn off in their mandibles. At first one, then a few, enough for him to hear their tinny drone above the cicadas. *Dear God*, he wondered, maybe these are sarcophagi, smelling his imminent death. His hands could not make a fist but he could thrash about like a baby in a crib to dislodge the feasters, and if they settled on his face, he could swing an arm up. When a couple tried to light on his eyelids, a tiny surge of adrenalin gave him renewed strength. One of his pulp mystery novels had detailed with sickening precision a family of possums that had burrowed through the decomposing corpse of a victim from behind and cored the body like an apple.

Finally, Herb could no longer deny his bladder and he wet himself. The stinging hot burn of his urine was the worst indignity so far. Tears of shame and rage welled up and flowed down his face, adding salt to the sting. Every nerve fiber in his brain was carrying the same message over and over: *this hurts, this hurts, God damn, thishurtsthishurts* . . .

More time elapsed and he heard sounds—people talking. The faintest drifts of chatter carried on the wind and just barely reached his ears. The wiener roast: *I am saved*, he thought.

If he could have summoned moisture from his dehydrated, exhausted tear ducts, he would have shed new tears. Herb strained to listen. He could not make out words but these happy sounds thrilled him to the marrow. He imagined the scene: food, beer, wine, hot dogs grilling, and prepared covered dishes just like last summer. Herb liked some of his neighbors, and for the few hours he could manage to be sociable, he even enjoyed a little gossip and talk of local politics.

He was one of Flaubert's rebels: a good bourgeoisie in his private life but a revolutionary in his art, although being a frotteur might not qualify as art in everyone's book. Loretta was the one who overcame her Appalachian roots to mingle first and kept him from withdrawing too far into what she used to call his "bear cave."

Herb lay back and let the ebb and flow of his back spasms tick off the seconds and minutes until rescue. Once he drifted off and recalled a gorgeous woman he had stalked for that one shining moment of bliss. His compulsion in those days was unforgiving; it ordered his days and nights. By his twenties he had put aside the common rubric of "pervert" and was as good at it as circumstances allowed. For him, those moments of touch were the fevered bliss of a communicant receiving the wafer at high mass.

He woke to the last yellow rays of the sun piercing his eyes. His face hurt and the undersides of his arms were sticky as taffy and burned as if fire ants were biting his armpits. He shook some sweat out of his swollen eyes. He must have dozed longer than he realized. He strained to hear the sounds of the party. Thank God it was still going on. The volume had ascended several decibels and was stereophonic: young people, maybe some of the children or visiting out-of-state relatives, were gabbling about the events of their summer in bright chatter, maybe some were flirting. Herb's heart skipped; he was dehydrated beyond anything he had ever experienced. His mouth opened and closed, but he couldn't make any sounds louder than a baby's gurgle.

He imagined himself speckled in red swatches from the sunlight poking through the leaves above. His skin was hot to the touch, and the dried-up perspiration left him with unbearable itching in places he couldn't reach.

Overhead, contrails of passing jets drifted in the frigid air. Now and then a squawking gull flew past. Red-winged blackbirds from the wetlands near the breakwall set up a noisy din beneath his feeder just twenty feet from where he lay. So many times he had watched them billing and jostling, wasting their energy, when they could have been feeding on the seed he provided. It seemed cruel that they were indifferent to his plight, as if the suffering of their benefactor meant nothing and seed would always be plentiful.

Ideas seemed foreign now but images intensified. He was observing them from deep inside his mind's own theater. Some left him feeling befuddled, confused by their meaning, like in his dreams just before dawn. An unbidden image of Loretta dying bubbled to the surface, from the time when she was wasting away in the upstairs bedroom. He wept all over again. So many times had he begged God to let the cancer take him, and he would have willingly bargained with the forces of darkness when God refused to negotiate. *I could spit in your face.*

I am dying, a voice from somewhere said. "No," Herb said. *Not me. Not yet. Not like this.*

He would gather all his strength and make one last great effort to extricate himself. All pain be damned. When he opened his eyes again, he saw the first stars of nightfall. Somewhere high above where he lay pinned in the dirt, the outer stars of the constellation Capricornus bloomed in the night sky. *Mocked by a goat now,* he thought sadly.

A sound behind him ended his self-pity; a snuffling sound accompanied by grunts. His heart resumed its strange arrhythmia. He strained to hear more. Some olfactory switch was tripped because he seemed able to smell everything at once—himself most of all, the pungent dirt, the spicy or musty green odors of different plants commingled with the acidic wetness of urine.

Then the whiskers of some small animal brushed his face and he almost levitated in panic. Herb bucked again and the animal—whatever it was—went crashing through the brush. His body shook with the first waves of nausea. *I might choke to death on my own vomit . . .*

He gasped and wrenched his head painfully around so that the bile welling up from his stomach would not double back down his esophagus and strangle him. A thin spume of vomit gagged him with a burning, horrendous pain that was like drowning in sea of fire. Herb thought the top of his head was going to explode from the pressure; when he lay back in total exhaustion, he felt a long ropy string of drool extend from his mouth to his shoulder.

His head pounded with a furious pain. The smell of frying

meat almost made him vomit again. He knew he could not survive doing that twice. Dusk lasted seconds and then a tropical blackness fell like a descending curtain. Herb could no longer see the roof of his house. Most of the skin around his eyelids was swollen. He felt bumps and swellings all over his body. The dried urine was a corrosive acid eating the flesh of his groin. Nothing above was visible and there was nothing his peripheral vision could detect.

Herb began to sing without being aware of it. *Yes, Jesus loves me.* Croaking sounds, but in his head the notes were fine, no sharp or flat notes, no quavering like Mrs. Tobias, the oldest member of Loretta's Jevovah's Witness church.

Herb smelled them before he was aware of them. It was hard to tell how many because they shuffled and bumped one another in the dark, rubbed up against him, no longer fearful. Once in a while a whiskered snout butted him in the head or chin, or he felt sharp claws on his calf where a couple of them had scrambled over his body. They were loud—a dysfunctional family. He had a vision of red eyes staring at him like the devil himself. They jostled and disappeared, sucked back into the dark. Herb knew they were feasting beneath the bird feeder. Their noisy mastication sent icy ripples down his back. It hurt terribly to twist his head, but he could discern their humpy backs milling about in a feeding frenzy; he imagined their greedy little humanlike hands scooping seed into their mouths. They came at night, summer or winter, these nocturnal raccoons who lived over the bank in their burrows beneath the grapevines and the black alder trees he always meant to cut back.

Their screeches, so close, were hellish. One would nip or attack another—so loud were they that Herb was amazed the partygoers next door didn't come running over to witness the pandemonium. *If I hold my breath long enough, can I die?* Herb wondered whether a drowning man in the Caribbean would feel the first shark's bite or whether he would be past all pain, the amygdala, or whatever it was in the brain, shutting down all sensation as a last merciful gift. Herb floated in his wet blackness and thought about it for a long time.

He remembered he had some deal—or was it some bargain?—he had yet to fulfill. That worried him terribly. He felt her breath on his cheek and he whispered, "Loretta, wake up, sweetheart. It's a beautiful morning." *What luck*, he told himself. Just the day before he had awakened in the cold light of a winter morning, dressed in the dark, and gone foraging for beauty, his everyday routine. He raised his right arm, a supremely confident conductor in front of his orchestra. He would summon this one, tickle it from its dark corner.

The red eyes of raccoons studied him while Loretta stood on his porch at the precise moment he had opened the door, her radiant simple beauty a perfect confluence of time and destiny. At that angle, and with the full might of the stars overhead, the eyes of the feasters all turned to him at once and glowed with an incandescence like molten fire, and Herb felt his soul sliding backwards.

Twins

"You lazy asshole," he fumed, not as angry as his words sounded. Paul could swear like the demon in *The Exorcist*.

"I did the last one," he complained.

"Fair enough," I said.

I started at Rodriguez's black scalp line and peeled through the stubble of his cheek fat.

One tough Mexican street kid. He never cried out once.

"We're just animals," my brother whispered, smiling, looking on; his breath smelled rubbery like skunk.

Last Match in New Orleans

When he asked at the desk for change for ten dollars, the young black woman said cheerily, "Don't spend it all in one place." The man next to her at the computer smirked. This was his first stay at the Drake Hotel, although he had played matches in San Francisco before. David remembered the last one at a condo in Pacific Heights, and the memory was pleasant.

It was a habit of his not to be caught on the street of any city without change. He didn't want to be somewhere in an emergency and not able to make a 911 call. David acknowledged the odds of this happening were slim—besides that, he didn't know anyone he would have been comfortable calling. Few people were gracious about losing huge sums of money. Nonetheless, he thought it a harmless compulsion.

He took a leisurely walk down to Fisherman's Wharf. The sun was cheering despite its being early spring. Back in New York there had been nothing but icy drizzle for weeks on end. He realized he had been mildly depressed all this time.

He ignored the surge of shoppers crisscrossing his path. He decided to watch the harbor seals cavort around the pilings or sun themselves, oblivious to the human beings tossing scraps of food. He remembered a restaurant down there with a lot of glass and sunshine streaming through. His appetite sharpened, the langostinos in their piquant sauce a welcome olfactory memory.

Standing a little ways from a crowd of Chinese-American children, he watched the seals twist their tapered bodies near the pier. He was slightly repulsed by the sight of a dozen of them packed together and sunning on a pile of rocks. Their thick bodies were jammed in a gelatinous mass. He could barely discern a snout here or a fin there. He forgot what families of seals were called.

A young child's crying disturbed his reverie about the last match he had played. It was the way she cried, not as bratty children cry for attention but mournfully, too old a sound for such tiny lungs. He turned away from the harbor breeze, with its reek, and saw a young woman reach down to grab the child by her hand. The mother's short chestnut hair was feathered off her head and fell across her face. The light breeze was enough to lift it. David was struck by the spectacle despite his desire to return to the chess game in his head. He noticed two other children, an older boy, maybe six or seven, and another girl who have been hers as well, clustered around the young woman's legs. She looked in her early twenties and she was obviously well along in her pregnancy. The older children looked on with blank stares while their youngest sibling cried. The mother caught the child by the wrist and gently pulled her away from the curb. Another breeze lifted her hair from her face and David was struck by the sheer prettiness of her distressed face in profile.

She did not look poor. The children were dressed well, a little unkempt, but not unusually so. The mother's clothes were neither fashionable nor worn for comfort, but once out of Manhattan, he was never able to distinguish between an expensive chic look that bordered on slovenly dishabille and a look that was aiming for the effect and missed. The child's crying revved itself up to higher tones and he felt his space invaded as moan became screech and then climbed the scale toward dog whistle. It made him feel squirmy, and so he left the jetty and headed for the shining restaurant.

Waiting, he wondered where the patriarch of this ragtag family could be. A good meal and a glass of Chablis, something with a steely edge, would fix his darkening mood. He had taken his Lorazepam upon waking at five, so there would be no abrupt descent into sleepiness because of the wine at dinner. He put the family out of his mind, as forgotten as the harbor seals, and allowed the subdued conversations, the wink of light on goblet or tableware to soothe his spirit. The gentle clack of spoon on saucer or glass was sweeter music by far. He consciously unwrinkled his brow and felt the tension in his face and hands unknot. He called these pre-match jitters, although his confidence was always high.

He enjoyed his meal and overtipped. Joey Silva's fifty-thousand was carried in a money belt in fifties and hundreds. For a match in Toronto, Silva had pressed a banded packet of hundred-dollar bills into his hand. David assumed this was the opponent's request.

He had never challenged Joey S. on the sixty-percent share of his winnings. After all, Joey fronted the money and had all the contacts. He did agree to splitting expenses, although David was disappointed it wasn't 50-50. He was no good at negotiating with Silva, who seemed to have a natural bent for it. You could drop him into the middle of the Arabian desert and he would bargain with the blue tribesmen a camel in fifteen minutes. He could easily imagine Silva's thick hairy fingers wiggling into the palm of some nutbrown Toureg.

He and Joey were not friends. Joey called himself a booking agent, but he never heard him speak of working with anyone else. David didn't believe there were others like him, a rogue class of chess champions roaming the country for private matches in expensive homes. He supposed it was possible. Once he mentioned to David he owned a piece of a fighter in Detroit being trained by Don Thibbodeaux. Another time he said he stabled a thoroughbred at Saratoga, but these were beyond the pale of David's business with him.

Even so, the money was good at forty percent because he had lost just once in nine years. He had picked up a virus in Beijing and wasn't able to concentrate. His Shanghai hosts offered to delay the match until he felt better, but he declined and informed them it should proceed as planned. As ill as he was, he should have won that, too, but a misplayed rook in the end game was too much to overcome. He slept for three days straight, unable to get out of hotel bed except to reach the toilet, and found himself ejecting filthy liquids from both ends and was so racked by stomach spasms that when he deplaned in Detroit he was fifteen pounds lighter and suffering from a vertigo that forced him to look no higher than a person's waist.

He had called Joey from the Renaissance Center downtown and said he would be staying there until his health returned. Joey shrugged off the loss and his illness both: "It happens," he said. Excepting that single seventy-five thousand dollar loss, David had made just short of a million in almost nine years, invested most of his forty percent in T-bills and money-market certificates. He was reading avidly on the subject of hedge fund trading, especially in money markets; he knew his desire to play chess was waning. He never played unless money was at stake. Meanwhile, he had traveled the world and stayed in the finest hotels. Aside from his chess opponents, whom he did not want to know, he had seen much of the world and vastly different cultures. It was a varied life, and David liked it.

By the time he caught the trolley, it was packed. He rode the strap outside back to the hotel. The passengers were mostly Chinese-American children just released from school and a few well-dressed Caucasian tourists, mainly middle-aged women and their husbands. Two seats over from some tourists sat a scruffy white male, shabbily dressed. A Chinese man who had boarded with David made an attempt to sit next to the youth, but he got up very fast with a sour look on his face. The seat was wet. It might have been urine from the young man, who was talking incessantly in a one-way conversation.

Once in a while he broke free of his monologue and urged the driver, whom he referred to as "Hop Sing," to get the trolley moving faster. The children were oblivious to the strange man's mutterings, and David assumed they were used to seeing him aboard this trolley because they were a long way from the street people of the Mission district.

He had once been to the Castro district for a match with a wealthy gay man; he had looked down on the Presidio from the bridge. He had been to the red light district on his last stay, but declined the offer of sex from a dancer at one of the clubs. He wasn't afraid of AIDS so much; it was the paid sex with its taste of worms in his mouth. He used masturbation for release, and that kept things simple, though unsatisfying, for long periods of celibacy, which he referred to as "droughts." The current one was almost fourteen months and by far the worst. He seemed to be invisible to young women. He had no trouble meeting these women five years ago. Perhaps this was a normal transition to old age and he must learn to cope with it. He saw many lovely women in their late thirties to mid-forties in every big city. He had to adjust his habits; it would take a little time, he supposed.

When he reached the Drake, he saw the woman again, with her brood trailing slightly behind. From the opposite direction, a maroon Escalade was approaching at a high rate of speed. David's heart lurched and his brain took a snapshot, freezing it just as the mother reverse-clutched and yanked her children back before the big car mowed them all down in the middle of the busy street.

When time resumed, the car had passed with a contemptuous toot-toot of its horn; they all stood on the median, mother and ducklings temporarily safe. David's thought was unkind. "Stupid woman will get them all killed," he said to the man out front dressed like an English beefeater with a tall hat, who grimaced politely, and nodded to David as he stepped past. Inside the air-conditioned foyer's cool embrace, David felt ashamed of his response to the doorman; after all, it could have been a grisly scene instead of a near-accident. The low sound of people checking in and out, the echoing clack of shoe leather against the travertine tiles returned him to tranquility. His lunch had been satisfying and he felt that a nap after his brisk walk and trolley ride would be a good thing. He liked the décor of his room—the burnished old furniture, a handsome mahogany armoire, and the striped sheets and patterns of his curtains. He avoided cheap hotels or surroundings where there was nothing for his mind to latch on to.

Back in his room, he felt a sudden edginess and decided against the nap. The vision of the young mother and her children had unsettled him. It wasn't the imminent danger that bothered him but a glimpse of her face in that frozen moment that irritated something in his brain. As he replayed the film of her crossing, he freeze-framed her terrified expression along with an additional detail: her breasts in motion. The eroticism was out of place, he knew. As he so often did in busy streets around the world, he indulged a secret and harmless pleasure in male voyeurism: watching women's chests bounce and disturb their fronts as they passed him in the street.

He mentally stripped the mother in the middle of the street, letting his razor-sharp memory fill in the background and foreground; he added sound effects, until his mind had recomposed her exactly right, with one breast higher than the other in the momentum of her backward-thrusting torso. He held the scene for a long moment and lingered over the face and breasts. He wondered whether her areolae were dark or light, how prominent the nipples, and that led him to speculate about her pubis.

He called Joey S. in New York. Silva said the match was canceled because his opponent had called off as a result of a sudden relapse of his thyroid cancer. He told David to spend an extra day in town, take the Alcatraz tour, and come home. He promised he'd have something for him soon in New Orleans. David said he'd catch a later flight back to Dearborn and be in Manhattan later that week, maybe Wednesday.

Joey said, "Whatever," and told him about his latest scheme, which was to bet on professional golf while he was watching it, by placing online bets seconds after a putt or birdie was made.

"Small potatoes," Joey laughed, but he was racking up a nice amount of change and enjoying himself. Although David had met Silva at a boxing match in Mexican Town, Joey didn't like sports much and didn't participate in any. He knew that golf tournaments were taped, however, and the hushed voices of the announcers while someone was lining up a tricky shot were faked. He wondered how you could cheat in the way that Joey described. He suspected he was Joey's only real source of income because he always answered his cell on the first or second ring. Joey said if he ever needed three rings to answer David should dial 911 for him, but the fact is he was overweight and red-faced most of the time.

Besides the scant information Joey gave him on the matches, David didn't know how much was truth or fiction. He'd been a union big shot at Ford once, but had fought someone with a hammer, was paid off, and subsequently took his buy-out money straight into

Michigan boxing at the time when the Kronk gym was flooded with champions and contenders. David happened to be back in Dearborn at the time and saw a flyer announcing a boxing show in Mexican Town. David had never been to the fights. After the eighth bout, David was enraptured by the spectacle of two skilled men trying to kill each other in that squared circle of light. A man came over to him and introduced himself as "the Priest." He took David around and introduced him to several fighters. David shook hands with "Sugar" Ray Leonard and James "Lights Out" Toney and remembered how soft his hands were despite the calloused knuckles. The Priest laughed when David told him his reaction and said those were a fighter's "diamond points." The Priest seemed to enjoy escorting David around and told him how the fight game worked. He pointed out a lawyer in the crowd who had lost a ton of money by supporting fighters who wouldn't fight. "I love lawyers," the Priest said. "You can screw them out of money faster than rats can fuck." The Priest called him a week later and introduced himself as Joe Silva.

The neighborhood where he lived with his foster parents was now an Arab enclave with ethnic restaurants, newspapers, and mosques. David didn't know anyone left from the time he had lived there. The brownstones were still there and the maple trees lining the street looked the same in the fall, but the surrounding neighborhoods had flipped long ago and were now all black, showing the ravages of poverty and neglect like open sores; many abandoned or boarded-up houses dotted both sides off the street. Joey always mocked these "sentimental journeys," and David would flush with an embarrassed grin. He didn't know why he kept returning. New York was home, if any city could be called such. His birth name was Schmeissen. His adopted parents had changed it to Boyle. A month before he turned thirteen, he wondered if he should bring up the subject of his Bar Mitzvah over dinner, but decided against it because his new parents were not religious people, despite what they had told the agency in his presence about preserving David's Jewish heritage.

Freed of the anxiety he always felt before a match, he found himself restless and unable to stay put inside his room. Going downstairs in the elevator, he could not decide between a long taxi ride about the city or a stroll down to Market Street where the sex clubs advertised their wares in a glitzy miasma of neon. The light was already turning that golden color most people in the North associate with autumn.

Another man with a white-trimmed beard had come on duty, beamed a kindly smile at David and gestured toward a waiting taxi. David turned left, however, and began walking, unsure why he had shunned the offer of a ride. At this time of day, there was something faintly embarrassing in a grenadier's costume which didn't strike him as odd in the morning. Now, just before the city changed its expression for the coming of night and exchanged its office workers for a different set of people seeking the fancier restaurants and bars, he felt again out of place. He had no deals to make, there were no sexual liaisons on his agenda. The warm air had gathered in its city smells of fried food and car exhaust, making him heady. He wished he had taken the costumed smiley man's offer of a taxi.

He was waiting for the light to change when he became aware of her, standing near him in the small crowd at the corner. Then she was suddenly beside him with her children clutching at her hands and legs, all in preparation to cross the intersection. David's pulse rarely rose, even in the heat of intense combat when he knew, and his opponent knew, that his victory was inevitable. His heart rippled with a strange blood rhythm like a ballroom couple bursting out of a saraband into a frenetic tango. His face burned when she accidentally brushed his side. He shivered and felt heat rising to his face. He felt at once edgy and excited. When they crossed en masse, he lingered back to watch her move ahead with her children.

He wondered if she'd walked the streets all day and to what purpose. She must be exhausted. As if she were aware of him, too, had in fact been reading his mind, she suddenly turned and looked him in the face. He almost staggered into a woman carrying several heavy packages. The woman clicked her tongue in dismay. But the mother wasn't looking at him at all, he realized at once; she was looking past him or through him. He took advantage of the moment to stare at her. Her handsome face was etched with worry lines and her eyes were squinting into the glare. She looked tired.

The children were listless, standing around, unlike before. But their willingness to be herded by their mother was offset by a stupefied calm that made them reluctant to budge and made her task all the harder. David would soon be past her, and his heart began thumping louder as he approached. She approached one well-dressed man in a suit with her hand out, palm up, and David realized with a shock that she was begging. The man made a brusque gesture with his own hand and picked up his pace to move past her.

David knew in the instant before she did it that she would turn to the next stranger, him, and make the same appeal. But he was wrong. She flicked her eyes to his and cut them to a group of three women chattering amiably just behind him walking closer to the curb. She was about to dash for them when David reached out his hand and caught her firmly by the upper arm.

"Wait," he said. "Please."

He began fumbling in his wallet. His tongue was thick. She stood there a foot from him, eyes downcast, shrunken a bit, enjoying the respite from her public humiliation. David was caressed by her unabashed femininity, her scent and her warmth. Her breath was minty.

He struggled to open his wallet and when he did, he realized he had no money in it. After his shower, he had forgotten to take some bills from his money pouch. It was sitting back in his room safe.

"I left my money in my room," he said. "I'm sorry, I—"

She was gone like smoke. She regrouped her children and moved off down the street. David stood rooted to the sidewalk and watched her recede into the swarms of late-afternoon shoppers entering and leaving stores. He felt as if he had been struck across the cheek with a whip.

He ran back to his hotel, oblivious to everything but the black mood descending over him. An older couple in the elevator moved abruptly to the rear.

Inside his room, he stooped over the tiny safe in the closet and cursed as he overshot the last number. Twirling again, he missed the three-number sequence and the tumbler refused to drop the bolt.

He tried again and a fourth time and still failed to open the safe. He kicked the safe and molten pain shot up his leg. A litany of filthy words he had never used in his life poured from him. These were, in fact, the same words generally hissed at him by an exasperated opponent he had defeated in mere minutes and stripped of forty thousand dollars. In those situations, David's demeanor never changed, and his calm never betrayed him; he didn't flinch because he wasn't a coward. On that battlefield, he could afford to be generous to his enemy.

Here, now, in his room, his rage blackened and he threw a punch at the safe. "Open, you piece of shit!" he cried. This time the pain was hideous. His rage spent, he fell on the bed weeping and holding his hand. His knuckles were puffed and red, but his blow had been glancing or he would have shattered the metacarpal bones. He lay there gritting his teeth and moaning in a tangle of bed sheets, his undamaged fingers clutching the bedding. His phone rang but he ignored it. He jerked his head up and listened but could hear no noises from the hallway. He felt exhausted and ruined. He had once played a twenty-four hour exhibition as a boy. The *New York Post* even did an article on him, and a photographer covering the event took his photo and wrote down his name with the words *David Boyle, chess prodigy* as caption.

David slept until four in the morning. He woke with a headache and a parched mouth. His clothes were still on and his shoes pinched his feet. He felt nauseated and ashamed, but even more so, he was baffled by the abrupt descent into rage and wondered why his lethargy had prevented him from moving.

He got off the bed and double-clutched like an old man waking up in the middle of the night. He bent over the safe and twirled the three numbers effortlessly and the door popped open. He took out his money belt; by now, he could guess the amount based on the feel of it in his hands.

He dressed and went downstairs, past the front desk. The same woman who had made change for him looked up and then back to her computer screen. Still logy, he almost stumbled down the steps. Fortunately, there was no man in ridiculous garb to greet him. The traffic was mostly made up of taxis and limousines. The streets were almost empty. A woman jogged past in a yellow-and-black spandex outfit. He watched her thigh muscles bunch beneath the shiny material; her white running shoes made a slapand-whisper against the pavement. Her tight firm bottom barely jiggled. David remembered an ancient biology teacher back in Dearborn who had said that anything in nature that's yellow and black will sting you, bite you, or try to eat you.

David smelled his rancid breath. A breeze full of pungent smells made his skin prickle with gooseflesh. Bile churned in his stomach, threatening to scorch its way up his esophagus. He began walking left almost by instinct. His swollen hand throbbed. He ached to stand on the spot where she had stood before him, her children in a loose orbit around them both.

He was afraid the episode from his youth was returning full-blown to claim his sanity for good. He would tip over the edge like that scruffy youth on the trolley yesterday, gibbering nonsense, wetting himself.

He returned to his room and stayed there. He took three Lorazepam, which knocked him out. When he awoke with a sharp hunger, he ordered a sandwich named for a famous comedian with a prominent overbite, once a guest apparently, whose name he didn't recognize. David's ignorance of celebrities was profound. He used to stun Silva by professing not to know who Oprah Winfrey or Angelina Jolie were, other celebrities like that. He ordered another. He ate the same sourdough sandwich with Hollandaise dressing for the next several meals, until he couldn't tolerate another one and switched to bacon and eggs.

He placed the *Do Not Disturb* sign on the latch. He stayed up watching television nonstop until, between three and four in the morning, management slid a bill under his door. He waited for it, revulsed, a familiar albino nocturnal insect making its entrance each night on cue. Until he saw it, he couldn't get to sleep. He ignored the phone. He was afraid.

It must have been a Sunday, because he heard church bells in the distance. He stopped pacing and drew back the curtains. He blinked at the intrusion of the light. He saw tourists and traffic—then something familiar coming from the opposite side of the street toward the Drake. His heart bumped. He felt her before he recognized her, a life force with a gravitational pull that jerked his entire body. She controlled the serotonin levels in his brain just by walking down the street with her pack of children, all tiny reproductions of herself.

He began to panic. He had taken his last pill days ago. He needed a shower and a shave. When he was sixteen, his adoptive father had once pointed at him abruptly during dessert and called him a Neanderthal. David brushed his palm along the three-days' growth on his face. No, he could not risk it. He rummaged through a pile of dirty clothing; he had pondered for three days whether he should call down for laundry service. Deciding against it, he had kicked his dirty clothes into a corner of the small bathroom. He threw on some pants and a shirt, found his loafers in different corners of the room. He did not curse and he did not let his thoughts scatter. *The money pouch, the money pouch*—where did he put it? He knew he smelled ripe. He fled through the lobby and dashed past the white-bearded beefeater, taking in his open-mouthed reaction. She was gone.

He screamed at the man, "Where's that woman with the kids!" The man stuttered something back at him and pointed around the corner.

David ran in that direction, and as he made the corner, he saw the older girl, trailing the rest, as she turned into an alley. A sob or a laugh burst out of his chest and he dog-trotted happily toward them. He had never sung since elementary school, never even in the shower, but he almost did then. He wondered what strange notes would have come out of his mouth.

When he approached them, he saw the panic in the young woman's face. A mother sensing danger for her young, no doubt. He saw the two bigger children slip behind her legs for protection, while the youngest crouched, half-hidden, behind a big square of cardboard propped against the side of the Drake's back wall.

He could have wept at the thought of a mother and her children hiding in a dark and filthy alley while he was a stone's throw away in his comfortable room, eating ridiculous sandwiches named for buck-toothed comedians. He did something he had never done with any child: he cooed reassuringly. He knew his appearance would alarm her, so he approached carefully and let soothing words tumble out of his mouth.

"W-what do you want?" she asked him. Her voice was girlishly high.

"I want to give you something," he said. "That's all. I want to help."

"Why?" Her face was smeared with alley grit and her clothes didn't look fresh anymore. The children whimpered and called out for their "Mommy."

He held out his money pack. "Look. For you," he said. "For the children. To get—to get something, you know, to eat . . ."

Her eyes were red-rimmed. The exhaustion of this small confrontation was enough to cause her to wobble. David rushed to her and caught her in his arms and they both went down to the ground in a heap. Before he knew what he was doing, he kissed her dirty face, and smoothed the hair over her brow.

How he did it, he didn't know, but he would laugh with pride in the retelling of it later on—both of them would. When she came to, he lifted her to her feet and half-carried her back to the hotel with his arm wrapped around her waist. The children, amiable ducklings who sensed the strange man was not going to hurt their mother, followed in their wake.

The old beefeater's expression elicited a yawp of joy from David and he had to fight an urge toward hysterical laughter at the expressions of the guests and staff in the lobby. The people in front of the elevator stood back all at once, as if David had commandeered it for his family with a wave of his fluttering money pouch.

Inside his room, he helped her over to a padded armchair. He asked the children if they would like to sit on the bed and he gave the bigger girl the remote. She was a carbon copy of her mother, with tiny blue veins showing through translucent skin. She took the remote and immediately scanned to a show that caused the boy to erupt in a yell of glee and then look sheepishly at David. David smiled at him.

The phone rang and he picked it up. Someone identifying

herself with a triple-word title was enquiring about his "guests" in a voice that was neither friendly nor rude.

"Mind your own business," David fumed, careful not to let the children sense his anger. "I'll pay for them. Don't call this room again."

David returned to the young mother, whose eyes were closed. He knew she was awake and listening to his every word. He asked her name and told her his. During the next hour Emma told him how she and the children had come to be abandoned. Children's Services was on her trail, she said wearily, and so she was forced to keep moving. Her husband was long gone, she said; he had abandoned her in a rage six weeks ago, after she told him she was pregnant again.

"I'm here," he said, slightly aware how false this must sound. "I'll do—I'll do anything for you."

When she asked to use the shower for herself and the children, David nodded, barely able to contain his ebullience. "I'll be outside," he told her. "I'll go for a walk." He checked his watch. "Will a couple hours do?"

She smiled kindly at him. She had put her sensuality in abeyance somewhere, but David felt it surge forth and wrap itself around him in an effluvia that was almost narcotic. They were all well fed by then, and the children lay asleep in different places on the bed. Silver trays were stacked outside the door, many still laden with untouched food. She had laughed when she saw what the three waiters were rolling into the room on trolley carts.

David went down to the lobby and paid for two rooms, although he didn't want them to leave his room. He paid for an extra week. He used the card key for his second room to shower, and because the Drake didn't provide amenities, he had to take a taxi to find a pharmacy. The thought of returning to the room and disturbing her after he said he would be gone for two hours was unthinkable. He bought what he needed at a drug store on Van Ness and tipped the driver fifty dollars. He was giddy with happiness.

When he was shaved, and noted that a full extra fifteen minutes had passed, he walked down the hallway to their room. He suddenly panicked at the thought she might have had second thoughts and left him. When she opened the door to his room, refreshed from her own shower, her dark blonde hair hanging in caramel strings along the side of her lovely face, David's tormented mind finally felt easy.

They talked nonstop for hours. David listened to her as if all power and mystery were being translated through her tale of grief and abandonment. David wanted to pledge his all to her but restrained himself for fear of frightening her with this bizarre and quixotic devotion to her being. Before he left for his second room, he pushed some money to her in banded wads of bills.

She took it in her hands and began weeping. She called him her "angel." They embraced for the first time at the door and he kissed her on the forehead. The children, awake and watching from the bed, shrieked with laughter.

Back in his other room, he called Joey S. For the first time ever, he felt he controlled the conversation. He found Silva's hysterics drolly amusing and provoked him into a screaming frenzy with his sardonic comments on his famous Portuguese temper. Before Silva slammed the phone on him, he called him a "fucked-up Jewish mutt." David felt light and free, as if he had removed all unwanted baggage from his life.

Something clicked in David's brain as soon as he hung up: the name of the residence in New Orleans where the next match was proposed: Belle-Garde or Belle-Grande—something Joey had let slip in their conversation before he left town. Silva was always careful to keep every detail of the contests between David and his opponents until the last minute; it was his way of ensuring David's servitude and justifying his bigger percentage.

He formulated a plan as he lay in bed. Emma and the children would fly with him to New Orleans. David would set up the match, his last. He had enough money to start a new life with her, and he knew it was important to get her out of the city where, if she were found by authorities, her children would be placed in foster homes. He knew he had close to a quarter-million dollars invested. It was more than enough. Joey S. wasn't going to see a nickel of the money he had provided for the San Francisco trip, either. David would need it all to organize their flight and, besides, he considered it mere recompense for the short money over the years. Persuading her to leave with him was going to be the most important thing he had ever done in his life. The alternative, to lose her now, was unthinkable, a black vortex opening at his feet.

He bought them all clothes and gifts. He and the children sang songs and laughed while they sat around the television set in the evenings. Once, he turned and caught Emma glancing at him, and he saw real fondness in her eyes.

The next day Silva called David's cell from a bar in Brooklyn, but he hung up as soon as Joey launched into a new tirade of threats and pleas. David made immediate plans to leave the city. Tomorrow he would ask Emma to go with him.

The hotel staff was glad to see them leave. He left a pair of fifty-dollar bills on the polished dressers beside the bed of each room.

* * *

In contrast to the brisk sunshine of San Francisco, New Orleans was humid and rank. Their clothes stuck to them as they took a taxi down Interstate 10 into the city. For the first time since he had left Dearborn at nineteen, he felt a dread of motels. He told Emma they would rent a house as soon as he had his bearings. The taxi took them to a Ramada at the edge of the Vieux Carré, where the smells were, if anything, ranker and the humidity close to unbearable. The girls, Sarah and Ally, quarreled and slapped each other until they both started to wail their misery.

Emma was morose and silent all the way to the motel, but once inside their rooms, she quickly bathed and washed the children. David left her to shower and called her from his adjacent room. After a few minutes' desultory conversation, they hung up. She didn't invite him over. He barely slept that night. In the morning over breakfast, things improved and moods were restored. It had been an exhausting flight, Emma said, and David understood that, in her own way, she was apologizing for spurning his company last night. She was almost as beautiful as his first impression of her, but something was still not quite right with her beyond the exhaustion and the maternal claims. There was a hollowed sadness behind her eyes. He knew it would take time for her to adjust. He scoured the *Times Picayune* for houses and found a tumbledown colonial on a street called Bos Darc. David looked it up on his map, and noted how close to the bayou it was situated. Desperate to get them into a house and seeing nothing better on offer, he called the Sun Chance Real Estate agency and agreed to meet a woman named Chima Benson that same afternoon.

It turned out to be a roomy, lopsided house where nothing was plumb or square, but it was more than large enough for their needs. They moved in two days later with all their possessions packed into a Mazda Protégé David had picked up cheap from the police impound lot. Sans furniture, but with electricity and gas and water turned on, they wandered about their new home. David contacted his New York bank for a wire transfer that morning to make the sale. He was determined to give Emma and the children their own house.

In three weeks they were settled in and Emma had begun enquiries about schooling for the two older ones. She and David had found an OB/GYN, recommended to them by the neighbors, the Johnsons. Curtis Johnson was a shrimper who owned a boat he moored to a jetty in the bayou. David felt all the tension of San Francisco to be far behind him. He considered his life with Emma a miracle. She didn't love him yet, he knew, but he would remedy that with time.

Once, while they were strolling the French Quarter and the children munched croissants, David saw a strange figure in nineteenth-century dress turning a corner just ahead of them. The man was strolling along and smiling vacantly to himself. David stood rooted to the spot, until Emma tugged at his arm and asked him what the matter was. David wondered whether he had actually seen him. One saw so many strange people and oddities in this city and heard so many strange tongues that it hardly seemed like America at all.

Emma's doctor required money up front for her prenatal care despite the fact that she was two-thirds of the way in her pregnancy, or *enceinte*, a word David had never heard before. David never talked money with Emma, but he knew that he needed to restore his shrinking income soon. The San Francisco money was long gone by then, and coupled with the penalties on early withdrawal to liquidate for the purchase of the big house, David began to worry about the future. Curtis slyly prodded out of him what he had paid and whistled. He said something in Cajun David didn't understand, but it was obvious Curtis thought he had been swindled badly. David never thought of negotiating the price. For one thing, he wasn't a mercenary like Silva. For another, the stigma of a Jew haggling over pennies and nickels was odious, an inherited racial memory; growing up in Michigan, he had heard friends unthinkingly use expressions like "happy as a Jew in a junkyard."

The match loomed more and more in his mind as each day passed. He didn't want more for himself, but he would never let Emma suffer again as she had. The thought of that sickened him. Besides, he was worried about her lately. The sadness in her face never left, and he caught her at times looking off into the distance. They had become lovers weeks ago. David desired her more and more, but she seemed less eager as the days and weeks passed.

Six weeks into their new life in Louisiana, she came home from shopping and David smelled beer on her breath. Her eyes were unnaturally bright and the pupils dilated. She told him she wanted to have sex right then. He followed her into the bedroom while she stripped as she walked—David anxious lest the children awaken from their naps. When she turned and held out her arms, he saw that her breasts were full and tipped dark with blood and her mons beneath her big stomach was full and bushy. The nub of her clitoris projected from the crease between her legs. When she stripped off her panties, the curly wedge of her hair retained a swirl and the sight of it jutting out like a dark chestnut flame excited him. Before he entered her, she thrust herself up from the bed and said, "I want you to try this for me."

She reached under the bed and rummaged through her discarded clothing. David's erection bobbed against the back of her thigh.

She came up with a folded envelope and tapped a white powdery crystal into her palm and snorted it in to her nostrils. "Now you," she said and held out her palm. Without hesitation, David leaned his face into it, smelled the lavender scent of her wrist, and inhaled the powder. He thought a volcano had gone off behind his brain. Then a hot, downward-rushing feeling flushed his entire body, plus a sensation he couldn't describe—at least not while it was happening. She took another snort and they began to make love.

David had never experienced anything like it. It made all their previous lovemaking seem like a pair of fumbling junior-high kids experimenting on a first date. David lost track of time, lost track of himself entering her. His cock was a piston that obeyed their every whim and desire. He took her from the front and behind. When she sunk her mouth down on him, he could not believe that he was still erect even as she brought him to another climax. A silver thread of his ejaculate hung from a corner of her mouth. Her lips were puffy and bruised from the passionate kissing and the hours of sex. The room had turned musky.

They used meth every time afterward. David was worried, but she said they could control it. Even if he balked, she would use it and the dose was always a little more each time. He didn't ask where she got it. When she needed money, he gave it to her. David knew she wasn't a novice at this and the thought made him queasy in his belly. He wondered if she had him told the whole truth about the abusive husband back in San Francisco.

A month passed, the unbearable spring heat had turned to a furnace-like temperature and the ancient air conditioner rattled and died. They baked in the heat, too hot for television or eating much of anything. She was relentless in sex despite being in the late stages of pregnancy and having horrible bouts of morning sickness. Thinking of the baby, David stopped taking drugs but his example did nothing to persuade her. He worried about the kids going hungry while she slept in all morning recovering from a high. Whenever he was out of the house, he feared she might be poisoning the unborn infant's blood with the toxic residue of her bloodstream.

The money was dissolving like sugar in water. Her habit followed its own parabola. David seemed oddly resistant to its addictive powers, but he craved it during sex. When she was a day without it, her mood turned black and she hollered at David and the children about anything that went wrong—the cracks in the ceiling, the heat and humidity outside, the stench from the distant bayou. It was all a personal affront to her. Yet he never felt his love slip or his desire for her diminish by a fraction.

He asked Curtis one morning in a roundabout way what he thought he might do if worse came to worse.

"She, like, fixen to be a dope fiend or what?" Curtis responded in his thick patois.

David, horrified he had given him that impression, protested mightily.

"Crystal, man, it's bad shit. She, like, scratching her face and all?"

David recalled a few blisters on her chin that had scabbed over and which she covered with makeup. She was brushing her teeth five and six times a day but David saw her looking in the mirror that morning, checking for caries.

"Shee-yit, daddy-o, them crank bugs is a bad sign. Ya'll got to do something. She can't be takin' no drugs expectin' a baby and all."

"I don't know what to do," David said.

"Ya'll better have the Bank of New Orleans to pay for her habit then."

Curtis spat a gob of tobacco. He swept a hand over his head and removed the greasy ball cap with the other, something David had seen him do many times. His dark curls were sleek as a ferret's.

Silva had lied or deceived him about the estate and the man he was to play in New Orleans. There was no Belle-Garde or Belle-Grande in the city directory and an online search at the public library came up zilch. He called every estate owner he'd found and came down to his last four choices. One across the river, one in Metaire, one near Algiers, and one out near Lake Pontchartrain.

The estate owned by a man named Ouellette was called Beaubien and existed well beyond the Mississippi, due south of Live Oak Manor and Waggaman Pond.

"Beaubien ain't on any map," drawled Ouellette, "because the snobs on the board the Historical Preservation Society deemed it bad juju. You see, it's an old slave plantation where hundreds of men, women, and children died violently. Hanged most 'em, whipped some of 'em to death, tortured a few dozen to boot. The master, who I'm not ashamed to say is my great-great-grandaddy, was apparently afflicted with some form of madness. He found himself a crew of Irish overseers, all hired on the basis of their malevolence or sexual degeneracy toward slaves."

David had reached him when he was down to the last quarter in his pocket change. A slender young woman at the research desk had told him of Beaubien's dismal history among plantations.

"They's still a whole buncha them runnin' around New Orleans, living in the swamps and bayous on the coast," she said. "All related by blood through their overseers. People in New Orleans started calling them high–yallers because even their eyes were the color of tea. None of 'em like to admit they carryin' Irish blood, naturally. Cain't say as I blame 'em."

Ouellette intoned more details, cultivating a banality alongside menace that he seemed to enjoy. "That's all very interesting, Mister Ouellette, but what about our match?"

"That uncouth fellow in the Bronx or Brooklyn, was it? He said you was off the reservation—words to that effect, and so I was to inform him if you called me."

"Is that what you want to do?"

"I don't take orders from dagos or white trash, Mister Boyle. Ya'll weren't offended perhaps by my little historical synopsis a moment ago?"

"I'm not Irish or Italian or Portuguese," David said.

"Tomorrow night. I serve dinner at eight. You ever had ortolans, Mister Boyle?"

"I'll be there at eight o'clock."

Ouellette's manservant draped them both in bone-white sheets. David felt idiotic but submitted without demur. Ouellette's conversation and diction ranged from backwoods illiterate to cosmopolitan and segued from subject to subject in a lazy circular fashion, but he always seemed to return to the starting point. He spoke three languages, he said, and was teaching himself langue d'oïl, the dialect of French spoken in northern France in the Middle Ages.

"I have a smattering acquaintanceship, you might say, with

langue d'oc," he added, as he smoothed the sheets in his lap and looked at David through what appeared to be a monk's tapered cowl. "That was spoken in the South and would evolve into Provençal, Mister Boyle. May I call you David?"

The ortolans were served in butter with feet intact. Lightly braised in a pan, they looked like skinned sparrows that could have been pecking for worms hours earlier.

"The sheets, of course, keep the gore and blood from spattering about. Now the trick, David, is to eat them whole, guts and all, and pluck the feet out of your mouth. See, watch me, and I'll show you how to do it."

David watched the spectacle. Ouellette inserted the solid object delicately through the hole in his covering and it disappeared into his mouth. Seconds later he heard the feet hit the plate. Ouellette's face was obscured but he suspected he was immensely pleased enjoying himself. David noticed that his own sheets had been spattered with blood and innards from the bird.

"I've done this many times," he said blithely, "and I assure you it's very difficult to do without making something of a mess, so go ahead and don't be ashamed. Bon appétit, mon ami."

David managed to eat most of one ortolan, but it was impossible to eat it the way Ouellette himself did and he made a disgusting mess of the bird. He watched four sets of bird feet join the first pair on Ouellete's plate, each hitting with a tinny rattle. When another male servant came around to pour, David firmly refused with his hand over the glass. By then, David counted four full glasses of wine Ouellette had downed.

David declined cigars and port. He wanted to get on with the match. A proposed first match of eighty thousand. Two other rematches at fifty apiece. David had emptied his entire account. There was nothing left.

Ouellette's eyes were that smeary blue that women's magazines called sexy. His skin was fair and his white-blonde hair made him look Scandinavian. They adjourned to the den where the expensive chess board was set up. It looked old and valuable, like everything in the house including the four sets of medieval armor. The massive earthstone rubble fireplace was alight with hissing chunks of coal. One-half of the room remained chilled from the morgue-like temperature.

"White goes first," Ouellette said. "And I'm always white. House rules."

Ouellette drank more wine and talked throughout the match. David played his usual aggressive opening game but avoided obvious gambits until he knew his opponent. Ouellette lost piece after piece but never became provoked. David recognized the London system: D4 Nf6. Then Bg5. David expected him to take the knight, but instead he pulled back for an outpost. He talked and moved pieces with a bravado that made David relax.

Then he saw it—that is, he saw it five moves ahead. In his prime, at grandmaster level, he could see ten moves clearly, eleven decently, and twelve when he was at the top of his game. This was clever, Ouellete's trap, but easily avoided. By the time Ouellette was set to spring it, David had easily moved his knight out of harm's way and with his next move with his rook, he would place Ouellette's queen in mortal danger. It would be catastrophic.

Ouellette hesitated a fraction of a second when his turn came, and David took that for a tell, a sign he had recognized David's elusiveness. Still he proceeded on course, chattering about the artifacts and relics the house possessed, and David, measurably relaxed, followed him to the inevitable doom.

But it was not Ouellette's doom, and when he realized it, David gasped. That evoked a smile on Ouellette's face, though he continued nonplussed with his inane lecture about medieval chivalry. David was going to lose his first match in more than ten years; there was no sickness to blame for this one. Rather than prolong his antagonist's pleasure, he tipped over his king.

"Next game," said David. He felt his face whiten. Eighty thousand dollars gone, gone, gone.

"Not even a restroom break, David?" Ouellette toyed with him, and said that he would need one himself "to wash his hands."

"Your hands look clean enough," David said, betraying something of his anxiety and anger.

"As you know, David, the expression 'to wash one's hands' is often a euphemism for doing other things." Ouellette left the room whistling a song.

When he returned an agonizingly long twenty-six minutes later, David was in an excruciating state of distress and trying not to show how ruffled he was. His fingers felt like claws.

"My, my, champing at the bit, are we?" Ouellette said as he took his high-backed leather seat opposite him and kicked a leg casually over the armrest. In his absence, David exchanged his own comfortable chair for a simple one without the plush stuffing.

"Ah, I see you are an admirer of the Louis quatorze."

"Get on with it. White moves."

Ouellette put his finger to his lips and moved a pawn. "A soft word turneth away
wrath." He would occasionally dab at his crotch as if to shift his genitalia to a more comfortable position.

David countered with his own pawn. He was trying to drown out the buzzing in his ears.

"You are Jewish, are you not? I reckon New Orleans must be something of a culture shock to you."

"You reckoned wrongly."

"That so? Ya'll have family?" He put a hillbilly twang into it—mocking him.

"A wife, three children. We're expecting our fourth."

"A family man," Ouellette said, and winked so salaciously with his hand resting over his bulge that David wanted to reach across the board and choke him.

He lost the second game in less time. The third game was destined to be a drawn-out pitched battle. Around one in the morning, Ouellette suggested they draw cards to decide the winner. David shrugged, all his resources depleted by the steady nattering of the man and the loss of his wealth.

"You're my guest, you may cut," Ouellette said.

"Jack of hearts," Ouellette said as David flipped over his card. "Oh thou knavish boy—"

Ouellette slurred and chittered nonsense as he shuffled and reshuffled the deck.

"Cut for me," he told David. David flipped over the next card in the deck.

"A queen of spades to me. So sorry, Mister Boyle. You can leave the check with my man on your way out."

David wrote and signed the check. Byron appeared from a vestibule bordered in stained glass and held a brindle Pressa canaris on a short leash. David handed him the check while the dog's massive snout slavered onto his shoe. He noticed his hand was shaking.

Ouellette appeared suddenly at the door, still talking.

"Ya'll take care of your family," he said. "Hurricane's coming. I can smell it."

David brushed past him. "You smell your own shit."

On the ride back to Bos Darc, David saw a serpentine glitter of lights spoking out from the city and stretching in all directions from as far south as Tchoupitoulas Street by the river. It looked as if all Jefferson Parish was on the move.

The house was dark. She had not left a light on for him. He checked on the two girls in their room and Michael in his. Emma lay asleep, a light beading of sweat stippling her white forehead. He knew if he were to brush the damp hair out of her eyes he would see her black pupils. She was high all the time. She lied to him and to the doctor but the last amniocentesis test said the baby was addicted and would have to be born Caesarean.

David's depression over that and now the loss of all his money exhausted the last store of his energy. He fell into bed beside her and slept until late afternoon. When he awoke, she was gone. The kids were not in their beds. He walked outside into the miasma of heat and noticed Curtis packing up his black Chevy pickup.

"Ain't you leavin'?" Curtis shouted to him.

"Why would I leave?" David saw that the entire Johnson family, like carpenter ants, were carrying goods from their house in a row and dumping the items at Curtis' feet. He secured elastic straps to the underside of the truck bed and climbed the mound of bric-a-brac and furniture piled high above the bed.

"Boy, they's a hurricane coming! It's bearing down on us from the open sea."

David's sleep fog had not yet lifted. That explained the caravansary of automobiles fleeing in one direction which he had seen last night.

"You must be the only person in No'rleans ain't runnin' for high ground."

"Have you seen Emma?"

"This mawnin'. She had the younguns with her. Some guy in a car, he swoop by and they all climb in . . . 'bout seven o'clock this was."

David didn't know what that meant.

Curtis jumped off the pile of furniture and walked over to him shaking his head.

"Look, man, I tole you when ya'll moved to Bos Darc that the levee holding back the water isn't worth piss on cotton if we was to get a direct hit. Got-damn city's eight feet below sea level as it is. Never mind it's a category four hurricane looking to be a five by the time it hits land. Fact is, a tidal surge might could bring 'bout twenty-five, thirty feet a water straight through here—"

David looked up at the sky and saw a mountain of inky clouds over the sea stretching from one end of the horizon to the other. The air was damp, saturated with moisture, and the light over the gulf was fast changing to pewter.

"—winds off a five can produce tornadoes, man. You got to get out or you and them kids and that woman, ya'll gonna drown like sewer rats."

"Curtis, did you see who was driving the car?"

Curtis stared at him, shook his head sadly, and walked back to his truck; he began tying off a rope to the underside of the chassis.

David went into the house for his car keys and raced to the Mazda. He ran through the gears until the little car made a wheezing sound. He tore around corners and nearly fishtailed into cars with U-Hauls. He bolted through stop signs. He didn't dare think she had gone, met someone, or maybe had called her pusher and talked him into picking her and the kids up. Tears and sweat made his vision blur. The city was almost empty. He raced from one end of the Quarter to the other. He looked for cops but didn't see any. He stopped people scurrying past him: "Have you seen a woman and three little kids—"

He sat on a curb in utter despair. He thought of suicide but banished the thought. He heard four lissome trumpet notes from a nearby jazz bar. He wandered up and down the streets where he and Emma had walked on Sundays. He knew people were staring at him, agog and wide-eyed. He remembered this was Paul Morphy's city, that utterly deranged chess prodigy who had wandered the streets of the French Quarter, smiling at his own conceits.

A last flicker of hope stirred in him: maybe she was out looking for him. He ran back to the car, soaked in perspiration. The wind had picked up and it fluttered garbage and papers; cigarette packs and condom boxes bounced down the gutters. The light shifted to a milky gray. He floored the engine, headed home.

Curtis and his family were gone. He noticed that all the houses on Bos Darc were empty. Very few had bothered to put planking over the windows. There was no one left on the street. He felt like the last man alive on earth.

When he stumbled into the big house, shaking all over, he heard a noise from the kitchen. They were all there: Emma was cooking a gumbo at the stove and singing some popular ballad about hope and sorrow. Michael and Ally were playing chess at the table in the nook and arguing over who had won the last game. Baby Sarah was coloring stick figures on the floor near her mother. Her tiny legs were crossed behind her and she was humming her own song—four bird notes, out of key.

David stumbled inside, brushing tears away, and looked over her shoulder to see her drawing and asked her, "Who are these, baby?"

She turned and flashed him her big toothy grin with its gap between the incisors. She would be a stunning beauty like Emma one day. There was a little moustache of sticky chocolate ice cream on her lip. She pointed at the largest figure, a woman in a triangle dress and loop earrings. "That's Mommy," she said. She pointed at two smaller figures and named them as brother and sister.

"Who's that one?" he asked her. There was a third small figure standing in the corner, looking away from the others, as if shunned; he was slightly taller than Michael.

"That's you, David," she said.

"Why is he sad?" David pointed to the purple wavy line of his mouth.

"He's not sad," she giggled. "He's happy. That's a smile, you silly."

"Oh, OK," David said. He felt tears forming again at the corners of his eyes. He saw Emma staring at him from the doorway with a look somewhere between a laugh and a sob. Her pupils were dilated; she had worked in a dope fix with the ice cream treat.

David didn't care. He would tell her about the money later. He would tell her he would never be cross with her about the dope. He would get a job and give her his money. He would ask her to try to love him back if she could. He would tell her everything about himself that he had bottled up for twenty-five years. An image flitted through his mind and disappeared; he would never wind up like Bobby Fischer ranting about Jewish "snakes" in the Reykjavik airport or Paul Morphy tapping along with his cane in the French Quarter.

The first fat drops of rain smacked the house. They all stopped and stared at one another. David's family listened to the wind's *a capella* soughing as it rose by decibels and curved with flats or sharps to a banshee moan, coming from far out in the bayou, way out in the gulf where the black sea was churning the waves to froth and the bruised clouds were rising miles high into the air, big dirty glaciers of swirling water vapor waiting to ravage the earth, eager to sluice forth their walls of ocean to carve out new scars on the land and the people below.

Phuket, Thailand, 2004

Christmas, Patong beach, sun, freedom, life—Raul's dream
come true. Slaving away in a steel-and-glass cage for years as a nobody, not even qualified to be a junior accountant. Just a coffee and
mail fetcher, basically, at Price Waterhouse. Dirty, gray Cleveland,
Ohio was light years away. The oil had pooled in his belly button; one
hand trailed in the aquamarine waters beside his inflatable raft. Ex-
wife, then ex-boyfriends, revenue lawyers, dreary rain and gloomier
faces—gone forever.

He had to make these years last . . .

He felt a stirring of lust for the almond-skinned Thai waiter
from last night.

Screams from the shoreline—What? Not gulls. They screech,
don't they . . .

He sees stick figures pointing at him, running, scrambling
past their bright umbrellas.

What are those idiots pointing at?

He paddles a half-turn, cranes his neck toward the rising blue
bump in the ocean.

Oh no—

Bright Sky, Blue Waters of Rio

The Present, forty nautical miles from Búzios, sundown . . .

Rio was my undoing. Beware of a thing you want, they say, because you might get it. I got it. I got it in spades. It was the guidebook in the window that started it all. If I hadn't passed that window at that precise time of day, I never would have seen it. Some secondhand, end-of-its-tether bookstore with stacks of dog-eared paperbacks by Agatha Christie and Jackie Collins scattered about. Very sad bait to lure the discerning passerby. I've seen more window sophistication in a porno shop. I know about this kind of thing, baiting hooks to lure customers, because marketing is my business. Or was.

Then I myself took the bait.

All two million six hundred thousand dollars of it. Plus change. All from three accounts in New York, Chicago, and Denver.

The Good Life was beckoning to me in that magic triad: *Rio de Janeiro*, Cidade Maravilhosa, the Marvelous City.

5 weeks earlier . . .

It took me five minutes to steal that much money, but they were the longest five minutes of my life. The money was transferred with same touch of the keyboard from which I had sent a company-wide memo about contributing to the condolence funds to buy flowers for Guy Charbonneau, who was now drooling onto his pillow, half his body petrified by a massive stroke, after twenty-nine years of screwing people over and conniving for every advantage. The money flicked past my eyes as a rapid blur of numbers into the dummy accounts I had set up that morning. Timing was all. That and the desire to commit a crime. I stared at the screen when it was done, an irreversible act. My electronic footprints were all over the deed, of course. *Transaction Completed* formed itself out pixels of light on my screen and was gone like smoke.

In the morning, instead of turning off the Shoreway, I stayed south on I-90, careful not to speed. I pulled into Cleveland-Hopkins by eight a.m. Normally, I would be in my twelfth-floor digs grinding beans for the first of seven or eight pots of coffee. *Not my office now.* Not my life either, I thought.

My heart thumped in despair and hope. Every second I spent in this silver bird as it cut through the air brought me closer to Paradise.

3 weeks later . . .

On the beach at Ipanema, I strolled past blankets where exposed flesh was basted to shades of golden brown. I heard the samba music of Rio, and now and then something American, my ears instinctively seeking out English in the babel of tongues. The native Portuguese patois, with its sibilance and the soft *sh*, reminded me of mothers crooning to fussy children. Carlos Santana reached me; was it *Maria, Maria*? Then another sound, different from those slithering guitar riffs, too loud, ramped up to offend the neighbors; thick air waves pulsated in my direction; it affected me where they say the blood runs cold.

I was lifting sand out of my rolled trousers when the thumping lyrics brought me to a halt. I was thrust backward to Tower City in downtown Cleveland, where black kids cruising the streets amped their stereos to ear-bleed decibels.

Nelly's rap booted me in the ass down to the shoreline until I finally heard nothing but wind playing over gentle surf. Urban ugliness in this pristine setting offended my sensibilities. My self-imposed exile was still causing me vivid dreams and nightsweats. Arriving jet-lagged, nerves badly frayed, I hailed the first taxi at the airport after a short but gut-wrenching interrogation at customs. Somehow, in this dizzying state, I wound up in a second-rate hotel in downtown Centro, off Rua Barata Ribiero. I stayed in the room for most of three days before hunger drove me from my shabby haven. I emerged, blinking in the hard sunlight, and made my way to the first *churrascarrias* I tracked down by smell in the effluvia-rich tropical air, the pedestrian-heavy street full of bus fumes and honking taxis. At a kiosk, my eyes cut to the headlines of the *Jornol do Brasil*, fearful I would see familiar English words trumpeting my name and crime.

Thinking of McCready's twisted, puglike scowl, I barked a laugh and picked up my pace. Life was going to be great in *Rrrrrio*. I trilled those *r*'s and smiled at brightly patterned passersby in the surging street, men as gaudily dressed as women, the women carrying baskets of produce, the little schoolgirls in their parochial uniforms and patent-leather shoes, the parade of faces passing me by, openly gawping at the stranger in their midst, cutting their eyes to me and brazenly assessing my face and clothes. The air was redolent of city smells, sweet and foul alike, sewage laced with fried foods.

Little by little, I obtained the confidence I needed to relocate to an upscale hotel in Zona Norte, the Hotel Meridien off Princesa Isabel. And that is where I found my spirits soaring on a chaise lounge on the beach, a chilled glass of vodka and fruit juice in my hand.

During my second week, I forget the day or how long I had been in Rio, I felt a shadow pass over me as I nodded under a straw beach hat. I opened my eyes to see whether a cloud had blocked the sun A young man, maybe twenty-five, was looking down at me. Because he was backlit by the sun, an odd corona of light around his tousled black hair, I could not see much of his features. He was not handsome, I could tell that much, although his teeth were perfect, his mouth opened in a smile that was obscenely wide. He had an aquiline nose, gimlet-black eyes, and when he turned his head, I could see the faint outline of a scar that began at one eyebrow and traversed the side of his face down to his neck, thicker as it serpentined downwards and disappeared into his collar.

Damio showed me Rio, not just the elegant restaurants and boutiques I could find on my own thanks to an endless supply of cruzeiros from my embezzled stash, but the Rio the guidebooks don't mention when they speak of scantily-dressed women at Carnaval and

Christ the Redeemer on Corcovado. I saw what even the *cariocas*, the local natives, knew of but didn't get to or want to see.

Damio made my descent easy. His oily charm, crude but easy grace, cosmopolitan chic and aura of connections kept people from intimidating him despite his slender physique. His Hawaiian shirt flapping open in the offshore breeze, his bony chest belied his deep, velvety voice. The day we met, he laughed so hard at my descriptions of Americans on the streets and in the shops of Cleveland that I could count his ribs. A combination of naïveté, worldly sophistication, and childlike innocence made him an attractive fellow to a man like me, alone and alienated by my crime, unprepared for the swirling sounds and colors of a people I did not know and a language I could not speak. I had prepared so hard for the crime that I had neglected the aftermath, the long days stretching out to infinity. I did not yet miss America but I disliked knowing I would die in a foreign country.

But I had crossed a line. I willed myself to change every day, to be different. To be what I had been in Cleveland made no sense. I might as well turn myself in to the American consulate. So I let Damio be my guide. At first it was all fashionable spots off Avenida Atlântica, good eateries, cafés where women with jazzy baubles dangling from their wrists and ears sipped wine, trendy bistros and nightclubs and Las Vegas-style samba showhouses, dinner theaters, trips to Botafoga and a cruise around Guanabara Bay. One serenely calm afternoon, under an opaque sky that looked about to burst into one of Rio's tropical rainstorms, we were sitting on the deck of the Sol e Mar speaking of our favorite subject: the habits and customs of Americans versus *Cariocas*.

I said, "I'd like to see something besides the surf rolling up on the beaches of Ipanema and Copacabana."

Damio responded, "So you are already bored with beautiful Rio and its lovely beaches?"

His English had the nasality of French.

"The women are beautiful," I said. "I'd like to see a different side of Rio."

"Why?" he said, half-listening while fondling the stem of his wine glass.

"No reason."

"What are your limits?" He looked me in the eye.

"No limits," I said. "Anything goes."

"In Rio," he said, "'anything goes' means something different from your country."

"Indulge me, then," I replied.

"Then it shall be done, my friend, as you command." He had the carioca's habit of snapping his fingers, hissing, and making *sshh*-ing sounds. This time he opened and closed his palm to the ground as if he were waving goodbye to the ground, as if there were no more to it than that.

That night he greeted me in the hotel lobby and we went exploring the city. A leather binoculars case dangling from his neck, he winked and asked me whether I had done as he had instructed and left my charge card and passport in the hotel. Brazilians never do anything alone. You're always surrounded by groups of people. But that is not where the danger is, Damio said. He didn't have to tell me what had been obvious since the day I deplaned: a very few citizens are fabulously wealthy; the majority are raggedly poor. The taxi driver who took me to my first hotel had warned me to stay away from the *favelas*, those shanty towns dotting the hillsides. We drove past the Hotel Nacional and a bus packed with a motley crew of chattering locals, which made him spit out the window of his cab. Later I asked Damio what he meant.

"It's bus five-five-three," Damio said. "It goes past the Nacional and Intercontinental."

"The riders are all from Vidigal," he added. Vidigal is Rio's worst slum, where an average of thirty homicides a month occur, nearly all drug-related. I recalled seeing photos of it in *Time* magazine many years before, when Pope John XXIII had visited. Now the new pope was expected and the city and its *favelas* were seething with excitement.

That night we went to the Jardim de Allah, an eerie, desolate park separating the beach of Leblon from Ipanema. The binoculars were night-vision goggles, US-military-issue, and were extraordinarily high-powered. We had gone a little ways into the park and

67

found a spot isolated from the path. Damio led me to a little grotto of stones and thick plantain with a view of a clearing. Insects whirred overhead; tiny clouds of flying ants streamed from the brush near our heads. Showy Lady's Slipper and Nodding Mandarins hung among the grassy sedge and swamp flowers. Moss dripped from the low branches of guava trees. The ground was littered with browned and dead palm fronds. Brilliant wild orchids sprouted from clumps of vegetation and overhung a broken cement retaining wall covered in graffiti and scribbled over with names.

Goza na cara

Goza na boca

"What does it say?" I asked Damio

"'Come on my face, come in my mouth,'" he intoned. "Music of the funkeiros." In the saffron light of gloaming he had metamorphosed, a drag queen.

Damio pulled a flask out of his pocket and passed it to me.

"What is it?" I asked.

"Drink," he said and handed me the flask.

Expecting the smooth, fruity cocktails I was used to from the beaches of Copacabana, I took a sip and felt my throat instantly close as the fiery liquid swept past and down my gullet. I coughed, gagged up some of the liquid, and swore. Damio laughed, his white teeth possessing a neon glow in the twilight. "You like it, eh?" He took back the flask and drank. His Adam's apple bobbed as the molten lava surged down his throat. His eyes were watery. "It's made from sugar cane," he said. "A real drink from gaucho country."

We waited an hour, passed the time in conversation, before he silenced me with his hand. I heard nothing. A few moments later we heard a noise of voices followed by footsteps ion the dry underbrush. We had both squatted low to avoid detection. Damio stood up and aimed his goggles in the direction of the sounds.

I watched his face for a long time until a smile spread across his face.

"What is it?" I asked.

"Look," he said and handed me the glasses.

It was a prostitute and her customer. She was fumbling at his belt and soon on her knees performing fellatio. I scoped the action but it was less prurient than I expected. All I saw were the sudden movements of her head bobbing in front of him and the man's face, a tightened mask, in response to what she was doing below. They finished. He put his organ back and zipped himself up, a little flash of white flesh like a tiny fish darting back into the coral. There was some haggling in rapid Portuguese over the cost and I saw him make a motion to his wallet for more cruzeiros. They left, she walking slightly in back of and to the left.

Another twenty minutes passed before the next show. This time it was a pair of couples preceded by crisscrossing beams of light from their flashlights. They were drunk and noisy, sprawled on two blankets. We passed the goggles back and forth. After an interlude, the couples exchanged mates, the women giggling in the dark, finding their new partner using the flashlights on the ground beside their blankets. One of the women had large, heavy breasts with thick nipples. The second lovemaking session was as unerotic as the first.I handed back the binoculars. "Let's go," I said. "I've seen enough."

"It gets better later on in the early hours," he said.

"This is not what I had in mind."

We took the Bondinho, open cars, to Santa Theresa. Years ago the experience might have been picturesque, the subject matter of postcards, but today the cars are squalid and seedy, filled with Rio's unwashed on their way home to the sordid catastrophes they call lives. I felt the eyes boring into me from all sides. I knew they were all wondering the same thing: *Who is this Yanque millionaire in our midst?* Although I had a wad of cruzeiros, nothing more, I was feeling like every bag-snatcher's dream. There were four tough-looking youths in the back. I didn't stare, but I glimpsed their crude tattoos, hostile faces with cigarettes dangling from lips or crooked smiles that implied an indifference that smacked of trouble. Their laughter grew more voluble as we passed one impoverished hillside community after another, entering their world. Even in a foreign tongue their language sounded brutal and their laughter obscene. Damio seemed oblivious; he chattered at me and even hummed a tune. I detected, and was grateful for, a transformation. He didn't look like the mincing caricature of that morning. He seemed all confidence and *machismo*. "It couldn't have come at a better time," I thought, because my guts were churning with an icy fear at the thought of a confrontation with this group of thugs.

Then, as if by some bizarre sleight of hand, we got off at Rua Dias de Barros, the city of Rio spread out below and glittering with lights. Instead of the ragged poverty of a slum, I found cool air, cobbled streets, and little bodegas where one could imagine Picasso meeting that wild bohemian Jarry for an absinthe.

Reading my mind, Damio said, "Artists, political activists, lots of radicals live here. That slut Isabel de Jesus used to paint here. Now the bitch's works hang in the Museu Chácarra do Ceu." Lush gardens, winding streets, old mansions redolent of antiquity, and stone stairways carved into the hillside made the place seem enchanted.

We followed a circuitous path of stairways that crisscrossed and cut to ease the long climb. Damio's youth and speed were hard to match. He skipped like a goat from one shortcut to the other. I broke a sweat despite the cool air, and my breath came in staccato bursts, but I kept him in sight and the distance between us grew less. There were fewer houses, older ones, less splendid, in this section. At last he stopped, sniffed the air, and took his bearings. I caught up with him and put a hand on his shoulder.

"Damio," I gasped. "Slow down! I can't keep up with you."

He gave me that familiar look. "Have a drink," he said. There was the flask from the night before. In the dark I could not see its design or the embedded rhinestones surrounding the engraving.

I took a small sip. "Jesus Christ, this brew doesn't get easier with practice."

"You have noticed, maybe, there is a myth of sexual equality in Rio."

I was getting used to his non sequiturs and bizarre segues. "But in reality only the Europeans have the wealth and go to the exclusive balls where the women outnumber the men by as much as ten to one. The organizers of the most coveted balls pay the women a great deal of money. But at the Samba Parade, everyone is equal. Only timidity is castigated."

Short of breath, light-headed by the powerful drink, I could say only, "By all means let us castigate timidity."

He smirked. "You have not been in Rio long enough to understand. Everything is a myth in this city. The floats turn back into pumpkins, the samba dancers go back to their cramped apartments and dreary lives. The maids return to their quarters. The affluent return to their pleasures. Men dressed as women return to male. But for one bright, shining moment, everyone is equal in Rio."

"That's why I came," I said.

"Rio is one vast illusion. Take women, for example. They are revered as in no other culture or place on this planet. That is why even straight men dress up like women. They want to be women even for just one night."

"I don't want to be one, Damio. I want to find one." I tossed the empty flask at him. "Where is this taking us?"

"There," Damio said.

He pointed at a lime-green two-storey house with a patio and a detached porte cochere. He turned away from me and headed toward it. I followed. Damio walked up to the door and tapped out a rhythmic burst of knuckle on wood.

A young mulatta opened the door. She was pretty, very feminine, and completely nude. Her thick, swept up hair and her careful mascara and eye shadow were in stark contrast to the trimmed Mohawk between her legs.

Damio said over his shoulder, "If you want, you can call her Jade."

Everything that happened was as soullessly pornographic as any X-rated film I had ever seen. She spoke no English except the filthiest words in a sibilant, accented voice that purred a tantric, hallucinatory language of its own. Damio disappeared. I never gave him a thought once I found myself embraced.

At dawn, a milky, roseate glow appeared in her bedroom window, and I thought I heard him in an outer room talking to someone with a high epicene voice. I showered and dressed while she lay asleep, her naked flesh partially covered by the duvet, her womanly derrière as exhilarating to behold in my exhausted state as it was when she had me take her with a mushy-voweled, obscene urging.

Damio was sipping *cafezinho*, the black, thickly sweet native coffee the city is addicted to. I declined it. I was sated. I wanted no food, no drink, nothing to clutter my senses.

We strolled back in silence, although I felt such a surge in my blood that, had Damio chosen to run, I could have outrun him. As we approached Rua Dias de Barras, I saw a cement wall with graffiti. "What does it say?" I asked more to break the silence than out of a real curiosity.

"They are advertising the next funk ball at Complexo da Maré," he said. He pointed at the words and translated each one: Funk Balls Every Saturday Night."What are they?"

"Kids go there to dance, do drugs, the girls wear these micro skirts without panties and they fuck each other in a sex game they call the chair dance. At midnight the DJ summons them with his music, funk music from America of the seventies, only with our samba laced with it, and they must fight. That is why the rival gangs meet. Sometimes they fight to the death and the kids get killed, so they toss their bodies into garbage tips or dump them in the ravines along the hillside."

"Why kill each other?"

"Slum kids have no choice. There is an old saying here, 'Your imagination must provide what your wallet lacks.'"

"Why don't the authorities get rid of them?"

"The cops are in with the dealers. Everybody knows this. Besides they are armed better than the police. Uzis and AK 47s, man. And they all carry guns. Besides, the drug dealers own the *favelas*—they're cities within the city. Hundreds of thousands of people in Cidade de Deos, Ratolândia. Enormous places, got computers there, beauty parlors, banks—all that wonderful shit from your country."

"People have choices," I said, and smelled the sanctimonious whiff of my own hypocrisy.

"Only one way in, one way out. There is no debate going on whether they should be here or not. They just are. Drug dealers make it easier by helping out the community. The opiate of the poor used to be soccer and samba. Now it's funk and cocaine."

"Take me to one."

He smiled and showed canines, reddish gums. "As you wish, senhor."

We boarded the Bondinho and looked over the verdant hill-sides. The clapboard shacks, with their tin roofs and slapped-up boarding, were a washed-out gray. I looked away toward the waking, now bustling, city below; out to sea hundreds of luxury ships and yachts were moored in the bay around humpbacked Corcovado and the statue of Christ where, the citizens of Rio say, birds never alight on the outstretched arms. I saw sea cormorants and gulls form a lazy gyre above the lagoon, descending to feed on a school of fish just below the surface. The diving birds would spackle the water with the silver backs of the fish that glittered like coins. There was a bluish mist of clouds on the horizon where the light was just breaking through and the last of the constellations were fading from the night sky—Cygnus, the Swan and Aquila the Eagle.

Damio sang softly to himself. Again, I marveled at the range of his voice, from the basso-profundo of our metaphysical debates to this new one, an altar boy's oratorio sweetly hitting the high notes and quavering just enough to draw you into its spell:

"A refavela revela o choque
Entre a favela-inferno e o céu."

I asked him what he had sung.

"It does not translate well," he said after a while. "'The re-favela reveals the shock between the hell-favela and heaven.'"

"There is much in your culture that is at war between the body and the spirit," I said, perhaps a little too smugly.

"The eternal duality of the human being, no? To be at war with your body and your soul."

Monday . . .

I had my first ménage à trois. The blonde girl was German, the brunette was pure Rio. They worked together as a couple. Damio sat on the gold ottoman with red piping brocade the Meridien provided. He rolled joints for all of us, kept the drinks flowing, and watched.

Tuesday . . .

I invited two couples up to my suites for a late dinner. Damio had introduced them to me and then to each other after several poolside chats at the Le Saint-Trop. The women were a dozen years younger than the men. One of the men, Roberto Cavalcante, I had seen working at one of the banks where I secreted my money in notes and bearer bonds. We had taken him sailing with us on the sloop Damio arranged with one of his many invisible contacts. Damio bribed the head chef to make us the Meridien's *feijoada*, normally reserved for Saturdays. The women, drunk on a magnum of chilled French champagne that Damio paid for with my bills, took each other's bras off while they danced. Damio sliced and chopped four lines of Rio's cheap cocaine with a playing card on the tiled glass coffee table. The girls performed while the men watched.

Wednesday . . .

Damio arranged for us to have the sloop to cruise the islands of Guanabara Bay with two women he knew from the Jockey Club. The sunset was magnificent. As it dipped below the horizon, I saw in the confluence of sea, sky, and sun a green wink of light just before it disappeared into the sea. A trompe l'oeil, but to me a sign that I had seized the moment and that it all belonged to me.

Damio gave me some kind of powder that gave me staying power with the women. We took several turns with each below decks.

Thursday . . .

I slept all day and into the night. I woke in the early hours of the morning to a tropical rainstorm blowing in off the sea. The lightning flashes created a bizarre chiaroscuro effect in my room. I struggled to rouse myself from the torpor of too much sleep, drugs, booze, and sexual exhaustion. Thunder boomed like the coming of *Dies Irae* my childhood catechism had spoken of. At the window overlooking the sea, the sheers whipped and tangled in the cold wind blowing into the room and threw the shadows into havoc. For one terrifying, heart-scalding instant, I feared my days of hedonism had caused this natural occurrence. Despite the cold air, I was sweating. The pillow was soaked with the sour effluvia of my recent debauchery.

I remained awake, teeth chattering, nauseated, drinking one cup of the strong Brazilian coffee after another until my stomach and bowels finally revolted and I raced to the toilet, unable to aim a stream of projectile yellow vomit which spattered the sink and bowl and nearly caused me to hit the tub. I lay my head against the cool floor tiles and groaned until I passed out from the sheer pressure in my head and nether region. At dawn I felt, rather than saw, the first of the sun's bars of gold lance through the pewter clouds. I struggled back to bed and slept another eight hours. I heard my cell phone ringing, ringing, ringing . . . Damio calling, no doubt. I let it ring and slept. My dreams were like those I first had on arrival in the Centro hotel where I had skulked in the shadows, fearful of exposure and arrest.

Friday . . .

The grizzled beefeater formally handed me a card with a riffled edge on the blue hotel stationery. It requested, first, in Portuguese I could not read, and then below that, in elegant but broken English, that I remove myself from the premises as soon as it was possible. There had been complaints from the other guests about the noise.

That afternoon I relocated to the Rio Sheraton in São Conrado. The taxi driver kept up an amiable chatter despite the fact he spoke little English, but the ride was soothing to my jangled nerves and oncoming paranoia. I had never been kicked out of anything in my life—that is, until I cut myself loose from society by my crime.

We drove for twenty minutes past Leblon on Avenida Niemeyer in the direction of Rio's bustling residential district, Barra da Tijuca. Vast stretches of beach where the population was sparse unfolded—nothing like Copacabana's seething tempo, where cars and pedestrians vied for the same space.

Damio greeted me at the door with a small crowd of people in their twenties and thirties, mostly women, Europeans and cariocas, clubbers from their look and many of them, armed with bottles of wine, vodka, and various Brazilian potables made from exotic fruits.

"A house-warming," he said. "I know you're feeling down about the move."

"How did you know I got kicked out?" I asked him with an edge to my voice. I was rethinking my relationship to my guide.

"This is Rio and I know everything that happens here," he

said waving the crowd into my room.

Maria and Cleice were among them, our two girls from the sloop. Maria spoke in that slow, sing-songy Portuguese from the northeast. Damio said that she had been a country girl from the Pampas, had even been a child prostitute in São Paulo until a rich tycoon had "adopted" then married her. Her rise to Jockey Club status was a Cinderella existence.

"W-wait a minute," I began—

Be careful what you wish for, they say.

The party lasted until dawn. I must have passed out from the coke and booze. I woke to the sight of couples asleep in chairs, on sofas, and on the floor. A young carioca from the *favela* whose body was so thin that his thick member protruded impossibly in front of him was being fellated next to couple who had fallen asleep in each other's arms. The room stank of sex and marijuana.

I staggered to my bedroom and saw a girl of twenty taking on three men. Her boyish hair was slicked to her head like a seal's fur. A flaccid bald man with a black mat of hair on his stomach and abdomen videotaped the action. I stared for a long time at the obscene tableau. Some scrap of self-reflection, long in abeyance, told me that now was the time for redemption. But I couldn't force myself to any kind of decision. One of the men took himself out of her gasping mouth with a plopping sound and replaced the man thrusting from behind. Like an eel, he slithered beneath her and displaced the thrusting man having vaginal sex. By some tandem communication they both penetrated her and a new rhythm of steady beats added to the cacophony of her groans.

The photographer began stroking his member and exposed a spade-shaped glans; without lowering the camera, he cupped her chin and forced himself into her open mouth. Just then I was aware of Damio beside me.

"*Tchutchca*, a pretty little bitch," he said. "Let's join them."
Saturday 8:17 p.m., in Rocinha, Rio's largest favela . . .

Another bus roared and clanked gears from the last winding hill to the entrance of a warehouse-sized structure slabbed with corrugated tin roofing. The bus discharged groups of teenagers. They wore the same outfits. The boys bare-armed and tattooed. Levis and Doc Marten boots, expensive sneakers, posturing. The girls slutty in Lycra, tank tops exposing budding cleavage, leather skirts stopping at mid-thigh, and platform shoes or spiked heels. They came by the dozens on foot and in cars. Everywhere you looked it was an army of teenagers from the slums, a few well-dressed and middle-class-looking in American ball caps and low-slung khakis, boxer shorts showing beneath belly buttons. Cigarettes and marijuana, heroin and crack cocaine—drug deals were going on frenetically in clusters of twos, threes, and sometimes six or seven at once. Security guards patrolled the perimeter and carried walkie-talkies as they moved through the crowd with Glocks in their belts or on their hips. Some inbuilt Darwinian sense of survival kept these swirling masses of teens, *galeras*, moving toward their peers and away from their enemies in a seething ribbon like grackles roosting. Damio was off arranging our entrance with a thick packet of my cruzeiros. When he told me how much the man Fernandinho wanted, I hesitated.

"Everybody wets his beak," he said. "You have to pay for organizer's permission, give the DJ something, the security guards."

"Just do it."

He went away again and came back in five minutes. I had to think about what it was I wanted, what new satori I sought, what new dish I craved like the taste for the local freijoada, once the slum-dweller's stew of leftover meat, now haute cuisine to the jaded palate. Damio's eyes were alert and his stringy muscles coiled with tension.

"Listen to me," he said. "Do everything I tell you to do without question."

When I hesitated, a fraction of a beat too long, Damio exploded in wrath. The words that shot out of his mouth first were not English, not even Portuguese but Spanish: "Eso es una coña! Que boludo! . . . véte a la mierda! Just do what I say. These babykillers will gut you with their razors and suck the pulp out of your heart. Don't fuck with them." He stamped out his Marlboro.

Inside we saw the mobs of teens divide along opposite walls. The music was already cranked to emergency levels—a mixture of pop, samba, hip-hop, rap, and salsa. "They call each other 'Germans,'" Damio said gripping my shoulder with fingers like talons; he had to scream above the. din. "The object is to kill Germans." I nodded, not comprehending, overwhelmed by the noisy assault that rattled my breastbone.

"There," he paused, screaming into my ear, "They call it 'the Corridor of Death.'" I saw a phalanx of security men with truncheons facing the two walls and separated by just a few feet in the middle of this barn. The swirling mobs of teens were like separate, angry hives, oblivious of the other side's doing the same thing as they were.

"Wait until midnight," Damio purred. "You will see the blood flow, my friend."

The walls were crusted and stained brown with dried blood. Words of anger and hate, fealty to one's gang, were scrawled onto them.

"What do they call this place?" I was clutching at his arm like a frightened child in the mall afraid of losing his mother.

"Furacao. *Tornado.*"

One of the security guards, an unshaven thug in a black polyester shirt with gold chains curled amidst chest hair, gestured to Damio and waved us to a corner. They spoke briefly and I saw more of my money change hands.

"He'll bring us chopp," he said. The local beer seemed an odd normality in this frenzied atmosphere. I saw a young man receiving fellatio while calmly talking to a boy his age. The second boy nodded but didn't speak. There were skeins of human bodies weaving in an embrace and swaying to the thudding beat of the music. The air was clotted with marijuana and tobacco smoke, perfume and cologne, a heady broth of sex. In a few more hours it would be rank, fetid, the bodies drenched in sweat and other fluids.

"Look," said Damio. He pointed toward a writhing coil of bodies. One of those pregnancy trains I had read about in *O Globo*.

It was the musical chairs of my kindergarten transmogrified into an obscene caricature. The music suddenly stopped, the girls ran to sit on the laps of the boys and squirmed into their crotches. I watched one couple caught in midcoital thrust. When she jumped up from his lap as the music resumed, a ribbon of ejaculate was released into the air.

"Look at that one," he pointed at a girl whose skirt was up to her waist as she ground her pelvis onto a youth below her. Glossy pubic hair parted to expose the lips of her vagina as it opened for the boy's shaft.

"We love a woman with a big ass," he crowed.

At our table in the corner, we were ignored because we were old men by youth's standards or because word was out that we were not to be molested. We were voyeurs of the human condition in microcosm. I saw a couple of fistfights broken up, resolved by some gang leader who chastened the malefactors with sharp slaps to the face. I saw random couplings against walls and on chairs, as banal as stable matings. Damio pointed out the straight line of dancers in a tight embrace—*trenzinho, little train*—another variation on the theme of group sex. At some point a black-haired boy of fifteen grabbed a mic near the DJ's booth and wailed out a couple songs that seemed, momentarily, to still both halves of what was more like a Roman coliseum than a dance hall. The music finally beat me senseless, stupefied me to the point of exhaustion. I could not talk and my mouth was dry.

"I have to piss," I said.

"These funkateers are dangerous. They use the stalls for ambushing Germans. Go outside."

I found my way to the exit door slowly—bottles of iced Brahma Chopp appeared unbidden at our table before I could refuse another. The groups of teenagers parted in waves as if I had a contagion. Outside, the air was fuggy and rank with jungle smells. I heard voices: security guards and their walkie-talkies. I remembered their guns and decided not to go far, so I let the lemon stream fly against the side of the building. Overhead, the constellation Hydra was illumined against a blue-black sky far from the glare of Rio's lights far below. The moon's murky haze appeared as an areola of shimmering light surrounding a wobbling disc. I heard the popping sounds of gunfire in the distance. I realized I was drunk. Drunk in a ghetto of a quarter of a million people at the other end of the world. Drunk in the midst

79

of a horde of teenagers waiting for the signal to attack one another. *More of these kids die in funk balls than in all of Palestine's Entifadas . . . girls grind their stiletto heels into the faces of their rivals to mutilate them.* Why, I wondered, did I feel serene in the midst of this vileness?

The luminescent dial of my wristwatch said ten minutes to midnight. I had an urge to masturbate but decided against it. I returned inside. Damio looked the same—bored and indolent, like a character in a Chekhov play. At midnight I saw it happen. The music switched from its pulsing samba beat with techno slithers of guitar to the theme song from *Bonanza*, the TV Western I had watched as a boy. Pa, Little Joe, Hoss, the older brother played by Pernell Roberts (Jesus, I thought, I remembered him with hair and his signature black shirt). It was surreal beyond belief. When the signal for Mortal Kombat came from the DJ, it was an all-out assault from both sides. In the middle the guards beat them back with their sticks (the penalty for hitting a guard is death, Damio told me). I saw bones broken, faces and arms slashed with knives and razors, youths knocked unconscious, eyes punched out, faces smashed with fists, heads stomped and kicked in a mayhem of violence that lasted until dawn. I saw gang members drag a victim, a German, off to their side and watched the boy disappear, flailing arms and legs, like a frog tossed into a pool of piranhas. *They'll find them dead or beaten into a coma. The girls will have their hair ripped out in hanks, and they'll be covered in feces and urine. In the morning, if they're lucky, their friends will take them to the emergency room. If they're dead—I could almost hear the snap of Damio's fingers—the garbage dump.*

I drank and watched. The scenes of carnage and revelry were a musical score with variations on mayhem's themes, this harsh urban dance, with its swirling tonalities and shifts in tone. If I had made a bargain with the devil, if Damio was my Mephistopheles, I rejoiced that it had come to this. I had no pity. I had an appetite that was being slaked with my stolen money. It was a bartering game and I was winning. I felt the skin of my past slip away in the bloodshed. I wanted to thank these youths, feeling like a sated Roman emperor, for giving me my life. These swaggering boys in Bermuda shorts, the buffed and glistening weightlifters, the slumming middle-class women and children, the girls in skintight clothes and knee-high boots, their Madonna faces rimmed with lipstick and come, feigning or savoring the lewdest, most intimate acts. These hard-partying revelers had conspired unwittingly to give me something better than Carnaval, and I was grateful. *Morituri te salve,* I wanted to shout and laughed so hard that I vomited a plume of regurgitated beer across the table.

I clutched my spasming stomach. "Take this," said Damio, handing me a joint he'd pulled out of his shirt pocket and lit.

I have no memory of getting back to the Sheraton. I have no idea how Damio managed to drag me past the black-muzzled but resplendent beefeater and his doorman accomplices at the lobby, how he managed to get me into my room or onto the bed. I must have outweighed him by fifty pounds. But there I was at dawn, disheveled, rank in my clothes, stained and spotted with the spatter of the funk ball; there was even a smear of blood across the back of my shirt. I awoke at eleven. My eyes were red-rimmed, my beard had thickened in the night, and my hangover was fierce. I spewed up the sour beer left in my stomach.

I showered, ate an enormous meal of Bahia foods from the room-service menu: xinxim de galinha, a chicken cooked with lime, dendê oil, onions, shrimp and nuts. Gulped down a full pot of black coffee. Instead of my usual dessert, I ordered a batida—a variation on the pinga-and-juice theme with a stiff measure of vodka to settle my queasy stomach. Then I called Damio on his cell phone and made plans to go boating with the same women from the Jockey Club. Their husbands were away on business.

I wanted to sail north to Búzios, an enclave of expatriates and bohemians, feel the wind on my face. Instead of the single-masted sloop *Canja* that Damio had rented for me on two other occasions, he had arranged for a twin-engined yacht, *São Luis,* to be moored at the wharf. Its big rumbling outboards made a throaty roar as we pulled away from the dockside. I had never questioned Damio's ability to get what I needed. I gave him the money, he delivered. It was an arrangement I wanted to continue for a while longer. I knew the day was coming when I would no longer need a guide. I had now the will to live on my own terms and I did not need a companion for that. I yearned secretly to end the relationship. I would be generous but I would make it clear that our paths were not to cross.

We powered past small craft anchored in the bay. The women went to change below deck. I shaded my eyes to see Cristo the Redeemer as we made our way up the coast. He was on his mountaintop, clearly visible in the noonday's piercing light. We would spend an afternoon there and in the morning I would rent a car, return to Rio, or if I felt like it, take an air taxi to São Paolo. I wanted to see the city, first alone, and then Damio would show me the scenes, the nightlife and its underbelly. It was said that child prostitution was an open wound that the government could do as little about as they could the drugs in Rio. But there was so much more to explore in Rio before staking out new territory. I felt myself growing hard as I leaned over the stern railing and watched the churning wake.

I was staring at the smooth mounds of Cleice's backside as she sunbathed nude on the yacht's forward end, where a diving-board-sized addition projected from the bow; it was bordered by a chrome rail on either side about eighteen inches high, utterly superfluous unless you planned to harpoon whales from this vantage. Cleice's tanned, rounded orbs were a voluptuary's dream. The small furrowed space between her legs, dark with its thick tangle of unshaved pubic hair, was a striking contrast to her bottle-blonde top. A carafe of Brazilian plum liqueur sat within reach of her small hands, her unusually long fingers sporting rings with large stones of various shapes and colors. Damio's nickname for her was "Hell Cat."

The engines cut out suddenly. I turned to see Damio, all white teeth and wind-blown black hair, Hawaiian shirt open to the hairy fringe at his belly and snapping in the breeze. In the glare of the sun, he was just as I had seen him that first day on the beach, standing in a halo of white light and looking at me as if from a great height, a pasha surveying one of his servants.

"Why did you cut the engines?" I hollered to the cockpit. I looked at my watch. It was just three o'clock.

"Let's swim," he said.

The water was so blue, the sky so bright.

We dropped anchor.

Damio's body broke the water off the starboard side with nothing more than a *sshh*ing sound. Cleice lifted her head lazily and stood up in a single movement. Her magnificent body stretched forward, and she abruptly leaped from the bow in a clumsy dive that must have stung, but she came up laughing and burbling water, a water sprite from a fairyland for sensualists. Damio waved to us from the water, beckoning. He laughed. He had been a champion diver at his boarding school, and I had often watched him preen on the diving board for the tanned women in their thongs at the hotel pool. They pretended to read their trashy books or hide behind shades, but he knew they were conscious of his every flex and move on the high board. I heard the sound of another body hitting water and decided, "What the hell, might as well jump too."

I watched Damio break the surface like a seal and tread the crystalline water, lazily moving his arms to and fro, his shape a blurred outline beneath the surface. I dove aft of the boat and swam lazily toward him. Just as I reached him, he twisted around and gave me a look of terror as I had never seen on his face; his tanned face was blanched, leeched of blood. Then he yelled something unintelligible, a throated roar like a wounded animal and swam furiously away from me, punching the water in a caricature of his usual grace. I treaded a few feet aft of the motor and watched him circle the yacht— stopping here and there, then beating the water in that ungainly way with his right leg kicking upward to propel him faster. The look on his face was pained and frozen in a twisted grimace.

"What is the matter with you?" I asked.

"The ladder," he whispered. Then he moaned again, a low baying sound like a small dog.

Jesus Christ, the ladder.

Neither of us had thought to drop the folded-up ladder before we leaped into the water. No one needed to tell me that this yacht could not physically be boarded by someone in the water. It was impossible. I squeezed my eyes shut. There was no aluminum anchor affixed to the aft end to let someone climb back up.

The girls were up by the bow laughing and splashing. They didn't know yet.

I looked into Damio's face.

"We're really fucked now, man," he said. He started laughing insanely.

Ten hours later . . .

No one is coming. The sea lanes are many miles away. I have been conserving my strength as best I can, but my arms ache with pain that has magnified itself to a level I am unable to describe.

Maria had sunk beneath the water after treading for barely two hours. I watched her pouty little girl's face disappear beneath the water, a look of puzzled surprise on it as if life had done the final, unforgivable thing to her. But she never uttered a sound. Cleice, true to her nickname, screamed a vile torrent of slum curses at Damio and me.

"What did she say?" I asked him a long time after to break the terrible silence.

"Bitch knows a lot of curse words. You don't need to know them now," he said.

It helps slightly if I can keep my arms outstretched. I think of this parody of Cristo Redentor and my gentle mockery of Him in these, surely my final moments. But if I do not do these absurd calisthenics periodically to loosen my suffering muscles, my body will sink like a stone. Even though that is certainly going to be my fate, I wish to prolong it because I have to think of everything that has happened to me very carefully and very thoroughly since I took the money and ran off to Rio—to live. Talking was sapping strength and so we stayed silent, within reach, but not speaking. Simply watching the other tread water, expending as little energy as possible, spit the salty water from our mouths from time to time.

The water is now black and I have not seen Damio in three, maybe four hours. You cannot tell time. It passes but you cannot tell it. I cannot see much of the yacht, so every now and then I listen for the sound of the waves slapping against the hull. These are tiny waves but after hours in the water you can make out things more easily than if you were onshore or dry land. I wonder if he attempted to swim toward shore. I wonder if he simply gave up and let his head slip beneath the water. My mind is not well-focused at the moment because I am badly dehydrated. Shivering causes me to jerk about, lose even more energy, and bring the end on even faster.

Drowning is not painless. I am aware of the suffocation that will occur and how painful it will be once I take that first deep gulp of water into my lungs. It will be very painful and the long moments I am now experiencing will become hellishly prolonged until I black out. There is no easy death waiting for me. Perhaps the last myth to dispel will be the one that says you relive your life while drowning. I will relive it now while my brain continues to work, although my mind has been prone to drift much in these last hours since I dove into the water and saw the shock-pried face of Damio. I am interested only in the events that began my journey to the Marvelous City. I see myself high above a different city, looking at the rush-hour traffic; my vision is blurred; then it sharpens to reveal a panorama of a violent city where gunfire and dope deals make the east and west sides dangerous, places full of crack addicts and the whores . . . but there, you see, how my mind drifts along.

That last bout of shivering nearly did me in. I took in some water but gagged it up. I am afraid that cramps will double me up and then, before I can tell my story to myself and get to the finish, I will die. That would be a meaningless death. I must have some way of making sense of it all, so I will continue my story. You, who know me so well, will understand what I am trying to achieve.

There is a moon, but the scudding clouds carry it off and yet, now and then, it appears and gives me some hope. *Death, as the Psalmist saith, is certain to all, all must die*. To slip into the black water, open my mouth to the rushing salt stream.

"Damio!"

I forgot that he is gone. My mind is failing. My arms ache and I cannot keep afloat much longer. Damio has been gone many hours now. He has left me to face my own death. Was he a demon who took me down to the depths? Was I his demon? I imagine him appearing out of the waters on the beach of Ipanema, blocking the light of tomorrow's sun, looking down with wry detachment at some other gullible tourist with a dirty secret.

I think: *Cuyahoga* means *crooked* in Iroquois. The sludgescummed river down by the Flats in Cleveland, which caught fire like thousands of candles burning as a sacrifice to an unforgiving god.

The Atlantic Ocean, forty nautical miles from Búzios, 2:00 a.m. . . . .

The moon is gone. Blackness surrounds me like a soggy cloak. I can't breathe, my legs are cramping, and my arms are numb to the shoulder.

I am as cold as I have ever been in my life. I cannot tell which direction I am facing—out to sea or toward the shore—not that it matters because I could not swim a dozen yards. My head slips under the water and I have to use all my strength to swim upward through this ink. The last time it happened—moments, hours ago?—the struggle was too hard and I almost let go until the burning in my lungs became intolerable, too much to bear. My brain is fast becoming a dead receiver to the messages of my tortured flesh and twisted sinews. I do not know if I am hallucinating or thinking. I heard thrashing in the water nearby, a shark maybe. I imagine the phosphorescent glow of its fin breaking water and the black eyes rolling back, those rows of jagged teeth to rend my flesh. I swallow more water. The salt burns my throat . . . when I was a boy I opened my mouth to the wind howling off the lake in January. I could not eat or swallow for days afterward. My fever was 105 degrees.

I must return to my story again and for the hundredth or thousandth time. If I tell it to the end, I will know—what? Something, I will know something.

"What does it say?"

"It says funk balls advertised every Saturday night."

"What is a funk ball, Damio?"

"Damio, fucker."

Familiar spirit, Mephisto. Get thee behind me, Sathana.

I remember now, how it dreamed to me. . .

Experience life.

Jesus Christ, they're just children.

"Bless me, Father, for I have sinned . . ."

The Walls of Jericho Come Tumblin' Down, Down, Down

No, no—

"Not yet."

Virgin Mary, Mother of God.
Now and at the hour . . . at the hour--
Dies Irae—Wrath of God, Doomsday, Day of Doom.
Iemanjá, Goddess of the Sea, accept my offering.
Ah, there, there, you stupid motherfucker . . .

Eating Blondin's Omelet

Arnold Odell, retired power company executive, yearned for some distraction. Goldie (short for Goldenrod) lay curled atop Odell's black slippers with half his body elongated over each one. Apparently the smell of new leather was an aphrodisiac because the cat sought them out every time he came out onto the porch, and butted them aggressively with his head. Goldie's motor generally ran in low gear, but his excitement at the seeing the slippers made the old tom come alive, and he went through vibratos and trills that reminded Arnold of a car going through gears up a street. From Arnold's vantage, the cat's position looked uncomfortable, but short puffs of air disturbed the cat's face whiskers and suggested contentment.

The ugly male cat with his single ragged ear had shown up on the day of Helen's funeral last winter. Odell saw him limp between his and his neighbor's yards. Looking out over the lake's waves crashing against the breakwall, Arnold saw a glimpse of ragged orange fur as the cat pulled his hindquarters through a crack in his neighbor's foundation. Arnold wasn't moved to pity; he was still taking stock of his emotions in the wake of Helen's sudden death. He expected the cat to freeze to death under that porch in the frigid, bitter weather. Three days later Arnold saw the cat haul himself out, stretch and shake each forepaw, as if awakening from a nap in the sunlight. Arnold didn't like animals in general. An animal in a house blurred the definition of inside and outside too much. Nonetheless, he grabbed his keys, got in his car, drove to the grocery store, and brought back a couple cans of generic cat food. He set one next to the foundation that night. In the morning he saw that the can had moved a few feet, a tiny crescent of congealed food pasted into the rim of the can by the cat's tongue. Arnold figured the cat did not want to cut its tongue by dislodging it against the razor-sharp rim. That kind of primordial thinking intrigued him for some reason. In any event, that can extended the invitation, and when he next saw the cat extricating itself from the frigid confines beneath his neighbor's porch, Arnold sealed the unspoken contract between man and beast. The cat beelined for Arnold's open door without hesitation and had never looked back. He sometimes resented Goldie for making him feel like an hotelier.

Arnold had been working on his will all morning at his desk on the porch. The weather was an eerily perfect temperature for the northern part of the state this early in summer. He thought grimly of San Diego's 75-degree average temperature—unnatural.

The air was serene and left a patina of haze like white dust over the lake beyond his window. It made him think of an advertisement for a film he had seen during yesterday's evening news. An anguished man dives off a bridge to try to save his girlfriend, who is trapped in a submerged car. He's too late. He frantically treads water in the murky depths but she's lifeless, floating away, her hair undulating bewitchingly in the current. Arnold imagined the motorized sled gliding her away in the greenish water while she held her breath in simulated death. We're gaseous things, Arnold reasoned. We're meant to float. It would take a perfect coalescence of pressures to combat the human body's buoyancy and make one hang in the water like that.

Suddenly, this chore of bequeathing angered him. He saved the document to a file he called Last Things. He italicized his prompt and at the top of the screen put the words that had been running through his mind like an itch:
What am I afraid of?
children dying before me, cancer returns,
falling in elevator, plane crash, fire—no escape,
permanent nausea, randomness, Alzheimer's . . .

Lies, all lies. He rubbed the skin of his forearm where hair didn't grow, an old boyhood injury received while clambering around a deserted building on Hulbert Street. The bolts in the fire escape had come loose and he'd fallen into the brick rubble and sumac below. It often felt like ants were walking over the scarred part. *Falling in an elevator* . . . Why not add ax murderer, or being tossed into a bronze bull and roasted?

—*stupid, puerile.* The bogeymen of an aging mind.

He had taken early retirement because of his cancer, now in remission. These fears were not windows to his soul, just tiny fissures into his boyhood psyche mostly, small cracks through which Bosch-like creatures, half-machine, half-demon, scurried and wriggled free like those languid nudes in *Visions of the Beyond*—blissful, yet a worried dissipation like a detectable smell on their skin. Sin not yet a grim knowledge, but sorrow imminent. Bosch and his own stupid demons, those busy trolls cavorting on rats, clutching babies or toys.

"My fears looking back at me," he said to Goldie. Lying on the windowsill, Goldie flicked a paw at a plastic bottle of fizz water. A gift from his daughter in Austin, it made tornadoes when you shook it. Odell shook it and set it in front of Goldie's tea-colored eyes. On the back was the Fujita scale. He shook it again with a hard snap and made a perfect Devil's tail for Goldie.

At his age, he had not yet managed to come to grips with the question of an afterlife. He wondered if his increasing age were blunting self-awareness, a carapace around the fear of not-being which had been so common in his uncles before they died. His Uncle Ernie awakened three days after a brain aneurism to inquire about the rain gutters. He did not believe in the bottomless pit any more than Bosch had, but he admired the notion of a tower under continuous construction as a push against the Christian convention. Arnold had lost his faith so many years ago he could not remember when he believed in anything spiritual or profoundly evil. A month before his wife succumbed to her disease, they had visited Voltaire's church in Ferney. She asked him what *Deo erexit Voltaire* meant, and he said something pompous about its being the philosopher's crowning blasphemy, a stiff finger poked in God's eye. The look in her eyes shocked him as if he'd slapped her face. As if their entire married life together weren't on the line, but she said nothing.

The lies we tell ourselves, he thought. All that drivel about our stories coming from deep within, these inaccessible places of "courage" and "honesty" accessible to those possessing great gifts. Utter drivel. The catechism he had learned from the blue nuns so long ago, who troubled his imagination with images of souls in hell like burning matches and the dark spaces beyond time reserved for sinners. Pascal's bet, nothing more.

He explained the first and second noble truths of Buddha to the cat. *Suffering is a fact of life; suffering is caused by attachment.* Like any parent, he'd had his share of belly twinges when his children were hurt or sick. "We're animals with the power of love in our minds, Goldenrod," he said. He used the formal name instead of "Goldie" whenever he felt the discussion between them merited formality or decorum. It was an old subject, however, and the cat curled around his feet in a ball of sunshine, not listening. "Every day crocodiles devoured Thompson gazelles. Five-hundred pound zebras fording rivers are snatched by the hindquarters while smarmy voiceovers talk about 'thinning the herd.'"

His scalp prickled from the heat; he hadn't shaved in two days. Once thin-faced and handsome, or so Helen had always said, his reddish brown shock of hair contrasted oddly with his round face and eyes that seemed too small for their deep sockets. His doctor had written him a prescription for Atavan, referencing his body fat index instead of calling him obese and making an appointment for him "to ride the black snake." Arnold had left the office depressed, thoughts of a camera snaking its way up his rectum like a possum eating its way up a corpse from behind.

Ante Ente. He hadn't uttered that musical pair of syllables in over forty years. The Finnish boy—a real Finn whose aunt in Helsinki had sent him to America—not like the regular kids in his neighborhood like the Ellerby twins. The twins were bad enough; he had once been attacked by both of them in his cousin's yard, but even they were scared shitless of tangling with Ente. Just a glimpse of his white-blond buzz cut coming down the street, sometimes with an older tough named Miller, a fifteen-year-old who weighed two hundred pounds, was more than enough to send them scattering like a hawk among sparrows. Even more frightening was to be caught alone by him sneaking up on you. It rarely ended in a beating, but being subjected to his whispered, sadistic threats was enough to give anyone nightmares for a week.

The stories about him were legendary, such as the rumor that he dropped from the tree limbs of Walnut Street onto the roofs of cars and scampered off howling like a white wolf. It was no legend that he beat up older boys, some from high school, because several of us had witnessed it twice.

Odell had seen Bobby Tarbot beat up Freddie Enriccio, who still held the county record for most TDs in a season for the Harbor Mariners. But Ante Ente hit Bobby with a roundhouse right, then came with an uppercut and Bobby's teeth went into his upper lip and blood sprayed the crowd of spectators. Bobby's mother told Arnold's mom it took twenty-three stitches to close the tear and they were going to ask Judge Larrambois to deport Ente back to Helsinki . . .

About a month after the fight, Odell encountered Ente down at the slip where Arnold and some friends used to dive off some abandoned stone structures nicknamed "the Pyramids" into the oily water a dozen feet below—everybody keenly intent on clearing the rusted railroad spikes that jutted a half-foot out like rusted penises in eternal erection. Odell had been fishing for bluegill and crappie when Ente sneaked up behind him.

"Hey, fuckface," he said slowly. His dog, a fearless black-and-white terrier, came bounding into view, shaking a muskrat between his teeth and growling. Ente walked on to whatever mayhem would attract him next.

Arnold heard a clatter behind him on the floorboards. Goldie was frisking with his favorite toy. His pointy fangs were embedded in the cotton mouse's head and his back claws spun at the belly like a prizefighter working a speed bag. Arnold picked up a scorpion cocooned in glass. The transparent coffin showed the scorpion's eyes discernible at the ends of tiny stalks and its splayed pincers perfectly articulated in its armor of chitin. Goldie often made forays onto Arnold's desk and with sweeps of his forepaws sent the scorpion skipping across the desk to ricochet off books or objects like a tiny space traveler frozen, oblivious in its fourth dimension.

The wizened, pale nun, her face so hideously white that it looked as if she had dusted herself with talcum, used to tell his class bible stories. When he was a boy, he used to sneak off with the family's Douay-Rheims and read it for hours. He liked the illustrations especially—a bald, ranting Isaiah, surrounded by young mockers, a bear in the background; the chaos of the falling Tower of Babel; the rich man Dives supplicating the beggar Lazarus, snug in the arms of Abraham; and Jesus in the Garden of Gethsemane with dark droplets of blood speckling his brow and a rivulet snaking into his cloak. When he discovered a packing crate of Erle Stanley Gardner paperbacks, he abandoned his bible reading and took up mysteries. He had also discovered his penis that year.

The night before Arnold had had his recurring dream of falling in an elevator. He was bored with it by now, wondered if it meant he had been thinking too much of Helen the day before. Even the ricocheting *klaaang* of the cable against the walls of the shaft was a familiar terror . . . His mother had become agoraphobic in her old age. A trip to the grocery store was an adventure that left her gasping for breath when they returned home.

"It dreamed to me again," he mumbled to Goldie without realizing the garbled syntax.

The other items on his screen were from books he had read. Robert Caro's tetralogy of LBJ, and images of the first settlers of the hill country of Southwest Texas, Apaches raping every white woman they captured. They tied the husbands to tree limbs, slit their abdomens with their knife blades and gently pulled the big intestine out until it hung down like a smeary blue rope. Then they watched the coyotes sport.

He imagined Apaches hiding behind rocks, drunk on whiskey, giggling like schoolboys on a desperate prank. The alpha male appeared with lowered head and bunched shoulder muscles. Would he jerk the victim's guts from side to side as Tony used to do with the muskrats he caught? (The name was acquired because he liked

spaghetti, which Arnold used to sneak to him—his mother's cooking was deplorable and that, he always suspected, was the reason
Helen chided him for his gourmand pretensions.) He remembered
how Tony whipsawed tiny rabbits and moles into a blur and then left
their carcasses behind. He wondered: did those frontier victims go
into immediate shock watching their innards spatter feces and blood
about their legs and meadow grass? Was the pain so mind-numbing
that they were spared from suffering too much?

He looked at the screen again.

Silly, stupid.

He had grown up by the water, still lived near it. The ore boats
passing by his porch windows still held a fascination for him. He had
sailed out of that harbor himself for the first time aboard the *J. Burton
Ayers*, his parents unaware that his car was wrecked outside a drive-
in. He and Helen had been clipped by a car full of laughing boys and,
panicked, had turned right into them. The cars kissed rather than collided and his front fender became an instant sculpture in front of his
eyes. He had never told Helen that he had slipped his glasses into his
pocket because it was an embarrassing signal that he wanted to kiss
her.

They were married in Monroe, Michigan, by a Justice of the
Peace when he got off the boat after Labor Day and hitchhiked home
from Gary, Indiana. He walked through the massive steel plant and
stuck his thumb out. A couple college boys from Notre Dame gave
him a lift. He rode in the back of a black pickup truck with a beagle
and by ten at night he had made it as far as the Memorial Shoreway
in Cleveland. Cars were bigger then and people drove seventy-five,
eighty. He was afraid one of the cars with black males might stop
for him and do something to him—those were the days of race riots
in the big cities of America. Finally, an aging homosexual stopped,
picked him up, and never spoke much beyond his vague, mumbled
innuendo. He had no fear of being hurt by this man. Helen was pregnant, and she had written to him in Sault St. Marie to come home.
In those days, you came home for a summons like that; besides, he
loved her and the idea of being a father.

Three weeks before Helen's diagnosis he was told by the ex-wife of a friend of his from grad school that her former husband had died of a cerebral hemorrhage while he was grading essays. He was a matchmaker with an MFA degree and used to pick up classes as an adjunct faculty at Macomb Community College. As boxing in Detroit declined, he returned to teaching with the same zeal he once had for matching fighters in club shows. He once said of a story he was reading at the time, "This burns in the mind!" Arnold recalled his last visit to see him. They went over to watch the fights on Don Thibodeaux's big-screen television. Don had once trained Tommy ("Hit Man") Hearns before he had a falling out with Tommy's other handlers. Don reclined in his La-Z-Boy and exposed the scar from his heart bypass. They were watching James Toney hand out a twelve-round pasting. Don laughed at Toney's opponent's harmless pittie-pat flurries. The fighter was one of a team of four assembled by a Detroit tort lawyer who picked up all tabs for his fighters. Don said they didn't like to fight. His friend and Thib talked shop about fighters they knew and what had happened to this or that one. So many Kronk fighters dead of violence or drugs or gone to prison. Arnold liked listening in while watching "Lights Out" carry his opponent through the rounds. His friend had introduced him to Toney at a small club fight in Mexican Town. Arnold shivered as the child-eating, testicle-stomping rant of Mike Tyson supplanted that memory. I guess *I'll fade into Bolivian* . . .

"Fucking lawyers," Thib commented, as they headed down-town to pick up his sculpture *Inner Man*. Thib was training another gangly black kid from east Detroit but still believed in the resurrec-tion of the great Kronk fighters, Sugar Ray and Tommy. "Like this," he said from his La-Z-Boy, high on Percodan one night while they watched some pay-per-view fights on his big-screen TV, his petite Philippine wife asleep on the couch beside him. He laughed and thrust one of those crocodile arms of his which he said kept from being a great fighter. "Like this, Arnie," he said again, twisting his wrecking-ball fist straight up into an imaginary jaw, a tai chi move in fast forward.

"You have to cock your left leg at the same time," Thib said soberly. "That's what gives those short punches their power. Like Joe Louis, see? These dumb fuckin' ghetto kids don't know that from watching those asshole rap videos."

Thib's chrome statue of Ali, welded from car bumpers he fetched from a junkyard when he could still move, was worth a hundred thousand and he finally donated it to the African-American museum.

Arnold rubbed his temples and squeezed his eyes shut against the glare. His desk was a mess of bills, papers, pens. There were cat hairs everywhere his fingers touched.

He needed a haircut. Up until the time he was seventeen and began growing his hair long, he saw a barber named Charlie O'Connell, who lived in the harbor and who was always drunk in the afternoon. Charlie jabbed him with the electric razor and apologized. A flashback to an old man with deep wrinkles in Charlie's barber chair, eyeing him with a mix of envy and disgust: "Christ Almighty," he said out of the blue—whether to him or to Charlie, he was never sure: "I can remember when my hair was that color."

They found Charlie dead in the middle of Bridge Street coming out of the Iroquois Club. Old Father McCafferty, himself an Irish whiskey priest, administered Last Rites right there in the street.

Father McCafferty—he was a demon to the sisters. He used to drive them crazy. Odell had served mass for him many mornings. The priest never failed to clamp- his hand around Arnold's during the Offertory when he poured from the wine cruet into the chalice. It was never enough for him unless the chalice was filled to the brim. The priest's mottled hand rippled with wormy veins over whitened knuckles as he gripped down. There was nothing symbolic about wine to Father McCafferty, who steadied himself at the top of the altar steps, and the altar boys trembled at the thought he'd take a drunken step backward and keel over. Yet the boys admired and feared him, even when he handed out report cards and said unkind things through sour breath.

Arnold recalled the day Father McCafferty freed the entire school at recess. Waved them off in all directions, and they scattered like fish. Odell smiled thinking of the poor bus kids—they ran too, knowing they had to come right back and wait for their buses. But the walkers like Odell fled lest the nuns corral them back into the classrooms.

They played King-of-the-Mountain on snow mounds as high as the school's rooftop. The seventh-graders against the eighth. One boy—he had not thought of him in three decades—a good-looking kid with a swarthy complexion and a mellifluous Italian surname, used to get beat up by a big eighth-grader, the biggest kids in school. The bully was retired now, too, like Arnold, and living in the harbor. His right leg had been amputated as a result of diabetes, and he wore thick, owlish lenses. His athlete's body long gone, he had to be helped in and out of his car by his wife or daughter. Arnold could not remember his name.

He wondered why the bully had chosen the handsome boy. The boy's white shirt was smudged (razor-creased slacks, white shirts, penny loafers—the *de rigueur* outfit of the middle-class Catholic boy of his day). He shoved him into the tarred playground surface. He saw the boy get up, smile, and brush himself off with a bravado that infuriated the bully: You wanna do *something* about it, hunh, hunh? *C'mon, chicken. You chicken, Condonella?*

What sprocket of memory had been suddenly unstuck to unleash that memory, he wondered.

There, got it, the name: *Pete Condonella.*

Boys didn't talk like that anymore. Black kids in Arnold's neighborhood were a new phenomenon, and their "motherfucking"-everything in sight used to make Helen anxious. The white- trash girl down the street hollered at two passing girls, boyfriend rivals: "You jackass bitch motherfuckers!" Her older sisters were notorious receptacles for black males and always pregnant. There was always a city vehicle checking out how clean their house was. The neighborhood rumor was that two infants had been found dead inside of undetermined causes within a few months of each other.

Odell leaned as far back as he could without tipping over until his chair creaked with stress; he laced his fingers over his eyes. He wanted some kind of epiphany about—*something, damn it*. He did not know whether God existed, but he didn't feel bitter about the lies they had told him in religion. They were believers. He was not into that kind of God-as-rewarder, God-as-punisher explanation. He had one print in his study: Winslow Homer's painting of a black slave adrift in the Caribbean Sea, alone, surrounded by sharks. He thought: *I am waiting around for death just like that.*

The whole harbor where he lived was blighted. Factories that used to poison the landscape had long since closed down or moved to Mexico. Flumes and vats that once spewed arsenic-laced clouds had crusted over decades before. The men who labored in the factories were dead or had moved to the South with their aging spouses, having sold off their houses. Many of those houses he could once name by family were rental properties held by out-of-state children. Everywhere else was filled in by tacky strip malls, Dairy Marts, used-car lots, a massage parlor or a check-cashing service. Weeds cracked the foundations of the buildings waiting to get knocked down or sold. Helen had lamented the loss of those old Victorian houses and the streets of laughing kids, the fathers who wore fedoras and ties to ballgames and mothers that smelled of cooking and perfume and whose breasts were used to the suckling of their babies, but he knew hers was a vision of nostalgia.

Behind the façade of his brainstormed list, lay another, and behind that, another *ad infinitum, ad nauseam.* His father worked on the tugboats as a wiper in the engine room. He was a big man with a great stomach from years of drinking beer on and off the job (his older sister, a Catholic nun herself, of the Holy Humility of Mary, once chided him for his big gut when he came to fetch her at the convent). He was a remote man, alcoholic and violent when provoked, which was a weekly routine and generally the climax to the Sunday evening weeklong binge that ended in a big, noisy fight and sometimes with blows thrown at his mother. Arnold's older sister would bravely round them up and they would try to stop the fight. He once found himself kicked across the kitchen floor by his father's foot—luckily his father wasn't wearing his steel-toed work boots at the time. His mother was intellectually superior to his father, often bored or disdainful of her own children, frustrated by housework and also a drunk.

All but one of his siblings married, had children, and moved away. One remained in town and lived in a sentimentalized past and really believed their parents were good people who did their best despite their drinking. He had escaped the house at a young age and moved to Florida, where he succumbed to a vortex of partying and drugs. He ended up with a prison sentence for forging prescription drugs. His son was raised by one of his sisters in another state.

He was aware of sounds and voices. He looked out his window and up to the roof of his neighbor's house. He saw three Amish men shingling the roof. All were in their twenties, two married (their beards signified that, he remembered), all standing on the apex of the steeply pitched colonial, taking a break maybe. They all wore clean blue shirts in different shades with black pants.

Their nonchalance drew Arnold's gaze—they were young, confident, insouciantly defying the law of gravity as they moved across the roof. Their joy was evident—was it being young or working under a blue, cloudless sky? He saw one of the bearded men scuttle along the roofline's flashing as nimbly as a goat. Odell felt pity and a pang of anguish wash over him, not sure why his observation of strange men working on a roof should inspire any feeling at all, much less something like ambivalence. Maybe it was sorrow he felt. It seemed wrong somehow that they should have no fear of an angry God, who could give them the night sweats.

Cosmologists now tell us that eleven parallel worlds exist at ninety-degree angles to each other, all separated by the thinnest of membranes, perhaps the collapsing stars of black holes, that spice in the universal stew that draws the Milky Way toward the Andromeda Galaxy at seven hundred thousand miles an hour and which in four billion years will annihilate this corner of the universe in one spectacular blaze that might even impress an indifferent God. Odell had an image of a painted circus clown whirling plates on sticks.

Christ Almighty.

He rubbed a crick in his neck. He looked down at his list and flushed with embarrassment, grateful to be alone and that Helen wasn't there to hurt him with her eyes. He hit delete. He got up, stretched his back muscles, and went into the other room to finish watching a documentary on the life of the Great Blondin, the Frenchman who first walked across the Niagara Gorge in 1859. Blondin later varied his stunt by carrying his manager, standing on a chair with only one leg on the rope, walking blindfolded, and by pushing a wheelbarrow containing a stove. The narrator said Blondin once stopped halfway across and cooked an omelet on the sheet-iron stove and ate it before continuing on. On another Niagara crossing, he lowered his omelet to passengers on the *Maid of the Mist* and waited for them to eat before going on.

Arnold wondered what Blondin thought about while he waited for them to finish and render applause. Unlike those unlucky Wallendas who seemed to tumble out of the air with deadly regularity every few years, Blondin would lead a charmed life. He performed over the transept of the Crystal Palace, where he turned somersaults on stilts seventy feet above the heads of the gasping onlookers. In 1861 in Dublin, at the Portobello Gardens, a rope parted and two workmen fell to their deaths from scaffolding. He himself was unhurt. Diabetes took him in 1896 at 72 and he lies in repose in Kensal Green Cemetery. The good burghers of Ealing named a couple roads for him: Niagara Avenue and Blondin Avenue.

Brushing Crumbs

My doctor said, "Keep only those routines that make you feel calm."

I've always been a neat freak. When I put the baby in his carry-all and set him on top of the Navigator to wipe away the crumbs, I remembered at once: his first birthday cake.

Why are you looking at me like that?

When Are You Ever Coming Home?

The green highway sign with the glitter said *Columbiana County*.

They hadn't seen a Youngstown sign since Canfield, and the traffic was thinning out. He'd said he was going down to Steubenville and they were welcome to drive along with him, her and her son. Kid was retarded and had some kind of nigger name like Tyshawn but he didn't look like no halfie he'd ever seen. Every so often she leaned over and gave his thigh a light squeeze and thanked him again for helping them out like this. The boy didn't look too retarded and didn't act it except for his nigger-loving music, that hip-hop shit that turned his white man's stomach sour. He told the boy not to go touching his radio again or he'd pull back a bloody stump. Kid was so stupid he didn't know who Shania Twain was, ass-headed little turd.

He brought the conversation around to what she had said in the diner to him, and she smiled shyly. He told her company policy wouldn't let him give rides, but what the heck, this time, and you such a pretty thing . . .

He'd throw her ass and the kid's out at the next exit if she pretended not to know what the score was. Guy Lee Fuqua was no Good Samaritan. The next sign said East Palestine but might as well have said East Jesus, way to fuck out here. Nothing out here for a hundred miles. He laughed to himself: stupid woman was going to stand out on the freeway in that skimpy outfit with her retard—*Jesus wheezus, broads are so fucking dumb. But she's got big ones, that's for damn sure.* The staties could drive by any minute. He wasn't sure if you could get arrested for vagrancy, but if he had to, he'd remind her of that, too. See if that jogged her memory. A deal was made across that table, and he was going to insist she honor it.

She had been quiet for a long time. Then she turned to him, and looked at him. She wore no makeup, kind of beat up around the eyes, and those strange gold eyes—what the hell.

"Why don't you take one of those side roads off of here," she suggested.

"I thought maybe we could find us a little place, maybe a motel."

"What's your name anyway?"

"Jill," she said.

"Mine's Jack," he said. "Jack Mehoff." He winked, but the dumb bitch didn't get it.

"No, no, a rest stop," she said. "Or just pull off the highway."

He liked that. This pig was getting right down to it now. His sac hadn't been drained in a few days with all this damned road work so he was ready, Freddy.

"I know one's coming up," he said with a wink. She was going to get a real pounding whether she knew it or not. He was truly sorry about her rough life and all, but once he had a peek at them big ole titties, pity took a backseat with junior back there. She was packing some man-sized funbags.

"What about him?" He nodded his head where retardo boy was picking a booger. If the little nose miner started eating them, he'd slap the shit right out of him right after he got done with Momma, but first, it was time to make that German soldier march.

"Don't mind him," she said. "Just turn off somewhere." He winked at her again. "He used to it, huh?" He'd go for the hat trick. Darlene hated it up the ass at first, most of them did, but he'd make this one take it up the dirt chute and then make her suck the shit right off it. He saw that in a porn rental last week and planned to do it—just didn't think he'd get lucky so soon.

"I keep a little stash under the seat," he said. "You know, for those times."

She let her hand brush across the bulge in his pants and then reached under his seat to find the baggie.

"I like a smoke once in a while," she said, and let her finger-nail trace his cock's outline on the way back up.

"Me too. Makes it all the better. Whyn't you scoot a little closer, hon?"

He took an exit off the freeway and then a left, no idea where he was going, didn't give a fuck, just wanted to get there fast before she made him pop. He saw a winding blacktop road that petered out into a gravel one about a quarter-mile in, just beyond a stand of trees. It looked like an old orchard. It would do. His off-road tires were the most expensive item on his Silverado—beat a shit-assed Ford Ranger Super Cab any day and could handle anything short of quicksand or a vertical mountain.

"How's this?" he stood on the brakes and skidded the truck into a juddering halt between a couple pine trees. He leaned back to unzip. He had to get it out of there before he had a permanent crook in it.

"Come on, baby, there it is."

She had one rolled and lit. She liked to do a little weed before sex. She took a hit and placed it between his lips. Then she went down on him with her whole mouth, took it all the way back to the throat. He placed his palms on either side of her head while she bobbed. She was good, all right, a real pro. Made it slick and gummy with her spit. While she deep-throated him, he felt his testicles shrivel, harden to walnuts.

She came up suddenly and looked at him with those glittery eyes. He forced her head back onto it; his cock frisking about like a windsock. He forced her back down it once again. She acted like she'd never seen one before, staring at the purple, velvety head, pumping it with her hand. But she was a born cocksucker if he ever met one—*what'd she say her name was? Fuck it*, he had something to tell the guys on the job—

He was sucking in smoke when he felt a light scraping of her teeth against the shaft, and then she bit him. He choked, gasping, and pulled her head free.

"Watch the teeth, you cunt!" he said. "Bite me again, and I'll beat the living shit out of you."

She smiled at him differently this time and took another hit of the joint before she went back to work. She blew smoke all around it, and he lay back in the seat and closed his eyes, the pain forgotten. This was heaven and he was getting paid too. When she bit him again, he thought he was dreaming. But the fire that shot up from his root straight up to his scalp was like having a scalding cup of coffee dumped into his lap. His hands clutched her head and tore into the hair to jerk her free, but she clamped down on his manhood with the full force of her jaws. He came close to passing out.

He didn't know who the hell was screaming like that, thought it must be the retarded kid, but the little fuck was all of a sudden holding him around the neck, trying to pull him backwards in the seat while she jerked her head back and forth like a terrier with a rat in its teeth. The pain had become a steady revving inside his brain and filled the entire cab with its sound. She grabbed his hands and tried to snap his fingers. The kid was holding his bicep or he would have ripped her scalp clean off her head.

He sucked air. He felt as if his whole body was wrapped in a blanket of fire. He whipped his forearm backward to get the kid off and heard him bounce to the floor in a heap—deal with her fast. He threw a short rabbit chop to her neck as she reared up, claws out, eyes blazing. He hadn't even stunned her. He knocked her back against the passenger door with a short punch. She was a big, fighting creature, and he knew this was the worst trouble of his life. He didn't dare look down at the pulpy mess because it was going to be bad and maybe past surgery, but he was by God going to kill this fucking bitch right now. Gouge those yellow eyes out of her fucking skull with his thumbs—

Instead of springing back at him as he expected, she twisted low in the seat and when she came up, he thought for a second she was covering up, waiting for the onslaught of his fists—

The bullet hit him in the guts. He said, "Ouch, that fuckin' stings."

Then another explosion, another sting, and he felt this gooey bubbling up inside him.

She looked at him, hard, mean and unafraid, with the gun pointing at his chest. He heard the next explosion and felt another one go in his arm, out the back. He raised his fist to strike her. She shot him in the wrist. The bullet ricocheted off bone and broke the window behind him. He'd once stuck his hand in a jar with angry purple wasps on a dare. This was like having a thousand loose on him. His chest cavity was filling with blood, and his breathing was hard like swallowing razor blades. He felt like a hollow man constructed of bones and wires.

Another explosion, another wasp. His brain was tripping on him. He was dotted with stings. Big red ones that leaked. His whole body felt slick. He pulled his brain free for a second and saw her staring at him with that bitchy-cunt look. The gun rested sideways in her lap. Her chest going in and out with every breath. His brain fogged up. He felt confused. He asked where were the stingers on them wasps, you know, you're so fucking smart, and don't tell me wasps not s'posed to have them barbed tails pokin' out their asses . . . he touched himself where the slugs had bored through, black stipple on his clothing and a marshy stink in the enclosed air.

He gurgled, tried to speak. Pink drool came out and poured down his chin.

"What you say, fucker? I didn't hear you."

He was immensely strong, had inherited a genetic peculiarity from his grandfather, who was said to be able to lift up those old-time, wooden railroad flatbeds and tip fifty-gallon drums with just his fingertips. While the wasps sizzled inside him, he had a flashback—some old sawbones in Moundsville his mother had taken him to when he was five years old after he had fallen out of a tree. The doctor used words like *sthenic* to her to explain how a little boy could sit calmly and try to fix his own broken leg. As a man, he understood what that meant because he could endure cold, heat, or long hours on the high steel under a broiling sun and then drink a case of beer at the end of the day. He had knocked men out with punches like the one he'd given her jaw. But he wanted out of it now, the wasps hurt too badly, and he was feeling warm, sleepy. He gathered in his last remaining strength and spat out the words with the bright pink gore:

"Ridge-running . . . trash . . . cunt . . . fuck . . . ing . . . hillbilly . . . whore—"

The next bullet tore a big jagged exit hole in the occipital bone after punching through his cheek and turning his brain to stew. His head knocked against the door. Another slug sizzled through his sinus cavity and made his right eyeball disappear in a red mist.

She unloaded the rest of the clip into his face and blew pieces of him out the shattered window, including teeth, bits of skull and nose cartilage, until the click of dry-firing was all the noise inside. The cab reeked of cordite fumes and smoke.

"God damn," Chyrone cried. "God damn!"

She let him remove the gun from her hand. He eased her fingers off, one at a time, slowly, careful not burn her with the red-hot barrel.

"Who's white trash now, motherfucker?" She spat. She sounded as if she had just awoken from a long nap.

They looked at each other. Her jaw throbbed with pain and one side of Chyrone's face was bruised.

It should have taken longer and been more painful, she thought. He died too damned easily.

Things were looking up, finally. They had his wallet and a pretty good roll of bills. "That fuckhead must have just got paid," Chyrone said to her while he kissed the back of her neck.

She was on Highway 39 coming up just below New Philadelphia. Chyrone wasn't saying much, in a sulk because she had given away that blowjob. He was just like the other boys that way, she smiled. He said he didn't mind playing the retard, and she told him he was every bit as good as what's-his-name? That actor in *What's Eating Gilbert Grape?*

That pissed him off more.

"That fag? You've got to be shitting me!"

"He's kinda cute," she said. In fact, she'd had exquisite sexual fantasies of him. Every time she read about some teacher being busted for having sex with a fifteen-year-old, her heart raced. Her favorite sex fantasy was a gangbang of young boys, she on the bed, all of them surrounding her, pointing at her.

"Next time, give me the fucking gun," he said. "I'll take care of it."

Blah-blah, on and on for about twenty-five miles. He could be such a baby. If she told him how much cock she'd had in her mouth or pussy since she was fifteen—why, hell, it would be one long dick stretching from here to the moon—but she asked him nicely to shut up, baby, please. Maybe she was nothing but a no-count whore like everybody back home thought, but she knew how to listen to men and boys, not just empty their loads, which was more than most women ever needed to know in their hot-shit lives.

She thought back to Christmas. Her husband had an open recipe book on his table and was blathering about something called *crabes farci*. No, she told him, she didn't like Creole food. For one thing, she didn't know what a Creole was, but from the way he was trying to impress his boss and the wife, it didn't matter. She did what Jerry said: "Show plenty of cleavage, let him talk, and leave the rest to me." Then he was going on about some island beach somewhere and its white coral sands, a rain forest on a place called Basse-Terre, something about how many bananas exported to France, membership in the EU, whatever, and snorkeling in the Réserve Cousteau. She went from stifling a yawn to keep from choking on her drink at the image he painted—his pea-sized balls and little stick of cock in a male bikini—a pair of undulating flippers behind the plump snorkeler among the bright reefs. She imagined him, all wobbly pink flesh, lowered by a canvas truss and pulley, like a baleen whale, into a swimming pool.

This was right after their first date, when he said something about the ways to cook conch. She remembered Jerry making a sly dig about her "conch" and then he started talking to her about Canada. His grandfather was born in a railroad encampment near Jasper, where he said tourists could walk on a glacier and ride up the mountain in a gondola. She heard him lecturing her as the miles blitzed past: *"The railroad built fabulous chalet-type hotels from Toronto all the way to Vancouver,"* blah-blah, but they never connected it, he said. She smiled at him, totally bored, and waiting for someone better to come along so she could get laid, at least, but he seemed in love with his own voice and preferred mental foreplay to the real thing.

All she knew about British Columbia was that hydroponic bud was grown all over the island like a cottage industry. She learned that thanks to that art professor from Sinclair Community College she met at the Dayton Swim and Social Club. Jerry was still bragging about the magnificent "old pile," as he called the Empress Hotel: ". . . *the last great hotel built by the Grand Trunk Railroad.*" He and his parents used to take tea there at four o'clock. She had seen through men's lies since she was a girl and didn't believe a word he was saying. It was all snob talk, seduction talk. Jerry was born with more smarts, was all it was. He grew up in Seattle and had a scholarship to Stanford. Interstate 90 dead-ended there. That was all she knew about any place west of Youngstown, Ohio.

Jill was short on book-learning, never cared for reading made-up stuff or things that already happened in the past. But she knew that you never escaped your family; she knew that what happened to you in your adolescence created the pattern of your life for all your choices from then on. Most people lived out those themes all their lives. It took a crisis to change you—something to make you depart from the pattern. Something to make you or break you. Jerry had never walked on the wild side until he met her at that party three years ago.

Chyrone slept beside her with his head resting on her shoulder. She mussed his hair gently. They'd have to worry about money for food and gas eventually, but she knew where the professor was going. He was a clever man, all right, but not in her class on this particular playing field. Besides, she thought to herself, she had a Ph.D. in males. Giving hand jobs in the restroom was her high-school diploma, topless dancing for cruddy-looking hill men was her bachelor's, rimming and getting cornholed by blacks in Cleveland was her master's, and marriage to a wealthy developer of gated communities was her doctorate.

She opened a window to let clean air whistle through her hair and wash out the cab and blow the scent of coppery blood out. Jill wondered if she could fall in love again. But she was certain she was never going back home again. Not to Bluefield, not to that manor house of Barré stone.

She popped another stick of gum from the endless supply in Chyrone's pockets. He was fiddling intently with the buttons seeking his music. Her breath was still scented with the redneck's semen. That one back there—well, call him a post-doc seminar.

Honey of Marrakesh

The sandstone rock face outside Marrakesh was a challenge. I had climbed all morning through the golden light until a black storm blew in from the wadi. Fissures gave good purchase. It turned out to be an easy climb, after all. The tribesmen call it Vendevale, the wind that blows from the Straits of Gibraltar all the way to the bulge of West Africa. It was becoming stronger and whistled like a train over the broken ridge of escarpment I had just crossed that morning. I scrambled inside a cave to wait out the winds and the massive rust-colored veil of sand it carried.

Suddenly, a miracle. The once-a-year rains came down in thick gray sheets. I see water sluicing past the mouth of the cave. Thick drops fill up my boot prints, crest and run over. No one besides me has been inside here for a thousand years. I was thinking that I would like my next adventure to be in the Lost Quarter of the Arabian Desert. I could easily imagine the hot Siroccos blowing their sand seas into exquisite shapes. I passed the time naming the winds of the world I had experienced in my travels: the Abroholos (Brazil), Alberta Clippers (western Canada)another near the old Yukon mining territory—What was it called?—Chinooks, the Inuit called their winds "snow eaters"the Squamish (British Columbia), the Williwaw (Straits of Magellan), el Zonda (Andes). I was deep in a pleasant reverie. The storm was abating.

I settled to the back of the cave so that the damp would not chafe my skin on the climb down. I touched something wet and gluey on the walls. They climbed out like tiny drunkards to see who has disturbed their combs. Yellow, black—the colors in nature that mean trouble.

The first wave strikes: face, neck, cheeks—acid burn. A dog-eared *National Geographic* left behind in the hostel flashed into my mind: "African bees," it said, "always attack the eyes first."

Dozens, hundreds. They'll keep coming—
Now they smell me, they know I'm here.

Desideratum of the Adjunct Professor

He came awake choking, his heart pounded like a bongo. He'd been dreaming he was caught in a rip tide, but his oxygen-starved brain had told him he was still swimming strokes on the surface when, in the upside-down reality of his dream, he was really drowning beneath the waves. He had been dreaming of Guadeloupe again. Not the sunny island he yearned for, but a different one, one where nature's forces were perverted and crawling things swarmed over the forest floor. His muscles felt as if a giant hand had been kneading him all night. The light flooding his eyes looked strained through dirty cheesecloth. The luminescent hands of the clock told him he had slept the day away.

Macbride lay back and shut his eyes. He willed his happy island back with its vivid colors, secret groves of lime trees and turquoise lagoons. He saw the bright cerise flowers, frangipanni and monkey's tail, shockingly red flame trees amid the lush green jungles, steep mountainous rock faces wreathed in blue mists. His bowels clamored for release, however, and he had to urinate with an exquisite urge. His broken toilet dictated the unthinkable. He grabbed a roll of tissue and stumbled to the back door, finding his slippers. The door opened on the same hostile universe.

Like a dog, he headed for a distant maple tree. With his robe bunched around him, Macbride squatted and evacuated his bowels; then he pulled his shriveled penis from the nest of his pubic ruff into the icy cold and loosed a lemon stream, which eased the ache in his lower back considerably, but did nothing for his humiliation and self-contempt. He had fallen so low so fast.

Macbride had come to hate winters. It wasn't possible to tell morning from afternoon for months at a time; the ubiquitous gray light ceased only at dark, which came too soon and then a pall of blackness over the land smothering him. Along the western horizon a marching column of nimbus loomed majestically, all backlit in hot pink and smears of yellows like pus in a wound, he thought grimly.

Inside, he immediately headed for the downstairs bathroom; his legs were blue with cold and he was shivering uncontrollably. His throat was coated with slime. He risked a glance in the mirror on the way into the shower. His right eye was a dark slit, almost Mongolian, where abraded skin puffed out around the socket. A chartreuse patch was overtaking the lavender bruise, blood coagulating while he had dreamed fitfully. His cheeks were roughened with gray stubble. His thick Vandyke, once a majestic sable with white tips, now hid a weak chin worsened by years of obesity. Fat rolls bunched at his neck. The sedentary years, the cheeseburgers ("heart bullets," his wag of a med-ico called them), the ennui of his depressing life—all were tolling a doomsday cardiac clock with the minute hand at ten to midnight.

Drying himself, he gazed once more at his bloated and pur-pled bruises. "I had pretty plumage once," he said to the mirror. His double replied, "No, that's a fib." It repeated the litany of cruel epi-thets hurled at him from the far past, those calling cards of his un-happy youth and the wives who betrayed him. Never getting the last word in, Macbride watched them all go in succession—wives, lovers, friends, colleagues.

Hunger burned his stomach, yet he struggled against a de-sire to return to sleep. He noticed the red light's telephone messages winking at him in the half-dark. He turned back to the kitchen and held onto the sink, drank deeply from the faucet. He'd spent a life-time constructing props to fortify himself against the darkness, and now it crowded around, wolves at a campfire. He had kept it all at bay, his squalid childhood and all the rest, but it was coming undone like a house of cards under strobe lighting.

Gray turned to ink. Night was pierced by a waning moon over the lake—a gift of beauty in the midst of his black despair. He thought of Helena at the piano, playing her favorite Chopin étude. He had left the West Coast for her when she accepted a professor's position at the Dana School of Music in Youngstown. His future, too, was golden then: a young assistant professor on the verge of early promotion at UCLA. Liquid notes dropped around him in Dolby stereo, an image of her long, tapered fingers blurring into a glissando. His uneasy mind segued to his last tawdry fling with the barmaid; her stubby fingers wrapped around his member—*disgusting. No, erotic*. Blood surged south of its own volition.

He hated this house, this miserable life, everything about it nauseated him to the deepest core of his being. He had plunged from one mistake to another in a long dissolute chain that led to this sorry moment. The phone rang with a shrillness that jolted him and made his hands shake. *I have too much past, no future*. He heard the recorder kick in, then a familiar, unwelcome voice intruded:

"Uh, yiss, this is Assistant Dean Shrivistava . . . calling for, uh, Douglas Macbride. Hello, hello, hell-o . . . I need you to sign some papers . . ."

Shrivastava was the epicene, bespectacled factotum of the campus dean, her hatchet-man for anyone she wanted fired. In a less civilized era, her victims would have been emasculated in full view of her court. Macbride loathed the dean on sight, a menopausal harpie on a power trip. Shrivastava, court eunuch, wielded those shears with giddy élan. Tenured faculty ignored him, but vulnerable adjuncts listened hard for his footsteps. Alas, he admitted, he had made himself a rather big target of late.

Gossip said Shrivastava had climbed out of ragged poverty in a fishing village near Madras. Macbride built the man around the disembodied voice: nut-brown skin and gleaming teeth with a clipboard permanently attached to his hand. Adjuncts had to grovel for their measly pittance. They were forced to attend orientation meetings at the beginning of every semester where the wretched little wog droned on at the lectern about such scintillating subjects as secretarial support, keys, and access to the Xerox machine. Macbride usually slept through them, sometimes inebriated. He recalled little besides the man's tonsured head gleaming under fluorescent lights whenever he bent down to retrieve his clipboard, which owing to some kind of dropsical lethargy, seemed to slip out of his hands every ten minutes. This brought forth a photo from Macbride's box of memories, one of his adopted mother, an alcoholic poisoned by uremia at forty. Forks and spoons would drop from her hands as if the floor were magnetized. She had died despising him.

His last encounter with Shrivastava had been a fiasco of epic proportions: Macbride's last class before the fateful night at the Wing Ding bar. With the booze fog lifted, he could recall every detail leading up to the débâcle.

He had been furtively eyeing the wall clock, slogging through the last lesson of this hideously long semester. He had trashed the syllabus long ago. The students stared ahead, none turned to follow his progress, all used to his peripatetic style. A row of umlaut Ü's with blank faces and pasted-on smiles. He despised the business majors in particular, their minds soft as clatch. The text had been chosen for him, a dullish tome that took the ludicrous view of managerial benevolence when it came to labor relations. The sound of prison doors slamming behind millionaire CEOs all over the country reverberated like skeletons fornicating on a tin roof, yet this idiotic husband-wife tandem prattled about business ethics—what a colossal oxymoron! Despite the rank tissue of lies from beginning to end, he was unable to convince the little dean to let him change texts. He left Shrivastava's office saying he would be happy to spoon-feed them uncreative drivel. That evening he had slipped into class at five after to avoid the dean on patrol. Macbride's antennae quivered; this was the day adjunct contracts were to be renewed—or not.

No sooner was he in the classroom than a loud yawn erupted from the opposite corner. It had to be Rochelle—the little trollop was probably sleeping off a high. She liked to cradle her head in her arms and snooze. He sensed the rest of the class, all white-bread types, expected him to invoke one of his thunderous rebukes. Truth was, the very sight of her evoked pity rather than righteous indignation.

She was a delicately boned creature with almond skin a toothy smile, and very bright, thought Macbride, despite an occasional crudity of prose—but she could think, really think—furthermore, during her infrequent visits to class, she had kept him on his toes whenever she deigned to pay attention to his lecture. She sported a garish tattoo of the kind girls favored down their lower backsides. Rochelle's was a winking, round-faced baby devil with a pair of horns and a pitchfork. Macbride had already had the benefit of the devil's countenance. Whenever he circled behind her, its leer gaped between sacral dimples. The tail was, no doubt, a rigid arrow pointing lasciviously between the crease of her buttocks.

He usually let her sleep, but his sense of the day's magnitude in his own life must have increased his sense of life as theatre. He snapped the book shut as an exclamation point to some Victorian pap of Carnegie's he was quoting. Rochelle shot up in her seat, startled.

"Miss Bryce, perhaps you could favor us with your interpretation of that passage relative to the Homestead strikers."

The class smirked, enjoying the spectacle-to-come.

"I'm sorry, professor, I wasn't paying attention."

A few light snickers about the room.

"But Hugh O'Donnell," he intoned, "and his advisory committee believed Frick was a man of reasonableness and good faith, did they not?"

"I guess so."

"You must have heard me quote Carnegie just now. His workers, he said, those tough Irish and the Czech immigrants puddling molten iron twelve hours a day in freezing cold and scorching summers, were his 'partners' in the corporation."

"That's bullshit, professor."

Gasps, a few guffaws. *Rochelle, class pariah, was in the house.*

Macbride had touched a nerve. She tensed with feline grace and her face glowed. Her first essay concerned a great-grandfather from Mississippi, one of the hundreds of black strikebreakers brought in to destroy O'Donnell's and "Honest" John McLuckie's fledgling union after the battle on the river with the Pinkertons. The blacks toughed out white hatred until winter and starvation came to the Monongahela Valley.

"Carnegie was a ff—was a two-faced liar," she said hotly. "When it came time to recognize the union, he lit out for his damned castle in Scotland."

"Indeed, indeed, and so he did, Miss Bryce. He left his capable right-hand man to handle the contract negotiations. His course of action was . . . remind me, would you?"

"He dissolved the union and he threw out the men," she said. "He had a twelve-foot fence built around the steelworks and razor wire barricading it from the workers who made him his millions."

Macbride pouted—big business's very own devil's advocate. "Was it all so one-sided, Miss Bryce?"

The wings of her nostrils flared.

"Didn't he tie their contracts to the McKinley tariffs of 1890 to favor the high price of steel?"

She grumbled something that sounded like "Big deal."

"Wasn't it the workers themselves and their Amalgamated Iron and Tin Workers who insisted on that?"

The tinny castrato trill of the overhead clock signified the end—*orationis magistri intermittebur*—*professor interrupted*, lesson ended—indeed, he reckoned, the end of them from his life forever. *Good riddance, wayfarers.*

The clatter of books slammed shut, laptops slipped into carrying cases, and papers being shuffled erupted in pockets about the room. He pointed to the board, where his email address and a date were written for mailing in the take-home final, another of his many violations of campus policy. He watched them troop out. A small perk there—watching Rochelle exit a room. It summoned forth a tasty paradox—Marilyn Monroe's entrance in *Niagara*.

"Miss Bryce," he said, not unkindly, "may I suggest for your academic good that you do your sleeping at night?"

"I wish I could, professor, but my baby have—has the croup right now."

Macbride had seen many of them, young women who bloomed early and blighted fast. They found themselves trapped by men and babies, soiled pampers, and WIC coupons. Most gave up their dreams and fell back into the ranks of the working poor. The lucky ones graduated with some kind of training, rarely an education, and fled the state with sparks flying from their shoes.

Macbride feasted on Rochelle's swiveling hips. Bookless, paperless, unhappy creature—just another Lolita destined to disappear into the gray pallor of the Midwest.

Macbride was so locked into his own escape that he only just became aware of a mild disturbance in the doorway. *Too late*, he realized—*trapped*. The little nabob was shuffling and grinning at him, clipboard at half-mast.

"I heard a bit of your lecture, professor. I love the interaction of students with their teachers," said Shrivastava.

You would, you cretin.

"Andrew Carnegie—my, all those wonderful libraries to help people better themselves."

Macbride saw the little dean was not going to budge from the doorway—a determined process server—so Macbride hoped to distract him with a barrage of piffle as he gathered up his scattered papers—a man in haste to get to an important appointment.

"Let me tell you something about Carnegie, Dean," he said. "That young woman was right. Carnegie and Henry Clay Frick were a pair of heartless bastards."

"Ah, yiss." Macbride in fact hated Carnegie; he saw him as a little boy in a squalid cottage in the old country, stuffing himself on porridge, spoons in both hands, crying to his mother, "Maire, maire!" Sickeningly devoted to her all his life, he evolved—pupa to parasitical moth—into the nation's richest, most avaricious businessman and finally into the white-bearded, myopic philanthropist of his idiotic portraits.

"Some of your students have complained, Professor—"

"It is in the nature of students to complain, Dean."

This was real trouble. He could not afford to lose this wretched job. It would mean longer on the road next semester, less money. Another barrage of wordshot was needed, but his magazine was empty, his quiver held nothing save a few broken arrows.

"Do you know that Frick took three bullets from an anarchist's gun during the Homestead strike and then went back to work in his office three hours later?"

"My, my, what courage—but about your absenteeism, Professor—"

Macbride, briefcase in hand, bore down on him, but the momentum had shifted. He was the insect, the little brown dean the heel.

"Frick despised Carnegie like the devil himself—" Macbride effused, hopelessly lost now, desperate, on the verge of begging for another chance.

Shrivastava sensed his advantage but retreated a cautious few dilatory steps. Macbride would have to physically bump him to get past—odious thought, but he was prepared to do it.

Up close, smiling nervously, perspiration leaking from his pores, he fired a last volley while his hands fumbled at the satchel: "Frick even refused to reconcile in old age when they were a pair of Park Avenue millionaires." He took in the beaming dean's happy, homunculus face and saw his fate etched there.

"'Tell him,' said Frick to Carnegie's messenger," Macbride finished with a wan hopelessness, "'I'll see him in hell where we are both surely going.'"

"You don't say."

Macbride saw a breech and bulled through. "Yes, well, good evening, Dean."

"I am sorry to say we won't be requiring your services next semester, professor."

Macbride heard the words, halted in his progress.

Fired. The *s*'s of the Dean's pronouncement resonating like poison in his ear from a tiny dropper, death by millimeters and fractions.

". . . our adjunct contracts—as-needed basis, as you know . . . despite your distinguished service—"

Take thy beak from out mine heart.

Hurried footsteps *tock-tocked* behind him on the faux travertine floor.

"I say, pro-FES-sor Mac-BRIDE, I say, I have papers for you to sign!"

But Macbride, long experienced with dissatisfied wives and students, clamped his hat on his pate and was already down the staircase en route to the side exit. He would front the wrath of nature by circling the entire building to get to his rattle-trap Volvo before he would sign a single paper for this bureaucratic wretch nipping at his heels. "One simply knows," he muttered, confused and fearful as the abyss opened before him.

It made small difference now. Let the wind flay the skin from his battered hide and disembowel him if it could. He thought of Guadeloupe, where fronds of palm trees wafted gently by the warm blue shore. His sacking by the little dean had broken something in him, finally. His utilitarian shield was already riddled with gashes and holes—a lame beast too far behind the herd. He could not ford the river with it any longer: too many crocodiles. Rebellious words and defiant tones he might have used rushed too late to mind. His wives never lost their tongues when it came time for the big get-even. Not even a phrase to throw in the little worm's face, no borrowed grandeur, not so much as a whimper of protest much less a grand *non serviam*.

The truth was bitter. Macbride would have begged him on his knees for the chance to serve in this shabby heaven rather than reign in hell, and he knew it in the deepest cockles of his heart. He reviled his doppelgänger for cowardice, his ever-faithful whipping boy.

Would a last-second bootlicking save him from financial chaos? He looked back at the building—an impregnable fortress with its drawbridge lashed behind the portcullis.

"*Acta non verba*," said Macbride, gaining a little courage, isolated and weary beneath the vast star-studded night. *Deeds not words.* Then: *I need a drink.*

The hot needle spray of the showerhead blasted away the rest of his Wing Ding memories and their squalid aftermath like so much water circling the drain. He washed his chest and face and tried to avoid the tender places where tissue and muscle throbbed beneath the dark patches. Still wet, he threw on a frayed and seamsplit terrycloth robe from a hook behind the door.

He brewed a cup of scalding mint tea and gave Tod his supper from a can of whitefish and shrimp. The label portrayed a piratical, chops-licking alley cat on this so-called "seafood feast." The scratching of nails on linoleum signaled the cat's awakening. Always hungry, he came hustling from one of his naptime hideout spots as soon as he heard the top peeled back. Macbride watched him nip a hollow shrimp tail from the glutinous debris in his bowl. Tod growled with happiness.

"There, there, old boy," Macbride said with a stroke of his fur. The limp tail shot up with pornographic fidelity. He had saved the cat from vicious little boys trying to dock his tail with a paring knife. When one of the boys' fathers came by in his pickup truck and demanded the cat back, Macbride stood firm and refused. He would not surrender the kitten—*no, not on his life!* The man, a steelworker from the looks of him, stared with malevolence; his big fists were wrecking balls. Macbride refused to be goaded into a fight with the brute. When he thought of the gun rack in the back of the driver's seat, his legs trembled all over again.

He sipped the tea and looked out the window at the brittle flakes floating past the window in a horizontal stream. Where was life taking him?

Last night's slattern of a barmaid and her womanly curves beckoned. He had been celibate so long that the recollection of his sexless life made him feel utterly woebegone. His students obviously knew nothing of celibacy. He didn't want to think of their reckless copulations. Life was so unfair.

He forced his thoughts to Shrivastava, a guaranteed anaphrodisiac. He looked at the phone in its cradle still semaphoring its single red pulse. He thought better with Debussy. *La fille aux cheveux de lin*'s saccharine chords smoothed out some of the wrinkles. Something else tickled in his brain: Suicide. What summoned this will-o-the-wisp to his desperate mind? No flaxen-haired, blue-eyed Jesus at the end of the tunnel would ever beckon him. Was this merely agitated brain cells twitching their last in self-defense before all light faded as it must? And wherefrom his ticket out of the Slough of Despond? Wherefrom a way back to warmth and light—perhaps even a kind woman's touch?

Why not, his mind said, at least, consider it? *It*, that. The unnameable, unthinkable deed, the church's unforgivable sin in a world reeking of malevolence. But as an intellectual idea merely, what harm could it do, he thought.

Macbride tallied his many deficits: bank account depleted, savings nil, credit zilch, all cards maxed—thanks to his latest splurge in the Wing Ding Bar & Grill. The challenges were equally grim: obtain more underpaid teaching assignments in other community colleges—force himself into a selling demeanor, print up his curriculum vitae like yard sale flyers and carry them about—smile, grovel, lie. Add hundreds of miles more to his already exhausting itinerary so he could scratch out a penurious living. The thought sickened him.

He saw himself competing for road space at breakneck speeds in winter gales while eighteen-wheelers guided by amphetamine-laced rednecks played tag with his clapped-out Volvo on icy freeways. Then having to find spaces in the frozen tundras of college parking lots between classes, hurry to get into the classroom by the scheduled time, hang his coat in a space designated for adjunct faculty, which amounted to a broom closet's width. Never mind the single ancient computer and a printer (both working simultaneously would be a miracle) and afterwards cram down his starving gullet a stale sandwich from a vending machine. Don't forget the time to prepare lecture notes, to Xerox, to make those transparencies that melted inside the infernal machine—

He stopped pacing. The law of diminishing returns squared off against Occam's razor. He was barely making ends meet with his current load at campuses and traveling across the state line. He had been doing this drudgery for nine long years at beggar's wages, and all it meant was one thing: an existence that was harried, fraught with worry, and shabby to the core. How long before he must face the expense of a new car or his body's health would revolt and break down? A single traffic accident could ruin him.

He wanted to cry out to the stone-faced Doomsters above that he had other needs as well—how to satisfy those? Without a primer, he thought morosely, he wouldn't even be able to recall how to have sex anyway—*does her leg go there, my leg go here?* It had been so long since Siobhan . . .

No, no, no, by God! It simply cannot go on like this—

You can't do it.

Do what? Who said that?

Or—

He could choose the simpler path.

He stood on his mental fjord, giddy with fear and excitement. He looked down from a great dizzying height—and pondered his Kierkegaardian leap.

Do it.

Do what?

"The big leap, *ignoranus*."

"The word is *ignoramus*, you moron."

"I meant 'ignoranus' because you're stupid and you're an asshole," said phantom-Macbride right back, mocking him for all the catastrophes and failures of his life. "All right," Macbride said, exasperated by the cruel whispers. "All right, just stop badgering me."

"All right, *what*, Pro-fes-sor Mac-bride?" Shrivastava suddenly jumped up to replace his devil's advocate.

"I'll do it," Macbride said.

His heart beat wildly under the stars. He was exhilarated, terrified, but very much alive at the point he had decided to die—a cruel *carpe diem* exuberance that vanished at once. Another figure stepped from the wings into the arena of his debate with the forces of darkness. Macbride conjured that medieval iconoclast and logician, an intellectual hero of his early youth, William of Ockham. He who had incurred Pope John XXII's wrath and been forced to flee to his sanctuary in Surrey. Hounded by the pontiff, he then fled to Munich where he ended his days in embittered, lonely exile. Forlorn, Macbride thought of this sage man shivering in his last days, impoverished, infected with the viscous buboes of the Black Death. Even then, lying on death's doorstep, reeking of disease and decay, the great Ockham had been ducking a relentless papal emissary chasing him with recantation papers to sign.

Macbride detested himself for carrying along the vestiges of superstition's rags—a fear of providence, one by turns malignant and benevolent, overseeing dim humanity. Macbride's adopted mother had forced him to attend a hellfire and brimstone Pentecostal church and there he had acquired the horrific notion of God as a vindictive boy with an ant farm. He openly scoffed at the cheap Christian framework of his times and the boorish middle-class ethos that propped it up. Every aspect of rational life was plagued by its nonsense. Christmas season was the worst. Look at the buffoons mumbling their sanctimonious gibberish in front of every plaster crèche in town. The blatant appeals for money, the pederasts in Santa suits dandling children on their knees in department stores—what a loathsome display of greed and concupiscence. It was as transparent and crude an homage as the pornographic drivel being poured into suggestible, empty-headed black kids in the inner cities hunkered around boom boxes. As the Midwest burned, Washington fiddled.

Yet, and yet—oh, he hated himself for his inability to wean his intellectual bastion from the clammy grip of religion. He saw himself linked to that great miserable Nietzsche. He was like that lonely curmudgeon who also admired and hated what he feared. Deep in his bones, Macbride knew the stars neither bless nor scold, much less rule—they just are. But he felt he was being watched by someone with a mocking leer like those Norwegian tales of a certain gnomic creature, a bodiless head on a pair of feet that scuttled out of sight just at the very moment you turned your head to catch it watching you.

He put Chopin on and finished the dregs of Glenfiddich from a bottle that had rolled forgotten under the sofa.In moments of grand despair, Macbride needed and craved an audience. He addressed his cat lovingly; the cat was his sole companion in arms against the world; he spoke fondly of the cat's youth, calling him his beloved boy, his *puer eternitatis*, and bade him a solemn farewell, *ave et atque*. The cat's belly was full and he was disinclined to remain still unless the noise issuing from the hole in the man's head was accompanied by a scratch behind the ears or a stroke. Tod looked at the man with suspicion while he moved a kitchen chair to the foyer, a piece of cord dangling around his neck. The cat watched him position the chair just so. Instinct prompted Tod to find a spot on up the stairs where he could perch between the dowels of the banister and watch from a secure position. The strange new tone of the man's monologue betokened something between threat and play and his action did not seem familiar enough to Tod's patterned responses.

A chagrined Macbride discovered his bulk was an obstacle to so ordinary a task as climbing onto, and standing upon, a chair. He puzzled it out with a few scrapes to his right shin against the latticed backing. The chair squeaked like bones where the stress of his shifting center of gravity was greatest. Finally, Macbride was able to stand upright on the chair—a spinning plate on a magician's stick. He wondered belatedly if these things were factory-tested for this purpose. He tried lassoing the bottom portion of the pear-shaped dowel post that jutted beneath the stairwell, but the dexterity he needed to cinch the slipknot tight was a task requiring far more skill than he had reckoned upon. After a few tosses while straining to maintain balance, his shoulders, wrists, and knees burned.

His impatience and exasperation overwhelmed his caution. He put too much torque on the delicate spindles supporting the seat. The splintering sound no sooner registered in his brain than he was flat-backed to the floor with a tremendous *whump* that sucked the oxygen out of his lungs. His head struck the carpet, temporarily blinding him. Time went down a black hole. When Macbride's vision refocused, he saw the cat's goldgreen eyes locked on his from above. Man and cat remained in that position for a long time; neither seemingly able to break the stare. Macbride mainly because he couldn't. His shocked nervous system was working to process the flurry of his body's messages.The brain, on the verge of abandoning the citadel, slowly resumed control over the chaotic traffic.

After a longer time yet, he rose—staggering gingerly to his knees and then drunk-walking to his faded red velour sofa, where he collapsed in a heap. He lay there for hours in the fading light of the shortest day he remembered. Soon, the saffron glow of the moonlight reached his windows. The quiet of the night was like balm. He could draw no sensible conclusions from his thoughts, and he assumed he was concussed from the fall. One thought did emerge from the tumult: he no longer wanted to die.

A swish of Tod's tail caught Macbride's attention, and the

professor said to the cat, "You motherless son of a bitch, where were you when I needed you?"

Macbride was able to prop himself on one arm and reach down for the battered leather valise. He poked a hand into its maw and plucked out the long-ungraded student papers he'd crammed inside prior to his craven escape. He was completely sobered and a little sad, but grateful for the temporary respite the world was granting him. He rooted among the papers and found Rochelle's essay. He skimmed it first, making a holistic assessment before he got down to the minutiae of a word-by-word analysis; he covered it with commentary, *diabolus advocatus* as was his wont. He praised her, penned a capital B and circled it; as an afterthought, he recommended some texts she might want to look up for future reference. He then took another essay from the pile on the floor where Tod lay curled in sleep. Macbride smoothed the corners carefully where the edges had rucked. He repeated the process of extracting papers throughout the night until the pale glow through his windows was replaced by the first streaks of another frigid, pewter dawn. In Guadeloupe, daybreak would come with salmon streaks and the air would be scented with lemon. Blue skies stretched toward infinity over the aquamarine waters from the lagoons to the sea. He got up to make a cup of green tea and feed Tod his first meal of the day.

Lagos, Nigeria

My son moans and says, "Five hundred thousand! Je-sus Christ . . ." Mark glares at me. He's exactly the spitting image of Frank: arms crossed, leaning to the side like a dope fiend. He wears that OSU sweatshirt with Brutus Buckeye doing obscene things to a Michigan cheerleader. *Spit and image . . . spitting image . . .*

"Lagos! Can you tell me how a Harvard cardiologist gets scammed by some raggedy-assed computer bandits from a shithole country like that?" My hand itches for a scalpel. One swipe and arterial blood would spout like a red geyser from here to the garage.

"I don't see what there is to smile about, God damn you!" he shouts.

I imagine Mark getting off his plane in Africa, a fresh-eyed Peace Corps volunteer, not this greedy, shouting creature from my womb. His first letter home: his first week in the tropical heat, sweating in the stink, guzzling Coca-Colas, tossing in his hammock from the fever dreams of blood and violent sex brought on by mefloquine. I time-lapse him through the decades until his skin is sallow and his eyes are the color of egg yolk from malaria. An old man's body raked by sun, bald and blind. I shrivel him to a withered fetus at my breast.

Mark stops shouting and says something about his inheritance . . .

I let him vent. I have a quadruple and two implants today.

The new med surg nurse keeps bumping me from behind. She knows I know it's on purpose. How I'd love to get behind her in the shower and reach my hand around to feel her pubic ruff and push my cunt into her bottom, hear her moans . . ."Mother, Jesus fucking Christ, are you listening?"

Alice and Bob at Play in the Zero Field

By the time I reached elementary schoolroom in 1950, thermonuclear hydrogen bombs would have been tested from Pacific atolls to the Nevada desert. Old Father O'Grady would loom from the pulpit with thundering sermons about enslavement to Communism. (He liked to smack his fist into his palm as he ended his oration on the evils of "the hammer and the sickle").

One morning, Fr. O'Grady came to our playground at recess while we were flipping baseball cards, horsing around, playing Rover, Red Rover. He had a head of shiny silver hair and a kind drunkard's face (but let an altar boy move the wine cruet away too soon and he would find his wrist gripped in an iron vise until the wine was emptied). The nuns despised him, but he paid them no mind. We ran to him. He extended his arms like the big statue of Christ the Redeemer above Rio de Janeiro. Undoubtedly intoxicated, he said we could all go home. We took off, breathless—all but the bus kids—and raced homeward in all directions, scattering like minnows.

My father, like my uncles and grandfather, worked for Great Lakes Towing Company. I myself sailed the Great Lakes and made very good money for a teenager. I didn't mind being on the water for weeks on end while moving up or down the lakes, because I liked to read. Religion and English were the two subjects favored by the sisters of the Holy Humility of Mary—or the blue nuns, as they were called.

When I was five, my mother took me down to George O'Leary's shoe store on the harbor to buy me a pair of new shoes. My family and all my cousins bought their shoes from him. He was a neat, tidy man who wore white shirts and a Navy blue suit. He was clean-shaven and completely bald, no Caesar fringe, so that top of his head gleamed under lights. His voice was soft, not like my father's, and had a musical, lilting quality.

My father worked below decks on the big diesels that propelled this 90-ton workhorse, the tug America. As a boy occasionally allowed to tag along for the day, I watched the men prepare to make a tow while the captain stayed in the pilothouse. My father coiled tow ropes as big around as pythons in loops back and forth on the stern. I loved those red-and-green tugboats as they cut through the water. High above me, in the bow of the lakeboat, an arm tossed a painter tied to the hawser down to a tugman on the afterend. The steamship's cargo hold was like a great monster with its belly stuffed with billions of taconite pellets, as many as stars, mined from the ore fields of Minnesota.

In Superior, Wisconsin, one summer in my sailing days to make money for college, a dockworker released taconite down a chute to fill up the cargo hold of the *Col. James Pickands*. I was nauseated and dizzy, probably from a hangover, and wasn't paying attention. The chute missed my head by inches and nearly sent me flying into the blackened hold of the steel-plated bottom of the cargo deck several stories below. I remember looking up to see the bottom of his boots on the iron grating. Not a man, just a pair of boots that didn't move.

There were three tugs tied to iron bits cemented into the dock. The men called them niggerheads. The *Idaho* and the *America* were my favorite of the tugboats. After a tow, the men would go to a bar and drink. I drank ginger ale or orange soda and played Skee-ball. The men had huge bellies from consuming so much beer.

Twenty-five years before I was born, sitting in his study in Göttingen reading the liberal *Berliner Tageblatt*, Werner Heisenberg dreamed of meeting Albert Einstein. His work with Niels Bohr at the University of Copenhagen would result in his appointment as the youngest Professor of Theoretical Physics at the University of Leipzig at the age of 26.

At 26, Einstein was living with his older Serbian wife, Mileva, and their infant son, Hans Albert, at 49 Kramgasse, Bern. Their two-room apartment was reached after a long climb up a steep staircase, but it was all he could afford as a clerk in the patent office. In what would be known as his "miraculous year," Einstein would produce five papers for the *Annelen der Physic*. The fourth paper of 1905 would grab the world's attention with its $E=mc^2$ formula, proving matter and energy were exchangeable concepts. His final paper, modestly entitled "On a Heuristic Point of View Concerning the Production and Transformation of Light," would set a course for modern physics that would change everyday notions of reality, nature, God, and the universe more profoundly than had Newton's *Principia*.

Gone forever was the notion of a gossamer ether through which light traveled and stars twinkled. (For Newton this pervasive condition of absolute rest was nothing other than the eternally enduring Almighty.) Einstein wrote to a friend in May that his light theory was "very revolutionary," but he did not wholly trust it, and he would never accept its probabilistic view of reality despite the fact that Heisenberg and Erwin Schrödinger in the 1920s were already establishing the validity for quantum theory with mathematical matrices.

Einstein philosophically desired a universe of causality, one comprised entirely of granular atoms or one existing in discrete, continuous bundles of energy (his quanta), these flowing, indivisible packets of energy, never at rest. "God does not play dice," Einstein would famously say—to which Heisenberg's Danish mentor Niels Bohr would respond—although no one is certain of the verbatim response: "Einstein, stop telling God what to do with His dice."

I sailed the Great Lakes for a couple years as an ordinary seaman, then I hitchhiked home from the Bethlehem Steel plant in Gary, Indiana where my boat, the *Lehigh*, was tied up. My girlfriend and I eloped to Monroe, Michigan. We bought wedding rings at a jewelry store near the statue of General Custer. Back home, I asked our parish priest to marry us at Mother of Sorrows, where I had gone through the eighth grade and served hundreds of masses. Father McKinney had a brogue and an unwavering sternness; he refused. I had stopped believing in God by then. My wife's face wet with tears as we left the parish house.

Three years before his prestigious appointment, Heisenberg had hoped to meet Einstein at a lecture to be given in Leipzig. Widespread anti-Semitic agitation at the time might have prevented this. Heisenberg was handed a leaflet on his way up the steps to the lecture by a student of a prominent German physicist of the day; in it, Einstein's theories were deplored as Jewish propaganda. Heisenberg and Einstein would meet three years later, in autumn, at the Solvay Congress in Brussels. By then, Heisenberg had perfected his uncertainty principle, based on Schrödinger's breakthrough experiments on wave mechanics. The meeting was cordial, but Einstein refused to concede to the theory of uncertain relations, arguing that unobservable quantities were essential to all theories. Future mathematicians, he hoped, would prove this so.

In 1935 Einstein and two colleagues published a paper on the strange nature of quantum superposition. A quantum superposition is the combination of all the possible states of a system. If, for instance, a laser-bombarded isotope of beryllium has a top-spin, diagonal spin, or a down-spin, its mate will arrive at its detector with a corresponding opposite spin. Researchers have sent these subatomic pairs down fiber-optic lines and discovered the same result every time. The isotopes—physicists facetiously call them "Bob" and "Alice" in these experiments—cannot communicate with each other en route to their detectors—unless it is at many times faster than the speed of light, which is the universe's automatic braking system, according to Einstein.

This brings me to Schrödinger's cat in the box. Schrödinger's what-if experiment works thusly: place a cat in a sealed box with a flask of hydrocyanic acid and a radioactive source in a Geiger counter. Isolate the box from any decoherence. If a single decayed atom is released, it causes the counter tube to discharge, releasing a hammer to break the glass tube of poison, which kills the cat. The cat's life is dependent on a single subatomic particle. After a short elapse of time, the cat, he argued, must be seen to remain both dead and alive to the universe outside the box. It's a classic *reductio ad absurdam* argument, but he never intended to prove that a cat could be *dead and alive* at the same time.

Schrödinger called it *Verschränkung*—"entanglement." Einstein called it "spooky action at a distance." When he and Schrödinger exchanged letters in 1950, Einstein was fulsome in praise of this so-called "Copenhagen interpretation." A system stops being a superposition at the moment of observation—one must look inside the box to see if the cat is alive or dead.

The problem with the cat paradox, as contemporary cosmologists have noted, is that the cat and the observer are necessarily "entangled" at the moment of observation. When opening the box, the observer becomes entangled with the cat, so states of observation corresponding to the cat's being alive or—as Schrödinger himself inelegantly expressed it, "mixed or smeared out in equal parts"—are not possible. At the moment of observation, the already split-cat has further separated into an observer looking into a box at a dead cat or an observer looking at a live cat. No single-state perception is possible to collapse into until both observer and cat are joined in a common system state where the information known is held by both the cat inside the box and the observer looking down into it. Different branches of the universe, in other words. Both real, both possible. Einstein insisted nothing could travel faster than light, but quantum computers will make today's computers (i.e., Turing machines) with their ones and zeroes seem like quaint Amish buggies shambling up to the starting gate at the Grand Prix.

At 26 I taught for a small college in Salem, West Virginia that underwent a transformation from Baptist affiliation to a private, Japanese-owned university. I remember a couple of cousins named Fordyce who played football. One of the cousins was illiterate and copied what I wrote on the board in his tiny, sloping penmanship.

On the day I went with my mother to O'Leary's shoe store, however, something was wrong. Shoes boxes lay strewn all over the store as if someone were piling them up for bonfires. New shoes were scattered about, still folded in tissue. Mr. O'Leary was dressed in his usual dark blue suit and his mellow voice was the same, but I sensed my mother growing nervous as he brought one pair after the other for me to try on. He set each pair next to my feet as gently as if they were swaddled newborns. I don't recall how long we were inside, but my mother hustled me out of there with a nervous explanation that I knew was a lie.

Did I read about his funeral or did someone tell me of it? I have no clear memory. I was too young to know what Alzheimer's was, and I would not learn of Newton's melancholic second law until high school.

In the zero-point field where all energy disappears, a single cubic centimeter of this emptiness (a "morphogenetic field" or "the thin stuff from which everything is made") has a density of ten thousand billion to the power of four more energy than all the matter in the known universe. We cannot measure it. Like Bob and Alice, "it" knows everything that happens in the universe, instantaneously and with absolute accuracy. It is where all action at a distance occurs in perfect synchronicity at ten thousand times the speed of light. Jung called it the collective unconscious. It is a field of information or, if you prefer, a field of pure consciousness. Some say it is God.

We move inexorably toward something, synchronicity, if not chaos. The light that reaches me here is always eight minutes old. In the "diabolical mechanism" of my brain is a box of memories where lonely misfits gather—but no cats, alive or dead. A man stands in an empty store, a boy watches his father coil a rope, and a vulgar-minded whiskey priest stretches his arms toward children at play.

The Rare Book Thief

A very large man named Lloyd Shibley was experiencing painful stomach gas in front of the steps to the Cleveland Public Library.

He blamed it on his last-second impulse to turn around just as he'd reached the revolving glass turnstile at the top of the library steps. Like a beagle with its nose to the wind, he reversed direction and headed straight to the street vendor on the corner of East Third where he scored a couple foot-long chili dogs topped with diced onion, jalapeños, and cheese.

He could not help it. Food nowadays held him in thrall like some bewitching domme in black Lycra wielding a whip against his plump backside. *Eat*, it commanded, *eat more, eat until you can't eat anymore* . . . .

Food was now his sole comfort in a world that had all too rapidly turned upside down. *I have fallen so fast*, he lamented to his inward spirit, his consoling voice—the true and noble Lloyd Shibley who resided within. *Alas*, Shibley thought, *there was so much more space for occupancy now, too.* Never svelte, he had ballooned to three hundred pounds in a matter of months, despite the vexations of travel, stress, and *them*.

In truth, Shibley's in-house doppelgänger was under siege. This delicate alter ego, so long in the making and self-created from a lonely boyhood through an adulthood of blighted promise to a shabbily genteel middle-age where success, fortune, and women had all slipped through his fingers like sand, was succumbing to the nightmare of his desperate circumstances.

The elevator pinged the second floor. He waited for the pneumatic hiss of the doors. He stepped onto a pomegranate-red carpet that baffled any sound from the reading room. His stomach rumbled again. He looked around to see if anyone noticed, but he was alone in the foyer to the reading room, which was a long carpeted extension of the exhibition corridor where objet d'art were sequestered behind their thick glass panes.

He passed slowly through the corridor that led to the reading room. He noted, as before, the rows of lockers where briefcases were to be secured before one could enter the reading room. Shibley's special valise was in there too, held hostage with the rest, but unlike the rest, his was engineered with panels, levers, and hidden compartments; these engineered devices were his modus operandi where valuable works were given a fast ride out the doors straight to the black market of rare books.

The life-sized portrait of the founding donor stared down at him from piercing glacier-blue eyes while one hand fondled his silver pocket watch, as if to say: *I have called the police. They will be here any minute*. Shibley withered under the ghostly stare, knowing he was about to violate the sancta sanctorum of this man's legacy.

Entering the plush rectangular room, he stopped briefly. His radar blipped the two witches behind the special collections desk, although neither glanced his way, busy as they were with that old scholar. Shibley had endured a long conversation with him already and tagged him the Melville maniac. Apparently one of the city's founding fathers, trudging through the bracken along Lake Erie's shore all the way from Connecticut, had a descendant back home who acquired a respectable collection of letters from the great novelist and his heir had bequeathed them to this burg's public library. According to the garrulous old man, every big academic library in the state had offered tons of money to extricate those letters for their own collections. *Fat chance*, the Melville maniac had chortled.

Shibley's vision swept the four other occupants of the room

at a glance; they were busy poring over their documents and books. He heard the faintest scratch of pencil on tablet paper. A gray-haired, attractively dressed woman seated at the table nearest him was busy copying something of her own. (Pens were of course *verboten* and white gloves mandated if one deigned to handle the delicate manuscripts issued by one of the joyless crones at the desk.)

Opposite him and a few seats away, the maniac had strewn his belongings before him as if marking his territory so that no one would think of intruding into his space. His paraphernalia included one outsized magnifying lens that Shibley, and everyone else in the room, witnessed him using that morning. It was the peculiar use of that instrument that made Shibley want to pluck it out of his freckled hand and crack him over the skull with it. A little reflection, however, suggested the old man's presence was fortuitous and he would be able to profit from the oddball distraction the man provided.

The maniac was a frail, white-haired man in his seventies, Jewish—judging by his surname and ascetic features. Shibley's technique was long-established by now; he knew he had to control his immediate environment as much as possible and that sometimes meant tedious conversations with his fellow students of antiquity. *Blend in,* they said. *Even if you are big as a house, don't cause people to look at you.* That was in his trainee days. Now he was proficient enough to teach post-doctoral seminars in how to steal valuable works from libraries.

That morning he had chosen his spot for the best—which is to say, worst—vantage from the desk staff's point of view. The Melville fanatic was ideal for the purpose, for the man provided distractions galore and kept everyone's eyes on him. Shibley rapidly pegged him as one misstep from an Alzheimer's clinic. Shibley loathed his type; these were the harmless drudges who always succeeded in academia, that Garden of Eden from which he had been expelled long ago. Now in the advanced decrepitude of their old age and pressed by the inactivity of retirement, without a cheering gallery of subordinates and graduate-school lackeys, they frittered time away with more useless scholarship, hoping the world would pay them respect once more. Shibley saw them as aging, punch-drunk boxers with the self-delusion of yet one more fight left in them. Shibley snorted. The world needed one more article on Melville's white whale as much as he needed a double-limbed amputation.—*Ye gods above, one of the harpies was focusing her laser stare right through him . . .*

The Melville madman was planted in his seat, ignoring Shibley's faint smile of acknowledgment, and he immediately plunged into his erratic investigation of the letter before him, the same one he extracted with gloved fingers from its cellophane like stale cheese from a vending machine's sandwich. He proceeded to mutter and fuss over it, a bomb expert looking for the right wire to cut. Then he would pick up his trusty lens and resume his exotic method of examining the letter's handwriting.

Shibley had seen enough of this weird action that very morning on his first reconnoiter, yet he was nonetheless fascinated by the man's bizarre habit of waving the lens about before targeting whatever word or phrase he sought and then letting his whole head follow the glass. He seemed to be trying to extract each sepia-toned word from its page with his peculiar motion. Now and then he jerked upright in his chair as if shocked. Shibley thought of a man who couldn't decide whether to haul in his fish or bob for another apple.

The other academic sat quietly hunched over his book. (Shibley so guessed from the *de rigueur* salt-and-pepper beard and other outré apparel, which included a mustard-yellow vest that looked as if it had been decorated with bottle caps.) Shibley watched him pore lovingly over a beautifully illustrated *Rubaiyat*. Shibley's disdain for his fellow occupants had nothing to do with their welcome cover; these two made an efficient team like a pair of planets sucking into their orbits space debris that might otherwise come his way. He could almost hear the clucking of tongues the other nuisance generated at the front desk.

Shibley took in the tableau with his peripheral vision once more and he reviewed his plan.

Once seated comfortably again, he slowed down his breathing. Before all else, he had to get this anxiety under control. He spread out in front of him a number of his own books and a notebook into which he scribbled gibberish whenever staff passed by. It was most irksome to discover that a piddling library like this—*Good God*, one that specialized in chess and checkers, orientalia, and the tripe of folklore—had the temerity to install security procedures that would have safeguarded the black stone of Mecca during Hajj.

Shibley subconsciously tensed. Without looking up, he knew the walking guard was coming toward his table. His heart fluttered. He realized he had not secured the tiny extension on his laptop, the only object allowed in the reading room besides the writing paraphernalia. He felt perspiration under his arms and beads gathering at his temple and on the back of his neck.

"Sir, turn that over," the guard said.

Shibley's stomach contents turned to instant liquid like tree sap hit by lightning.

This was it: his last few breaths as a free man. His mind reeled off the coming hours in fast-time: shackles, prison orange, public shaming, a trial, a long bus ride to some desolate compound which might look like a college campus from the outside, except for the encircling razor wire, but inside contained thousands of savages, barely literate men, violent miscreants and the dullards, scores of daily humiliations to be borne and—*horribili visu*—terrors and degradations beyond the mind's imagining. He blanched at the mere thought of prison rape. A real Dantean circle from which no one like him ever escaped unscathed in mind or body. . .

"Sir, I asked you to turn that letter over."

The Melville man looked up from his scrutinizing and blinked at the guard like a baby bird.

"The letter, sir. Turn the letter over. Documents are not permitted to be set face down."

"I'm just checking the watermark," the old man replied.

"Those are rules of the reading room, sir."

Shibley, his head bowed and still as a stone monument on Easter Island, perused one of his own books with watery eyes that saw no words. He silently cursed the old man's obstinacy with a fury that made his body tremble. His stomach resolved the standoff by gurgling so loudly that both the guard and aged scholar ceased their exchange in mid-word and looked right at him. The old man's face was all annoyance, but Shibley shrugged his shoulders and smiled—what is one to do?

The guard's tone grew more impatient, but the old man hotly persisted in his "right as a taxpayer of the state" to examine the letter as he chose, rules or no rules. Tiny pinpricks of light like fireflies appeared in the room and Shibley realized he was on the verge of actually fainting! The fake door of his computer would be discovered and all that he had just imagined would come to pass.

No, no—fighting off his wooziness, he recovered his wits and his breath and slid the panel shut. He stood up.

Out of the corner of his eye, he saw the old man grudgingly flip the letter over. The guard said, "Thank you, sir," and turned on his heel, no doubt glad to be rid of the old fart.

"Melville didn't write this letter," the old man said to Shibley with a triumphant leer.

"Oh, you don't say?" Shibley barely managed to be intelligible.

"You don't look good," the maniac said. "What's wrong with you?"

"I'm feeling—I'm feeling . . . pardon me, I'm—"

"You're pardoned," the old man said, "better go get a drink of water. The fountain's in the hallway out there." He dismissed Shibley and returned to his precious discovery.

Despite rubbery legs, Shibley made it to the desk and mentioned that he was stepping out for a second to go to the men's room.

"I'll hold your I.D. until you come back, Professor Duncan," she said. She had mistakenly used the wrong surname from Shibley's fake business card he was currently using, but he let it pass.

Up close she was much older than he had realized and singularly unattractive, with wide-spaced eyes and a russet wig that perched gaudily on her head. Faint-headed, Shibley stared at fissures and tiny cracks radiating in all directions from her red lipstick. He casually mentioned he might "step outside for a breath of fresh air."

"Whatever," she replied and continued making notes on an index card.

Shibley almost barked a laugh, so close was he to all-out hysteria at that point. He was an inch from reverting to the mentality of a little boy with uncontrollable giggles during high mass.

His wobbly legs required a Herculean effort to get him out of there. He somehow tore his vision from the ludicrous wig and scarlet circumference of mouth and ambled toward the door.

Like a horse with blinders, Shibley stepped off the elevator and found his way to the restroom on the floor below. He splashed cold water on his face. *He whom the gods would destroy they first make mad.*

"Hunh, man, whatcha'll sayin'?"

He did not realize he was not alone. A black teenager in a burnt orange Cavaliers jersey with a hand-drawn X across LeBron James' number stitched on the front stepped out of a stall at the end and loomed in his vision. Shibley looked at the mocha face surrounded by dreadlocks secured by tiny bands of brightly colored beads. The youth stared into the mirror right at him as if he were as out of place as a balloon-blowing goat.

"Cha'll say, homes? I dint catch that, yo."

"Nothing, nothing," Shibley muttered, still flustered, "I didn't say anything."

He stared back at the boy, or rather, at the boy's face next to his in the rust-spotted mirror. The boy dusted invisible crumbs from the front of his khakis and Shibley saw about four inches' worth of BVD exposed beneath the popped navel button.

"Ya'll better put that crack pipe down, fool," the boy said with a lot of topspin, street-thug style. He walked out with that exaggerated stroll of city youth everywhere. Shoulders rolling, he glided to the door and without any discernible effort from a well-muscled arm, popped it open.

Shibley heard its sibilant hiss fade and looked back into the mirror.

"Fool," he repeated to his mirror's image. He wanted to escape, just walk out the door and keep walking until he collapsed. He could head straight for Lake Erie at the end of the Ninth Street pier and step off, let the waters close over his miserable head. Unlike those rare books upstairs, there would be no elaborate printer's rubric to mark his life's sojourn's end. Fish food. He imagined lampreys and zebra mussels covering his bloated corpse . . .

Time was passing. He had to steel himself for the next phase. The face in the lavatory mirror told him he was all right, his fears were unwarranted, and the time to act was now. *Acta non Verba*, as the sage Romans counseled: "Deeds, not words."

So far he had gone through works by Balde, Delille, Juan Huarte de San Juan, Rabelais, Tegner, Vergilius and Girolamo Vida. Each slip request filled out, turned in; then he would wait until the book arrived, sometimes escorted by another staff member, walk the tome over to his table under the watchful eyes of the staff. By now the guard was used to seeing him, which would allay any suspicion he was someone other than what he sometimes called himself: book thief *extraordinaire*. Shibley forced himself to peruse the work, which invariably meant nothing whatsoever, and jot occasionally in his notebook, which consisted mostly of his personal lamentations about his miserable existence in a stream of consciousness interrupted with an occasional obscene haiku. After a reasonable interval, he would return the book and proffer his next request. They had to be as sick of him as he of them by now.

It was time for the next stage of the mission. Shibley thrilled with a giddy delight that reminded him of his pubescent days of pilfering *Playboys* under his windbreaker from the Rite-Aid pharmacy in Seattle.

He strode back to the elevator, punched two, giving himself a pep talk. He banished fear, all doubt, and ordered his beating heart to be still. This was the old Lloyd Shibley.

He made a last sweep of the room to ascertain the position of the personnel and then made his move. With skills practiced in seedy motels under the tutelage of his Russian thugs, Shibley secreted a very rare edition of *The Courtier* in a pocket sewn inside his suit coat. An even more valuable *Gesta Romanorum* went down his pants into a pouch twenty minutes later. He could maneuver it with a drawstring until it settled against his thigh. The final phase of the operation required a surgeon's dexterity; he withdrew false cardboard covers for each book from square flaps cut into the back of his suit coat. Shibley could pop them loose from the false darts sewn there.

He made a little show of taking off his coat and whipping it over the seat back and pretending to straighten it out. Covers in hand, he had only to attach them to the books he had brought for the purpose. Their design would fool no expert, but the crones weren't experts. They were paper shufflers and book handlers. If it looked like a book and it felt like a book, it would pass muster.

Shibley's moment of terror was always that brief exchange of the book-manqué for the genuine article, but he had become so artful at engaging the attention of staff at the moment of transaction that they barely acknowledged the phony book in hand.

It was the stuff of movies and Shibley almost snickered at a romantic image of himself in a Zorro costume, though he could never envision his bulk astride a horse, much less leaping from a balcony onto one. He firmed the false covers snugly around cheap editions bought in bookstalls in Sofia and Budapest or wherever the Russians claimed to find them. Shibley told Boris that any neighborhood garage sale would yield the same result for the same purpose, but there was a routine to follow and follow it they would. He had long wondered why it was that the people behind his Russian mentors insisted on shipping books to different sites along their itinerary. On the one and only occasion Shibley had the temerity to voice his thoughts about the "extravagance" of waiting for shipments of old books, Boris, the cousin and boss of their operation, had ceased his pacing and fixed on him such a black look that he had never dared to speak about this part of their mission again.

His other two books were added for subterfuge. His week's long correspondence with the library staff from a Wi-Fi accommodation at the Double Tree Inn in North Indianapolis had prepared the ground for this mission. He was Professor Richard Hosmer Adams Blum, formerly emeritus professor of seventeenth- and eighteenth-century literature at the University of Arkansas. Shibley had taken his name from the same reference work he used for all his aliases, once ensuring that the man himself was deader than Julius Caesar. It wouldn't do to be caught borrowing a *nom de service* that one could trace back to a living soul. At that time, Shibley recalled, he was already fully occupied in lightening the William Charvat collection of American fiction at The Ohio State's special collections archives.

Columbus, alas and alack, was the beginning of his run of bad luck. For one thing, his goal there had been to acquire Cyrillic manuscripts from various monasteries on Mount Athos, Greece, and all his correspondence and false identity were designed for that purpose. However, Boris' mysterious Russian sources back in New York had not done their homework, because the library had recently microfilmed their entire Slavic collection, including the prized Hilander Monastery manuscripts. They were forced to improvise or waste the mission.

Even so, a priceless John Foxe's *Book of Martyrs* proved impossible to steal because a staff member stayed at his side the entire time he possessed the book. After several minutes of delicate thumbing through the leaves in gloved hands and writing some cryptic nonsense in his notebook, he thanked her for the "wonderful opportunity to hold that treasure in his hands" and returned it. For reasons of pique perhaps, or acclimating to his dubious role, the next day he returned to the library and walked out with a Nelson Algren and a William S. Burroughs in one sleeve and a pair of James Thurber letters and drawings in the other. It was no coup like the Foxe he was hoping for, but he was delighted he hadn't come away empty-handed.

"It was mere child's play," he bragged to the morose cousin of Boris, one Vassily Shostokovich, as he handed over the tomes.

His reward for initiative was to see Vassily smile. Then the smile disappeared and the Arctic frost of his normal visage returned. His black eyebrow bent slightly between his eyes and he ripped the books in half and tore the pages out in fistfuls. He did this without straining a single muscle. While he undid his belt buckle, his eyes never wavered from Shibley's shocked face even when he dropped his pants. Snatching the Thurber letters and sketches from Shibley's other hand, he wiped his backside with them. He wadded the papers into a tight ball and placed it into the palm of Shibley's hand and closed his large hand around Shibley's fingers, squeezing until Shibley gave out a yelp that could be heard from one end of the motel to the other.

Shibley awoke later on the floor of the room—how much later he still didn't know. He must have passed out from the excruciating pain. Boris was looking down at him with an idiot smile. "You just made my cousin mad," he said.

He and Boris disagreed often on the so-called training regimen. Boris constantly dinned into his ears not to call attention to himself once he entered the premises. "Be normal," he warned, "even if you are as big as a mountain." Shibley stubbornly refused to concede the point. For one thing, he told the Russians, it was moot.

"What is moot," Vassily snapped. "You're not a cow. Make sense."

CCTV would usually capture him entering and leaving any special collections, no matter what he did, said, or wore. Unless he wore bells on his shoes, it wasn't crucial to keep a low profile once he entered the special collections area. Watchers comprised the staff at the reception desk, circulating guards, surveillance cameras, open areas and cleared lines of sight—all of it, he knew, designed to prevent book mutilation or theft. If he had to use the restrooms, he'd have to leave his briefcase in the carrel and pass by staff, and whether hawk-eyed or indifferently regarded, he was constantly under someone's gaze. It was the accumulated effect of this continual scrutiny, all these eyes boring into him over the last few hard weeks that was giving him such stress and affecting his GI tract lately. . .

* * *

Shibley burped. Belatedly he attempted to cover his mouth with his fist.

The wizened Melville academic ceased his suctioning motions to fire a look his way. Shibley tried another weak smile, but received back a look of curled disdain. He felt the top of his head flush and immediately cut his gaze downward to the papers in front of him, hoping that no one else heard. The words jigged in front of his eyes. He maintained his vacuous perusal for five agonizing minutes before he dared to look up again. Everything seemed normal except for the twisting in his guts. He was so close to completing the mission with his prizes safely stowed and now this . . .

Another, lower temblor deep within his bowels settled the matter: *Oh dear*, he had to find a lavatory. *Right now.*

He pushed the chair back and stood up. The carpeting, however, had not permitted as much room as he required for his ample girth, and he found himself stutter-stepping with the chair somehow bumping against the back of his knees. Shibley corrected only to find his center of gravity now overcorrected—once again and forever, the fat boy in gym class—while his right shoe heel snagged against the chair's other leg, which had pinned itself into the carpeting like a dart.

Down went Lloyd Shibley, all three-hundred pounds.

After his vision cleared, he struggled to find purchase—first, with the upended chair to prop himself to his knees—and when the crack of wood made that an unwise decision—he threw one hand out on the carpet for balance, a Sumo wrestler tossing rice outside the ring, and then by dint of a heroic effort to gather all the strength in his outsized body, he rose to his feet.

His pate glowed crimson from the huge embarrassment and he wheezed from the effort. The aged academic was staring at him as if he had just witnessed a volcano rising from the seabed floor. It was a soft landing thanks to the plush carpeting, but if he had ignited a bar of Semtex, he could not have drawn more attention in the place. Every eye was fixed on him and every human being in whatever tiny motion had stopped to gaze at the commotion created by a large man extricating himself from the floor's humiliating clutch.

Shibley knew he had to get out of there at once. He could not go back into the lion's den thrice. *That mackerel-eyed, bewigged woman and her red-rimmed gape too much--simply too much for him to bear right now . . .*

He felt eyes touching him everywhere, his humiliated psyche probed by their sticky fingers, each eager to tear the scab off his still-bleeding wound—namely, that Lloyd Shibley, Ph.D., graduate of the University of Pennsylvania's prestigious Wharton School of Economics, MBA Stanford, *magna cum laude* University of Seattle, was nothing more than a lousy book thief who had just taken a pratfall.

But this too: always the tag-end of his prideful reminiscences of what he had once accomplished, the other side of the coin to what he once was and had lost: from tenured professor to adjunct faculty at nondescript community colleges. From a man sought by intelligent, good-looking women to a morbidly obese buffoon, love-smitten with food and terrified by a pair of twins more formidable than Castor and Pollux in the night sky.

Worse always came to worse in Lloyd Shibley's life, which had more twists than a pretzel factory: stealer of rare books, absconder of rare manuscripts, pilferer of annotated and limited editions, ransacker of incunabulae, and last and worst of all his self-hurled epithets: gutless pawn of oafish Russian scum. As always, he ended his litany of woe with an imprecation to the one he blamed for putting him into this morass of fear and despair: she who once lit his fire with her own unquenchable flame: the beautiful, cruelest one of womanhood's perfidious race: Siobhan of the red hair and red fingernails. Destroyer of men—in particular of *him*, her former lover and intellectual mentor. In the end, he was no more to her than a Helot to a Spartan, something to be killed for sport.

That lad back there in the restroom mirror was a prophet, he realized wanly. *But I had pretty plumage once*, he might have wept to that forlorn image staring back.

He stood up and patted down the Caesar fringe of hair spiking up from his ears; he hitched his pants higher up his great round belly. He tucked the wrinkled end of his shirt into his pants with stiff, pudgy fingers. In short order, he retrieved his I. D. from the disapproving harpy at the desk, fetched his valise from the locker, rode the elevator down to the first floor lobby. As the elevator creaked its descent, he was tortured by the accompaniment of music from overhead speakers, some kind of epicene-voiced pop singer vaguely familiar to his memory of riding in other elevators. The words were the usual half-intelligible gibberish of love-smitten pap but accompanied by freakish whistles, squeaks, and abrupt yawps as if the singer had Tourette's.

Shibley waited an eternity while the guard at the turnstile stuck his hand perfunctorily inside his valise and drew out various objects. He asked Shibley to remove the lap top and Shibley handed it to him. He had already assessed the Achilles heel of this library right there: a minimum-wage employee who wouldn't react to anything less than a leghold trap he stuck his mitt into, and even more important to Shibley, no scale for weighing the difference between what came inside and what left. Some library scales could detect as much as a gram of weight difference.

He headed down the steps to the street. It was necessary to get a taxi and go straight to the cheap motel to face his Russians. One foot in front of the other, the way mothers teach toddlers to walk, but in his case more like the way those poor captive bastards did it on the Bataan death march.

Shibley walked aimlessly away from the library without direction or purpose. The late-afternoon sunshine was a balm and he was just grateful to be free in the open air after his imprisonment upstairs. He was the wretched prisoner released from his oubliette by a dropped rope in those old French Foreign Legion films.

Cleveland's rush-hour pedestrian traffic was just then commencing. *Oh, to be nothing more than a frotteur*, he thought. Just to rub up against the rumps of these perfumed professional women in their fine attire would be all the risk he would ever desire henceforth in this life. He was aware that the same insipid tune as in the elevator was playing somewhere nearby . . . a young black male in a beret passed close by with an MP3 player and earbuds. An improvement from the boombox days when they blasted their hideous music everywhere, but Shibley had no doubt the same mawkish or infernal lyrics were being retailed. He experienced a sudden pungent whiff of rotting fish. He wondered if this was an olfactory or an aural hallucination—or both? Had the enormous stress of late finally cracked him like a walnut? Had he finally, completely, lost his mind?

He stopped. He let the wave of people pass around him like a rock in midstream. He looked down the broad avenue of traffic and watched these well-dressed men and women move on, bright with their lives' hopes and ambitions. He had once been there. Their lives and careers were normal and they were as oblivious to his misfortune as the rats dodging beneath their feet in the sewers. For the second time that day, he uttered words of a wasted education. This time, however, it was Milton he summoned from the depths—but not for any words of solace from the blind genius:

Whichever way I fly is hell, myself am hell.

It was a double dagger in the hymn book of his life, a mad cadenza played on a piano out of tune. Shibley wallowed in his self-pity, but he yet feared one thing more to the accumulated litany of his personal woes—the big reckoning, the *Dies Irae* waiting for him because he had failed to complete his mission. *The Russians—oh, yes, the Russians were waiting.* And they would not be pleased.

* * *

They had booked Shibley into the Embassy Suites downtown—at his firm insistence. He stubbornly refused to take a room with them at their lodging in some pastel-colored firetrap called the Shangri-la, a destitute-looking place with a neon palm tree sheltering a cobalt blue parrot in its leaves.

The whole lopsided structure was a shabby, two-toned affair in faded pink and turquoise which offered HBO and adult movies. The smaller sign below showed gaps in the letters like an old man's missing teeth: "Conv ie nt Mi mum Walk Dis ance to Q Loans," no doubt one of those greedy monopolistic corporate entities sucking up the taxpayers' gelt in the latest economic crisis.

Shibley, who disliked acronyms as much as enigmas, asked a nattily dressed black man in his sixties passing by the lobby what a "Q Loan" signified. The man gave him a long stare before replying: "Dude, that—that the "Q" arena, man, that used to be the home of King LeBron James before he fucked us and went to Miami! How you not know that, my man?" He walked off with the same studied hip-roll as the youth in the library.

Beside the motel was a Greyhound bus terminal and a seedy brownstone converted from an office building. Derelicts of the city, some with liquor or beer bottles in paper sacks as a concession to the roving police patrols, ambled about in no certain direction. Like dogs at an electronic fence, they never strayed past a certain point on the sidewalks. All the buildings on the street reminded him of bad architectural compromises between metropolitan morgues and European student hostels.

He had timidly explained to Boris (ignoring the black looks of Vassily altogether) that it wasn't so much that it was an insult to his person (it damned well was, of course) but because, he said, he needed to operate from a psychological vantage that was—well, *crucial* to the success of their missions. He had to appear to be a professional scholar, a man of worth and culture. He would not lower himself to their argot to explain what to him was perfectly obvious, but these low-rent numbskulls (his thugocracy, in effect) wouldn't know the difference between a bock and a dunkel, however much cheap beer they poured down their filthy gullets.

Their rooms over time in every city they had visited always stank of body odor, unwashed clothes and the remnants of greasy fast food; add to that heady broth their beery exudations and Shibley waited for the nausea to boil up in his stomach every time he went to check in with his masters.

When Boris opened the door, saw him, and turned his back to him, Shibley debated whether he should discreetly open the balcony's sliding door to carry off some of the noxious vapor. He hesitated and stopped, fearing he might offend them, not that these brutes had such delicate sensibilities . . .

"Sit the fuck down, professor," Boris barked at him as soon as he opened the door.

Shibley sat down on the nearest unmade bed and locked his fingers together in his lap to keep them from twitching, another sign of his growing unease with these two.

Boris glared at him and thumbed the cap off a St. Pauli Girl. The sight of his bobbing Adam's apple reminded Shibley of that shopworn academic and his piston-like magnifying lens. At least the brand of beverage seemed to be improving over their last motel stay in Columbus, where he had counted sixteen Coors strewn like dead soldiers near a basket overflowing with more empties.

Vassily, as usual, said nothing. He leaned against the dresser and bored into him with those dark baleful eyes of his. An empty green bottle dangled from his fingertips. The man was inhuman or subhuman, Shibley thought. One thick black ridge of eyebrow extended across his prognathous brow. Proof, Shibley thusly reasoned, that Neanderthal man had mated with modern man's remotest ancestor. But there was nothing of the knuckle-dragging, stolid brute in his movements. He glided like a vampire in a Hollywood movie. Vassily Shostokovich was as graceful and silent as a big cat on the prowl in the veldt. He was by far the scarier of the two men.

"Tell me again, God damn it, and use English this time," Boris said.

That cheap wit garnered a razor slit of smile across Vassily's normally frozen lips.

"You see," Shibley began, "as I said, I knew right away the guard out front was suspicious—"

Shibley cleared his throat and hoped this new tack was more credible than his first version that morning.

"How did you know the guard was suspicious of you?"

This might have been the longest utterance from Vassily in weeks. Although his syntax and vocabulary were superior to Boris', he almost never spoke to Vassily despite the fact he often heard them talk about working in the same beet-growing commune in the Ukraine before the collapse.

"It—it was while he was checking my identity at the—at the door, you know," Shibley stammered.

"You mean these," Vassily said, pointing to the identity cards and documents Shibley gave Boris. As Shibley knew by now, he had to get and return his forged papers every day; no doubt they feared he might use them to abscond.

Vassily casually tossed his empty onto the same bed. Shibley watched it roll toward him; his weight sucking it into his orbit like a rogue meteor in the space-time continuum. Vassily riffled through the papers, furrowing his single brow in concentration.

The big oaf has no idea what those papers signify, thought Shibley. He flinched at the slight contact of the bottle against his hip as if it were left molten from Vassily's touch.

"These, you mean?" Vassily repeated.

He swept up Shibley's fake identity cards and forged letters in his big paw, and with a theatrical flourish, licked his thumb before riffling the pages.

In fact, Shibley had not even needed to show his forged faculty I.D. from Loyola University or the letter from Ecole des Beaux Arts attesting to his scholarly credentials. These and similar ones, backed with email exchanges with the special collections staff, had always prepared the way before.

"Those are first-class forgeries, you lying sack of shit," Boris fumed.

"Boris, I know that! Believe me, I appreciate the fine work you—your associates in New York are providing, but there's been a spate of—" Shibley wanted to avoid the word *thefts* —

"I said English, you—"

"—of removals from several libraries in the last few weeks, as you indeed know, and perhaps he was suspicious of that."

Shibley thought that sounded right, but he swallowed under the high-powered beams of Vassily's stare from the periphery. Even with his eyes, the man could hurt.

"Bullshit," Boris spat.

"Boris, haven't I secured almost every item on our list so far? Haven't I accomplished every mission to date without fail, barring of course the occasional but unavoidable *contretemps*." The word slipped out.

"—fuckup, you mean," Boris said.

"Er, well, one might infer, that is—"

Shibley considered silence his best response at the moment. He had no reservoir of courage to confront this goon or his less amiable cousin.

After all, it was no more than the truth. He was more afraid of failure and facing the wrath of these two than he was of any bored-to-death guard asking to check his briefcase. Those two biddies today, for instance; what could they do to him compared to what Vassily and Boris were capable of? When moved to speech, Vassily's vocabulary could be as loathsomely crude as his cousin's: *Bring back the goods this time or I'll rip your testicles off* . . .

The goods *in situ* varied from one university town or one metropolitan library to another as they traversed a meandering path across the Midwest like bandits in the Old West. The differences, however, were striking: they robbed libraries, not banks, and did it without guns blazing or galloping horses. But the money was real enough. *My God, if only he could pry his share of it loose from these two* . . . Shibley's fee was apportioned at a flat rate of twelve percent, of which he had yet to see a solitary nickel except in figures scratched into Boris' notepad. New York always planned the "heists" and arranged for the documents. Shibley had no idea how all this was done. Boris always did the advance work because, even in a suit, the massive-shouldered Vassily looked as out of place in a library—to use Boris' less-than-fetching description—"as a rat fucking a grapefruit." Between Boris' foul-mouthed expressions and his military slang, a carryover from his Afghanistan service, Shibley had to ask Boris to repeat himself many times.

But one thing never changed from the day he had signed his Devil's pact: the cousins' words rarely varied regardless of the mission, or whichever book, document, map, translation, illustration, or sketch was to be stolen: *Here is what you need to get. Don't screw up. You know what'll happen if you fail. One call to New York.* Usually, one or the other cousin would accompany the threat with a hand across the throat—two Siberian tigers having fun with their staked goat.

Long before his honeymoon with this dangerous pair had ended, he knew that when that ominous call to New York was made, he wouldn't be privy to it. What he knew, in that way knowledge arrives, by slow degrees of accumulation like the layers of snow that precipitate an avalanche, was that when it was all over it would probably be Vassily's knife blade across his throat and then it would be as many seconds of life as it took for his already overburdened heart to pump out its arterial blood. Grim scenarios of his death at their hands—sometimes in a car on a deserted road at night, sometimes in a field overgrown with cattails or a putrid drainage ditch outside some anonymous town—were stretching his bouts of insomnia to the breaking point. Every day, upon waking in some hotel or other, he had to face this astounding horrific fact: *it might be today.*

What had begun just six months ago, almost as a prank (he told himself), had evolved into a sophisticated criminal enterprise with precision timing and vast amounts of money at stake. The shadowy criminal network that his Russians owed fealty to was pulling everyone's strings, and it made all decisions at every point as ruthlessly as any Wall Street broker hijacking an arbitrage. Despite Boris' bluster of being in charge, he too was a cog, and when this New York machine decided to end the operation, their book thief would be the first item to be dispensed with.

Shibley's blood chilled; he wanted nothing more than to fall asleep right here on this vile unmade bed and never wake up in this world again. In fact, if he were to lay his head back right now, he might will himself into permanent sleep like some ancient tribal shaman . . .

Fortunately Vassily distracted Boris with something in his native Ukraine and the two began an animated discussion. He knew he was the center of it. Cleveland was shaping up to be the *götterdämmerung* of this whole wretched business. It was a choice between years in prison or a horrible death, all because he had made one bad decision in a moment of inebriation. Now, because one corrupt oil baron in Kazakhstan fancied himself a grand master, he might not live to see another sunrise. He needed time to plan his escape. Hoods like these two didn't just shoot their wounded; they shot everyone.

The tone in Boris' voice snapped him out of his reverie more than his reverting to English. "Did you get the chess card?"

"No, uh, as I said, the woman at the desk—"

"What woman? Two minutes ago you said a guard was suspicious. Now it's a woman. I think you are lying to us. Isn't he lying to us, Vassily?"

"I think he's lying to us," Vassily said in his other voice, not the flat affect but the one Shibley had learned to call his sociopath's tremolo.

That morning he had indeed clapped eyes on the Fischer-Szabo scorecard from the 1970 Torneo Internacional de Ajedrez. One of the younger staff handed him the single sheet in her white gloves.

Shibley was amazed how well done the facsimile in his suit coat's hidden pocket was to the original. The Russians in New York had given the fake just the right patina of aging and random spotting. The scrawled word *Resign* opposite line 39 was at just the right tilt to the signature below it. Bobby Fischer's ghost wouldn't know the difference.

Shibley, long used to unhappy students and administrators, used his old trick of turning a negative. "I was wondering if, you know, we might square up the books a little," he suggested. After the Thurber episode, Shibley always addressed his questions to Boris.

"What—what are you talking about?"

"He means he wants his money," the bored Vassily said from the corner, yet his eyes never left Shibley. "He's a greedy pig."

"By my reckoning," Shibley quickly resumed his voice, "I—I do believe, uh, I'm currently owed one-hundred-fifty thousand and some change at this, uh, juncture," Shibley stated with as little quaver in his voice as possible.

"What do you want to buy so badly that you need your cut right this second?"

"Maybe he wants to buy a treadmill so he can fit into his pants," Vassily said.

"Not that I'm in any hurry to spend it, you see. I just thought I might make—make a few purchases while we're in town." Shibley coughed out of nervousness; he could see he was going too far now.

"You might make a few purchases . . ." Boris smiled at him; it wasn't a pleasant smile, and it didn't reach his eyes.

Very slowly, almost mincing the words, he said, "You'll get your cut when New York sends us ours. How many times have I told you this?" Shibley could see Boris' face darkening with blood. "And the reason we're stuck in this shithole is because you insisted on being put up in a luxurious hotel—"

"I wouldn't go quite so far as to say *luxurious*—" In truth, it was a Michelin 5-star compared to this filthy bear cave.

Vassily checked his watch. "We have to go, cousin."

"—and because you turned into chickenshit today, here we are and here we stay until you find your balls," Boris said and concluded the discussion with another black look.

It seemed difficult to turn his head away from Boris to look at Vassily, as if he were having some dialogue with him below the range of human hearing. Whatever it was, Shibley deemed it prudent not to exacerbate the mood of the volatile cousin.

"We'll be gone a few hours," Boris said. He looked normal again, which was somewhere between malevolent childishness and a spot close to the top of the sadistic psychopathy scale.

"May I ask—"

"No, you may not *ask*," Vassily hissed. "We have to go." Boris preceded Vassily to the door and turned around abruptly. If it weren't for the cat-like reflexes of Vassily, they would have collided. He took out a pair of twenties and tossed them in Shibley's direction. Fluttering green butterflies floating to the carpet.

Lloyd Shibley, antic fool of Russian slime, tried to catch them before they reached the carpet.

It was clear as sea ice their boredom with chaperoning him from city to city was in the steady barrage of verbal abuse and stupid little games. Before, they always tried to speak a polite, if broken, English. Now it was a constant shifting among corrupt English, slangy Russian from their Moscow days, and their native dialect from the Ukraine. Shibley was no linguist, but *Yop tavaya mat*, hissed or uttered forty times a day, by one or the other, was, he knew, the American ghetto equivalent of doing something unmentionable to one's mother.

A brief wolf smile creased the face of the bigger cousin at the doorway. The hulking Vassily missed nothing.

"Take a taxi, go back to your fancy hotel," Boris ordered. "You're going back inside and you're bringing out that scorecard—"

"Please, Boris, I can't go back in there. My nerves are shredded—"

"Fuck your nerves!" Boris shouted. "I'll personally stomp the yellow shit right out of you!" His fists were clenched, the size of wrecking balls. "Lock the door on your way out."

Vassily sauntered out after Boris and looked back once; he smiled wide at Shibley, showing lots of teeth. Shibley, a rotund mouse, stayed rigid while the hooded cobra's eyes zeroed on him.

Boris's words rattled around in Shibley's skull with a forlorn fatalism; he could taste copper in his mouth. He wanted to go back into that library as much as he wanted to climb the north face of the

Eiger.

Boris and Vassily must be testing him—they were lingering outside the door, waiting to see what he might do. Hoping that he would stick his hands into their possessions or search their drawers—for what, exactly? He knew they both carried money belts. Boris doled out a small allowance to him for his food and they always paid his lodging by the week in cash. He was no better off than a pimp's prostitute; he made the money with his work, they took the proceeds. This was a far cry from what they had promised six months ago in that wretched little tavern where he met them both in a moment of his most vulnerable weakness.

Share and share alike, Professor . . .

How stupid to have believed these criminals . . . How gullible I had been!

He burned with shame at the deeper memory of her, that tramp who led him down the primrose path to this misery. Shibley's hatred for the Russians was nothing compared to his hatred for her, the red-haired minx from hell whom he had plucked from his advanced Microeconomics class. What kind of Pygmalion delusion had he been under? *Ah, the booze. Of course, the booze. Many a good man's failing . . .* What else could have made him think he could teach refinement and grace to a boondocks hussy?

The cruelest blow of all was Siobhan's departure as he stood, mouth agape, in the driveway of his house on Lake Mosquito, having trundled home brain-wearied and demoralized after a triple back-to-back marathon of classes filled with dullards to whom he had spoon-fed the tripe of whatever textbook he was forced to use—to see her on the back of her new boyfriend's motorcycle giving him the finger as they drove off. Inside, he found the house destroyed—rooms ransacked, drawers pillaged as if Caesar and Vercingetorix had fought their famous battle from one room to another—all his furniture smashed, couch set afire with cigarettes, their engagement photos lay in ripped pieces amid the broken glass, along with his diplomas. He wept when he saw his degree from Leland Stanford's excellent institution converted into a crude origami beast with a spade-shaped penis. It was like rat poison trickled in his ear—one drop at a time—

drip, drip, drip—until his brain refused to go further.

Easy, mine heart, Shibley cautioned his inward man. *Best not think on the wretched girl now . . . .* Time was too precious when life was parsed into days, hours—maybe moments from where he sat contemplating doom. In a zero-sum game like this, he had to win. He hadn't read a copy of *Barron*'s in months, but he knew to the centavo or groszy what the value of the US dollar was to the world's currency—baht, rupee, drachma, Deutsche Mark, ruble, cruzeiro, thaler— his mantra in times of stress—anything to drown out the terrifying image of Vassily and his knife.

Forty bugshas to a riyal in Yemen. One hundred mongos to a tughrik in Mongolia . . .

He could have wept with frustration, but he had known plenty of adversity in his life. A boyhood growing up in foster homes in Seattle. One photo from Shibley's box of memories fell out—of his adopted mother, an alcoholic poisoned by uremia at forty. Forks and spoons would drop from her hands as if the floor were magnetized. She had died loathing him. Even before these Russian bullies took him over, body and soul, he had been skinned of all his worldly possessions, bank accounts, modest savings, and even furniture by his three wives.

He eyed the duffel bags lying against the wall near the open bathroom door. The thought of going through their things was odious. Clothes were strewn about the room along with cartons of food wrappers and paper sacks with the names of fast-food franchises or pictures of loony-looking cartoon animals. The whole room reeked of boiled onions and unwashed feet.

Disgusting. Better a tortured intellectual than a contented pig, eh, Wolfie?

Shibley sat immobile on the bed for long minutes and waited, torn by yet another pang of angst in his indecision. He watched dust motes swirl about his face. He was unable to move or to think. The overwhelming lethargy of his soul crushed him into the cheap mattress.

He wished he could fall right through the mattress, sink through the floors, and penetrate into the earth, far out of human sight. He had been taking shallow breaths to avoid the room's stink but now he sucked in a lungful of viscous air and felt the bile rise in his gorge. Lloyd Shibley, fifty years old, was not even worthy of calling himself a tethered goat. He was not a sheep, just a mouse like the one in the Scotsman's poem, whose burrow was turned over by the plow. He too had nothing to look back upon that didn't fill him with loathing and nothing to look forward to that didn't fill him with fear. In his throes, Shibley fancied himself a modern-day Faust—a tormented soul alternately hounded by the black dog of despair or teased by the red mouse of lust.

He got up slowly with an old man's hitch in his step and contemplated how far he could go on the forty-some dollars in his pocket. Then what? The internal debate raged between calling the authorities and throwing himself on the mercy of the court or waiting for the ever-receding hope these Russians would pay him the hundred-fifty thousand he was owed.

He opened the door cautiously and peered both ways down the empty hallway. No Russians waiting to pounce. He found the directory inside the bedside table drawer. He looked up the office of the local FBI. The number stared back at him. His destiny, his life to be decided at this very moment . . .

He dialed the first five numbers and stopped.

He was a coward through and through. He would crawl back to his burrow and hope the plow's edge would spare him. Hope was such a slender reed, yet the bitter reality of a life without money was its own hell. He had been there too long. Three broken marriages and a failed career, no teaching positions he managed to keep beyond a couple years. He could not go back to that life. Wearily, he knew, in the deepest cockles of his fat yellow heart, that he would pick up his broken rifle and head for the barricades. One feared the flying death squads of the S.S. coming up behind one more than one feared the Russian tanks.

He meekly dialed for a taxi and gave the hotel's address.

The driver was young with moist eyes. Roseate patches of acne scarred both cheeks. Shibley could not bear to hear more human speech after such a disastrous day. He wanted to get inside his room, pull the curtains closed, and unplug the phone. Sleep, just mindless sleep for as long as he could.

"I can't believe it," the driver stated as the taxi passed Chester. "I fucking can't believe it!"

He banged the steering wheel with his palm and spewed out a cacophonous string of profanity in his native tongue. Shibley jumped in his seat, startled from his reverie of blackness and silence.

He noticed the bedeviled stare in the driver's eyes, filmy with grief, and wondered what blow of misfortune had overtaken him— or had he somehow psychically peeked into Shibley's tortured heart? The boy's polyester shirt was unbuttoned to his navel. A gold crucifix dangled on his bony chest. Despite the no-smoking ordinance sign taped over the passenger side sun screen, he held a lit cigarette in one hand.

"I'm allergic to, uh, cigarette smoke," Shibley said meekly.

Perhaps, Shibley thought, if he were to show some solidarity of sadness for whatever bedeviled the young immigrant, he might gain his cooperation. The driver took a long drag of his cigarette. Shibley could see his eyes bugged out and wondered if he were high on something.

Shibley's stomach, so long in suspended revolt, finally had its say in one long eruption of passing gas.

"Hey, what—what is that? Hey, hey, you, you—fartin' in my taxi? Hey, man, no farting in my taxi! Are you crazy? You crazy—"

Shibley shifted his buttocks to relieve the searing hot pain; he craned his head toward the window and watched the eastside numbers roll past in that same miserably slow cadence that began at the library's elevator—East 70th, East 71st, East 72nd, East 73rd, East 74th, East 75th on and on into ascending numbers toward the infinity of quantum mechanics . . .

The driver's cursing subsided, then it rose again on a fluctuating wave of English and Polish, sine and cosine intertwined in a rotating dance. Shibley saw himself shrink, nothing but an insignificant node along the eternally moving tangent of Shibley's dismal life.

He would grow old in taxis like this for all eternity. He would wear a white beard and the only sounds he would ever hear again were the bawled curses of taxi drivers ringing in his ears while the smell of his own corruption wafted around him. The cruel gods had decided on something worse than his Russians. He knew himself, finally, as one of Dante's lost souls, cursed by entombment in filthiest excrement.

The Kneeling Veteran Recalls Korea

Weeks of mud and frozen hell endured—for this? We survived, called ourselves the "Cho-sin Few" for those days in that ice-cold miserable reservoir. I saw fingers and toes blackened from frostbite. We leaned together in threes, our helmets touching and slept in fits and starts.

The ormolu clock on the mantle tick-tocks, tick-tocks . . .

The Meals-on-Wheels woman has been sick for ten days. My knees are soldered into the floorboards. I can't feel my legs anymore. My kneecaps aren't where they're supposed to be. If they find me, they'll have to cut the floorboards to free me. My skin is like paper that's rotted away in a dusty attic. I wish I'd died in that reservoir with my friends.

White and Red: The Colors of My Youth

West Virginia white trash boy with glossy white-blonde hair. He lived on Third Street where the hillbillies drank and fought. He was a white wolf of the Siberian taiga, stalking and preying. He jumped onto cars from tree limbs. He beat up older boys. He put cherry bombs in the mouths of dead carp down by the slip. He called me *fuckface* and pointed his buck knife at me. Only my dog growling at him saved me . His relatives sent him back to Europe when he was fourteen. At the end of Third was a house with a porch. I followed a crowd of people to see what was going on. Rubberneckers from the middle of the street cried: "Cop got killed, boyoboy." "Brains are stuck on the ceiling . . ."

I watched the police officer's blood follow the tug of gravity down to the end of the porch and drip into a red puddle. I thought it was paint. I was ten. When I went to the county courthouse twenty-five years later to pay a fine, I saw his name on a memorial stone.

Years later in class I learned that the mind cannot tell the difference between the memory of an event and a perceived event. At the subatomic level, nothing touches. Hundreds of millions of neutrinos have already passed through my fingernail before I could type this sentence. I am nothing, not my words. Not my memories. Just this, like a love letter from Keats to his girl tucked away, forgotten in a book.

The Wine of Violence

Joseph Tuttlebaum reached across the night table to see what time it was. His wife grunted in her sleep and twitched. Another sleepless hour passed before he tried again; this time his groping fingers found the wristband and, stretching out a ligament in his shoulder, he pinched the button that activated the fluorescence: *Jesus*, three minutes to three o'clock. He lay back heavily into the pillow. He rarely had trouble getting to sleep. At 55, he considered a sound night's sleep a birthright, one of the few perks of middle age; sleep always came fast, and sometimes he would wake in the morning with a rueful feeling that these rapid descents into unconsciousness were bewitchingly easy to achieve

But not this night.

Sonnenstein's response was curt to the point of insult. *Nazi prick*, thought Tuttlebaum. *The presumed documents you refer to in our archives do not exist and have never existed at this institute.* Tuttlebaum envisioned Sonnenstein's dismissive sneer above his ego-trip signature; his imagination transmogrified the short letter's typescript into dagger-shaped serifs of gothic Plattdeutsche . . . *because Herr Doktor Otmar Freiherr von Verschuer burned them sixty years ago–that* would have been an honest reply.

He knew in his bones the Mengele documents existed because he had picked up the trail from a million-to-one chance remark— a visiting German professor named Lange had told a strange story of a nurse's brief encounter with a Nazi war criminal. Lange said the nurse had lived out her days in her home town of Schwabingen. Mengele had been screwing her. He had given her his Auschwitz files on twins from the "Zoo" while he was on the run from the Americans and the Russians. Tuttlebaum knew she must have sent the documents straight to von Verschuer in Berlin. Mengele would have insisted on that! Yet everyone believed Mengele had taken the documents to South America—documents that had never turned up to this day. Who else would he have trusted on the run but his mentor, the man who had groomed him right out of the SS and who championed his infamous Auschwitz experiments?

Joseph Tuttlebaum certainly knew Germans. When von Verschuer was given a clean bill of health by his colleagues and restored to his faculty position at the Karl Wilhelm Institute, the Americans were de-Nazifying Germany.

How tragic, he thought, *that only handsome young Werner Rhöde's neck was stretched for war crimes by physicians at Auschwitz of the many who practiced the Aryan life-unworthy-of-life philosophy across Hitler's 2,000 camps.* Unlike his many KZ colleagues, Rhöde had to stay drunk to tolerate the horror. Mengele, *natürlich,* volunteered for extra duty—he loved to swagger and pose before the frightened masses, shouting for his twins, *Zwillige, aus! Zwillige, aus!* Joseph could hear the ragged band of inmates playing their signature tango to ease fears. Ghastly German humor—he hated them, one and all. He wept when he thought of Herr Doktor's vile experiments on twin boys and girls in his specially built medical barracks at Camp F. Never mind his aplomb at the *Selektion* ramp, where the sound of trains steaming in at the railhead at five in the morning was music to his ears. This was truly satanic work, beyond all salvation.

Tuttlebaum passionately hated the Mengele relatives still thriving in Günzburg above all other Germans, especially their detestable Bavarian accents. Three years of searching archives and begging embassies sanitized by these smug burghers had exhausted his little stock of forgiveness. He knew they either feigned ignorance or were secretly proud of their infamous relative. But they knew, *they knew.* Their attics were no doubt stocked with Mengele's letters from

South America. *Like your archives, Herr Doktor Sonnenstein.*

Joseph lay back and thought of all those packing crates labeled Urgent War Material in the late spring of 1943-44. Among the fetuses expelled from their mothers' wombs (Mengele would jump on their stomachs) and *in vivo* specimens were gypsy heads packed in dry ice. He chafed at the notion that they were cloaked under some nondescript file coding by those abbreviation-loving Germans.

"I know Germans," Joseph muttered to his sleeping wife.

Just as blackness was about to enfold him, the Angel of Auschwitz himself materialized from the tormented mist of Joseph's brain. An incubus with gimlet eyes in a dapper uniform, Waffen SS cap tilted rakishly and white baton flicking to the left or right, Mengele looked down from his majestic calm at the exhausted, terror-filled wretches pouring out of the cattle cars.

One board high up on the staircase made that distinct *creee*ing sound.

Someone in the house —

Joseph threw the covers off. His eyes boxed the room's blackness, but could not make out the familiar surroundings—the sunburst clock from his in-laws on the wall, the dresser at his side, the chest where the duvet was stored for winter. A tiny vein ticked in his neck as his hearing sharpened like a rabbit's.

A moment passed, then the same sound was followed by a whispering noise like a hand brushing cloth. *Someone is bracing himself against the wall to mute the noise.* The body's alarm bells of incipient panic were gathering into an all-out, full-throttle adrenaline rush.

A brilliant light sent a shock wave through his optic nerves to his neocortex. A fuzzy figure in a hooded sweatshirt appeared against the wall, his arm extended to the light switch. He seemed outlined in a black and crimson penumbra. Something shiny extended from his other hand.

"Rise and shine, Jewboy," the dark figure said.

Joseph threw his aging, uncooperative body at the form. Time warped from laser speed to molasses.

He propelled his body at the figure's arm, knowing instinctively this is where hurt would come from. His helplessness stretched out before him like a drowning man's . . .

* * *

When his daughter called, her anguish throbbed in his ears, and he could not force out the words to say what he was feeling and any so he spoke of banalities rather than his healing wounds.

The scalp wound had taken 200 stitches. His skull was fractured in two places. Part of his earlobe was missing. Three of his upper teeth had been knocked out by the pommel, and two ribs were broken as well as his clavicle. When he looked in the upstairs hallway mirror, he saw a stranger with slightly familiar features beneath the congealing yellow and black splotches.

The homicide detective Zingaro said, "You bled out so much they never made sure of you. He used a Marine Corps officer's decorative knife from a pawn shop on Brookhaven. Easy to trace. Like I said, real dumbasses."

The youngest of the three, a 16-year-old, had admitted to being the one who had done the carving. A crude swastika with broken left arms was cut across Tuttlebaum's chest. His right nipple became infected and later had to be removed. When he opened his bathrobe, he saw a puckered starburst of purple flesh, a grotesque punctuation to the purplish tracing of the Nazi symbol. He stood in the mirror to see its true shape. A thousand years of accrued benevolence, that symbol, he mused, undone in a thirty-year span of time. Now he would wear it to his grave, a cattlebrand of unregenerate hatred. It was also the youth's idea to make it appear a hate crime once they came down from their high and realized the full extent of the mayhem. Last spring some high-school dropouts had shaved their heads and run amok in the neighborhood. So all three dabbed bloody swastikas on the walls and wrote hate slogans before they sloped out in the smeary dawn light.

"Can you believe it?" Zingaro fumed in his slow basso-profundo. Tuttlebaum could not recall much of their conversations because he was constantly drifting from the morphine drip next to his bed. "You expect even skinheads to spell 'Jew,' right?"

"Yes, you expect so," Tuttlebaum said dimly. He could not

attend his wife's funeral. His children flew in to handle that, so he never saw his wife in the casket, never said goodbye.

His children returned to Iowa and Missouri and California. They called him every day on the phone until gradually he learned the details of the funeral. His university condolence fund had sent a wreath. His son broke down entirely, and said, "Those evil sons of bitches . . ." His love for his mother was fierce despite the aloofness of his adolescent years in the house. When the silence became too awkward, the calls diminished and gradually ceased. Joseph was secretly relieved and guilty.

It turned out he wouldn't have to testify. He opened the paper one day to see a front-page photo of the prosecutor holding the evidence of the officer's sword and staring grimly toward the camera. There was a small white tag hanging from one end.

* * *

Zingaro called him to mention where the three would begin serving their sentences. The two adults, including the man who struck him, a 20-year-old from the projects, were in a holding facility until places opened up for them in the state's maximum security penitentiary.

"They're both LWOPS in that urinal down state," Zingaro said. "Lifers without parole." * * *By summer's end, he felt physically stronger except that clenching ache in his stomach and a ringing in his ears. His medication now included blood-pressure stabilizer to help with the tinnitus. "The tingling down your arms and legs is nerve damage," the doctor said. He wrote a prescription for Percodan, but it left Joseph with a debilitating, muzzy feeling.

While his students were taking an in-class final, Tuttlebaum sat outside in the reading court with the *New York Review* folded to an article titled "The Secrets of Easter Island"; his mind was uneasy in the late-August breeze under the blue sky, lacking the soothing habit of routine, like an aging athlete whose muscle memory was failing him. He had not spoken to his children in several weeks, but Zingaro had called to say the case was closed and that he hoped Joseph was getting on OK with his life.

"Take care, hoss," said Zingaro. "There are a lot of bad hats out there."

Six weeks into the fall semester, he found a note in his school mailbox and learned he was invited to meet with the newly hired provost. Her title had something to do with faculty affairs; she signed her girlishly neat signature with looping letters and used three names.

He felt he owed her the courtesy of a meeting, so before his ten o'clock class the next day, he rapped on her door and was summoned inside by a bright, bell-like voice. As he pushed open the door, he beheld a fortyish, attractive black woman. She shook his hand with a firm grip, and he noticed her slim figure in a navy-blue business outfit, her pleated skirt beneath a bone-white blouse. He smelled fresh coffee and was embarrassed by a sensation of spit in his mouth. He broke the silence by smiling and mentioning that he had class in a few minutes. Her mocha skin glowed beneath her makeup, but she did not return a smile. Instead, she said: "I'll come to the point. I've had two complaints about your teaching so far this semester."

"I'm sorry," he said, trying to restrain an agitation that coursed through his skin like molten shock, as if he had probed a light socket with his finger. "What—what complaints?" he managed to get out without spluttering. In twenty-eight years of teaching history, he had never been formally grieved. His student evaluations were always superior.

"Specifically, Doctor Tuttlebaum, there have been two accusations by students that you are making racially derogatory remarks."

"That is prepost—that is simply not true," he spluttered. He could not believe what he was hearing from this woman's mouth.

"These students both say that you are–let me put it this way— they say that your World War II class preaches Nazi doctrine."

"That is utterly ridiculous! Why would I—a Jew–espouse the most hated philosophy to my people ever known! That is so absurd as to be offensive." Tuttlebaum's neck vein ticked like a writhing parasite beneath his skin.

"Let me finish, please. I have a tape of your lecture. In it I believe you are extolling the virtues of Nazi ideology. You called it 'life unworthy of life.'"

"I was merely explaining Himmler's four-point genocidal program—"

"You intimated that there were members of our society whose removal would constitute a—and I quote from this lecture—'a beneficial population adjustment.'"

Tuttlebaum listened grimly to his own words filling up the space between him and this idiotic woman, this bureaucrat. She thumbed it off.

"That was a joke. Perhaps in poor taste but it was not meant—"

"I see," she said coldly. "Since you have not allotted sufficient time for this discussion, perhaps we might meet later on this afternoon."

The blood in his temples was pounding like a tom-tom's call to war.

At the door, she fired a last volley: "The First Amendment, Professor Tuttlebaum, does not protect hate speech on college campuses."

He gave an insipid lecture, mixing up the Fourth Marine Brigade's actions at Belleau Wood with Hürtgen Forest. Wrong war, wrong battle. Flushed with exhaustion, he dismissed class fifteen minutes early and heard their shuffling feet troop past, a few snickers from the last to leave. He felt ice in his solar plexus.

A week later, he discovered that the class had been taped by one of the complaining students. She brought the tape to Dr. Frazier-Jones along with a transcript. At the bottom of the page, she requested reimbursement from the university for the cost of a stenographer.

The ombudsman's letter was sent directly to Joseph's house. It set the date for a formal hearing and mentioned that chapter representative of the American Association of University Professors had been notified "as per protocol" (Joseph knew him to be an amiable nitwit). The letter affirmed he would be allowed to continue teaching but that all his classes were to be henceforth taped by "neutral parties."

He immediately thought of calling one, or all, of his children, but he changed his mind. What could they do except commiserate?

Why add more pain to what had been the worst year of everyone's life? No, he couldn't do that to them.

* * *

Tuttlebaum discovered that he didn't miss teaching. His life in the two months since he had penned a bland letter of resignation merged one gray day into another. The skies were full of pewter clouds that scudded across the horizon without letting the sun through. He slept late, never ate a meal that didn't come out of a can or wasn't frozen, and slept as long as twelve hours a day. Even then, he abetted his nightly sleep with long naps in the afternoon.

"I'm tired," he said to Sang-Froid, his wife's cat.

Tuttlebaum pointed the remote at her warm brown face and said, "Lies, all lies."

He clicked her into oblivion. He found a cacophony of ugly music and uglier language in a music video and was aghast at this slithering choreography of gyrating bodies accompanied by some kind of chant in unintelligible English that mixed anger, hate, and lust into one. The trio of rappers, spangled in outrageous gold jewelry and athletic jerseys, sported jailhouse tattoos or fraternity glyphs branded into their glistening flesh. Toward the end of the song a pelvic-thrusting blonde with a lot of cleavage insinuated herself among the black women.

"Animals," Tuttlebaum sneered.

He felt an icy burst of panic in his guts. He shut off the television, but he was too agitated to read his journals. His mind began churning with frightening images. He wandered around the house seeking out items that had belonged to Beth. The doctors told him not to be surprised if he lost some memory from just before the trauma. It was normal, the neurologist with the goatee had said.

He gave up trying to recall and decided to walk to the corner store for the *New York Times* and the few groceries he required. His torn ear burned in the stinging wind. He was surprised to notice that the old Italian owner had been replaced by a younger man, an Arab with dark probing eyes and several days' growth of beard. He took Tuttlebaum's money without thanking him as the old Italian used to do. Looking around, Joseph saw a new plexiglass screen separating the counter. A handwritten sign announced a new check-cashing service.

When he returned home, he noticed he had left the computer on and the email icon winked redly at him from the next room.

He opened it to discover a long message. The owner of the website thanked him and praised his insights.

He signed himself *Malcolm*.

Unbelievable, he thought. *I'm a Jew.* Joseph's right eye twitched. His fingers tapped out, *Have we met? Do I know you?* He sent it.

The answer came back instantly, as if Malcolm were sitting there with his fingers poised above the keyboard waiting for Tuttlebaum's email.

"I am an autodidact," it said.

Joseph: *Why does a self-taught man want to get mixed up in race-hatred?*

Malcolm: *Because I must.*

Joseph: *Must why?*

Malcolm: *It is your duty to follow the truth as well as mine.*

* * *

Tuttlebaum found Malcolm to be a willing student.

"My mission is different," Malcolm wrote. "I just want to know, to learn from you, to understand. *Teach me*," his emails begged Joseph.

Malcolm read everything Tuttlebaum suggested and asked intelligent questions. No graduate student was ever as eager to garner wisdom as Malcolm seemed intent to learn everything he could about the nature of the world. Tuttlebaum had started by taking him to task for his grammar, the fallacies of his reasoning, and his flimsy arguments.

Tuttlebaum's vanity was piqued and his spirits improved. He once caught himself whistling an aria from *Tosca* and realized with a jolt that he was acting out a fantasy, being a second-rate Rollo May playing to a rube Carl Rogers out there in the hinterlands about the nature of evil. He chided himself for this foolish diversion.

He entered Malcolm's website. His heart was throbbing and he felt the ache of his unhealed wounds. Tuttlebaum scanned quickly, eyes jumping from one piece to the next, taking only dollops of the foul-tasting cud of Malcolm's poisonous verbiage. It was a torrent of mockery, hatred and abuse, and ended with a passage from Psalms 14: "They are corrupt, they have done abominable works, there is none who does good." At the bottom, it was signed by Emeritus Professor Joseph Tuttlebaum. It gave his degrees, his former university and, worst of all, his email address.

Tuttlebaum groaned, leaped away as if bitten, ran down the steps to the basement for his son's old baseball bat, a Ted Williams.

He panted up the stairs, gripping the banister because his legs shook, and raised the bat high over his head. *Traitor*, he thought. *How could you?* The bat fell from his hands as if someone had merely plucked it out of his hands.

"All right," he said. He sat down with an old man's weariness and began typing. *Lose my address, you white trash hate-monger.*

* * *

Every day the mail came in, the phone never ceased ringing with invective until he jerked out the cord. He could not bear to read anything Malcolm put up under his name and he screamed curses with such fury that the cat hid herself as soon as she saw him go to the sewing room. He, an honorable man, was now linked to this odious nom de plume, this "Andreas" creation in the minds of these white supremacists and white-power fanatics who wrote sickening tributes and sung praises for Andreas's truth-telling style. They likened his "genuine voice" to Tom Metzger and Parson Richard Butler. He could not escape the fan mail and every day brought dozens more to his screen. They surrounded him in a viscous grip of admiration.

The list was depressingly long and included the most organized—the Posse Comitatus, Knights of the White Kamellia, White Revolution, Mystic Knights, Christian Identity, and the Order of St. Andrew. Something calling itself Sigrdrifa wanted a monograph on "the Rabbinical responsibility for anti-black racism"; the publisher of Volksfront's newsletter in Grove City, Ohio asked for a study of "that great mystic" Heinrich Himmler; Panzerfaust Records asked him if he had ever written any patriotic song lyrics, and 88 Enterprises asked for a book-length manuscript on "the pernicious virus of multiculturalism."

* * *

At the post office he had to run a gauntlet of eyes and wagging tongues. The first time he took the bag of mail from the postal worker, a red-haired woman in shorts, who averted her eyes when he thanked her, was one of the worst days of his life. Like a fleck of gold in a dung heap, however, lay his salvation: a delicately penned letter from Freiburg in formal English from Margaretta Schoenbein, a cousin of Mengele's first wife. The cousin had recently found some letters, forty-three in all, intact and undamaged, about 300 pages total from Josef to Irene that promised to fill in the gap from Mengele's life on the run in South America during the 1950s. It was the breakthrough he had been waiting for. If Herr Professor were willing to reimburse her the costs of photocopying and postage, she would be happy to send him copies. She insisted on no acknowledgment, however, should he publish. Joseph suspected her modesty was owing to the influence of those Günzburgers.

That night he drifted off to sleep with happy memories of Beth, when they were young and dating. He missed the sound of her laughter with a keen ache; his eyes brimmed with tears.

He woke before dawn when the muffled sound of the floorboards in the dining room signaled danger to his half-sleeping brain. *Oh Almighty God, not that.*

He crept down the stairs, a hand tracing the wall for guidance, careful to avoid the places where he knew the boards beneath the carpeting would give that betraying *cree.* As he rounded the banister and inched his way into the living room, a shaft of scattered light from the L-shaped room off the kitchen revealed a man in olive green examining a figurine from the China cabinet; it was a porcelain dog, one from Beth's collection.

The head swiveled gently in his direction and Tuttlebaum

glimpsed even white teeth.

"Better for you if you'd stayed asleep," the voice said calmly.

Joseph saw the glint of his buck knife, like a gleaming dragon's tooth, curled in the man's black-fisted glove.

"Take what you want and leave," Joseph said. His voice quavered with fear; his eyes were fixed on the man's knife, which was now held loosely at his midsection.

"You've got nothing but ceramic pottery."

"Leave," Tuttlebaum whispered. "I can't go through this again."

Joseph found, all at once, he couldn't breathe. He thought it was a heart attack–he had collapsed in a heap to the floor. But no–Joseph saw the gleaming teeth again. *Close, so close*–in his very face now. He smelled the man's rancid breath.

"I'm a doctor," he said nonsensically, gasping out the words as the man shifted position. He must have blacked out.

"I myself am a geneticist." The man knotted his fist into his Joseph's bathrobe and exposed the livid scar of the swastika.

"You see? We both wear the symbol, *hein*?"

"I can't breathe. Please," begged Tuttlebaum.

"We're the same, you and I," the man repeated. Joseph could feel the bristles of his moustache on his cheek as he turned away from the stench of his breath.

"Who–who are you?" Joseph gasped out.

"Don't you know me?"

The man gripped the frayed edges of Tuttlebaum's bathrobe and drew Tuttlebaum's face up to his own.

"Look at me. Look at me!"

Joseph whimpered, begged this dream to end, and opened his eyes.

"Now, then," said the man, as he got off Joseph's chest and stepped back into the shadows of the room. "That's much better."

Tuttlebaum sat up holding his chest. "I–I know who you are," he said. I know you! Josef Mengele, Angel of Auschwitz!"

"Don't be foolish, Andreas," said the man from his corner, "Mengele drowned in 1977 at Bertioga off the coast of São Paolo. I could not possibly be that man."

"What did you call me?" Joseph was unwilling to believe what he had heard, what his own eyes were telling him.

"You're Andreas," the man said calmly.

"Did he tell you . . . who I am?"

"I know who you are," the man said with the same bored insouciance.

"I'm Joseph Tuttlebaum."

"Yes, I know, Herr Doktor," the man said again. "I know who you are."

"Tell me . . . who you are," Tuttlebaum pleaded.

"I have a name, but it is not important. What you wish to know is important. That is why I am here."

"You're not . . ." Joseph couldn't finish it.

"Real? Is that what you were going to say?"

The man laughed. "The knife I hold in my hand is real enough. Would you like to feel it against the skin of your throat?"

"My head is pounding with such unbelievable pain," Joseph covered his own face with his hands.

"What does it matter how I appear?" A spike of annoyance in the voice. "I could be charged particles of your weary brain. I could be a thief stealing your silverware. I could be   anything."

"I must wake up," Joseph said into his hands.

"Better for you if you wake up, I suppose."

"What do you want with me?"

In the stillness between heartbeats, Tuttlebaum had not dared look toward the shadows, but he felt the man still there, quietly observing him, waiting for something, exuding his foul breath. Joseph felt the world turn upon its axis. Beyond the dirty kitchen window, a single star dominated the false dawn. Just beyond the lip of horizon was the last strand of trees in this neighborhood. That star's light came from hundreds of millions of years of travel, Joseph thought, to reach me at this very moment. The star was Sirius, the Dog Star, largest in the cobalt sky. Joseph knew this star was cherished by his guest as a lucky star, for it had brought him safely away from those who hunted him in the jungles or in the archives of West Berlin offices—

those Jews who wanted to see him hanged like Eichmann at Ramale Jail in Palestine.

"There is no justice," the man said.

From Joseph's vantage it looked as if he were leaning his back against the wall, only his boots and tunic buttons visible.

"I know," said Joseph eagerly.

"Only revenge-seekers," said the soothing voice.

"Yes," said Joseph, thrilled to the deepest marrow of his bones.

"You think you know," the voice whispered from afar, the merest lilt of a Bavarian accent. "But you don't know anything yet," he said.

"Yes," said Joseph. He felt release from the solitude of his excruciating anxiety, those terrible doubts about his own bitter existence. He was as gleeful as a child opening that one wished-for present that would make bliss out of blasted hopes.

"What shall I call you?" asked Tuttlebaum.

"You may call me Andreas."

Tuttlebaum's brain flipped through the Rolodex of aliases he had known the man to use: Fritz Ullman, Helmut Gregor, Peter Hochbichler, Juan Lechin, Pedro—so many during the more than thirty-five years on the run. Joseph thought of his guest's lonely sojourn across Europe from the rubble of Germany, his release from the American detention camp followed by his boarding of a steamer to Buenos Aires and then to Paraguay and finally to the jungle settlements of Brazil.

Joseph's mind drifted sleepily. *What was he saying?*

Joseph thought: "I understood his melancholy and his solitude."

"Let us begin your education into truth at once," he said. He wanted to weep from joy.

"I did not create Auschwitz," intoned his guest. "I found it there . . ."

"I know," Tuttlebaum said. "You tried to save lives . . ."

"Exactly," said Andreas. "Germans and Jews are the world's greatest peoples. I have always maintained that."

"You could not save everyone," Joseph urged him on. "You had to send the women with young children to the chimneys, the old who would not survive—"

"Yes, yes, you understand me precisely," Andreas interjected. "I was merely there to ascertain those who were able to work from those unable to work."

"But those experiments . . ."

"I shall show you my research. The case files do exist. You were right. That is what you are after, is it not?"

"Women and children," muttered Joseph in a strange kind of void. "Thousands upon thousands, never ending."

"I once had dreams of academic fame and success," said Andreas.

"They are all at peace now," Joseph said.

"Alles ist Wellen."

All is waves, agreed Joseph.

Tears formed at the corners of his eyes, and he knew with absolute conviction that this stranger, this enemy and friend from afar, was going to unlock the secrets of that terrible night from the very moment when he heard that other stranger climbing his stairs.

The Flush

Colors so vivid you thought you were entering a different world. DayGlo greens, fluorescent oranges, and reds, although my memory becomes less reliable with the passing years. Yet I am sure that what I recall is true, all those Kelly greens, lime to Jade, and especially the bright reds that ranged from fire-engine through shades of rose to salmon pink, all visible in shimmering water just a few feet below the surface. Somehow these algae, plants, and ferns managed to grow despite the torrent of water out of that pipe that turned the small pond into a frothy waterfall twice daily. Slime algae with their fuzzy beards would flatten against the rocks, but we would see them looking none the worse for the wear right after the water ceased to flow.

My friends, cousins Frankie and Billy, and I would take turns hanging on the bars when the water company flushed. The flush happened twice a day, early in the morning and at midafternoon. If we were close enough to hear the signal, which sounded like a pistol shot followed by a thunderous chugging and then a roar of wind as the water rushed through the huge cement pipe, we bolted toward it just to see the water gushing forth. If one of us was able to grasp the bars over the mouth of the pipe, he would hang on for dear life while his arms throbbed from the pressure.

No one was brave enough to try this stunt until the water receded to the half the height of the pipe's mouth, which was somewhere at the level of our belly-buttons, because the torrent was too strong. I don't remember any of us torn loose by the water's force roaring through the pipe, and even if we had been, the worst of it would have been a mouthful of water and a few scrapes from being knocked across the rough cement apron extending over the pond.

The water overwhelmed the pond like a tsunami and flowed downstream toward a lagoon that acted like a holding tank. In summer both sides of the stream that fed the lagoon were lush with vegetation. Trees grew easily here, especially the water-loving kind like black spruce, tamarack, gum, and willow. The fungi was amazingly pretty here, too, where the water lapped the sides of the stream: star-shaped, Whiffle-ball, phalluses, which of course gave us no end of wicked delight in snapping them off and holding them like neon erections between our skinny legs. On the hottest and most humid days, the air was musky with a variety of cloying scents. The small biting flies and midges filled the air in swirling clouds. The insects gathered on the rotted corpses of dead fish and small animals. Bright-colored mushroom spores grew inside tree trunks and the flies ate the slimy spore mass, flew off, defecated and created more spores in the nitrogen-rich soil. Every kind of freshwater grass grew there: pondweed, cattails (the smaller, fan-tailed phragmites would eventually drive them down to the edge of the lagoon at the breakwall), musk grass, coontail and stargrass, tapegrass, and horsetail with its segmented green links that you could snap off and crush with your fingers until your fingers turned green and smelled rank. Not many flowers grew there but plenty of weeds like Queen Anne's Lace, milkweed with its pods excellent for throwing, and a few trumpet vines that looked like tiny bursts of flame in the midst of all that green foliage and wheat-colored saw grass that we called elephant grass.

The mud along the banks was a tan sludge that we often walked through barefoot to feel it squish between our toes. When the sewers backed up during summer storms, the edges of the lagoon would be filled with all kinds of debris, an unusual kind of rip-rap like the bloated bodies of drowned rats, and lots of plastic. We didn't know what the plastic applicator tubes of women's tampons were, nor did we realize these "beach whistles" were being flushed down toilets to reach us in the wetlands. We used them as convenient ammo in our war games. The rule was that they could be thrown as hard as possible at any part of the body, although we tried to avoid the face because we didn't want our mothers to get involved in our business. Sometimes we'd try to catch frogs, so slippery in their goldgreen bodies like the eyes of cats, with their singular gold coin of an ear at the side of their heads. Toads, on the other hand, were easy to catch and those we didn't release were sometimes smashed with rocks as "enemy soldiers." We'd push over the bigger rocks to catch garter snakes. Mickey's older brother Johnny was terrified of snakes. If we managed to catch one before it whipsawed through the underbrush, several of us would gang up on Johnny to hold him down so his brother could torment him with a snake dangling over his face.

In summer the grass and trees would arch over the stream and we could wade it with our socks and tennis shoes held high, like soldiers fording a river; the jungle canopy overhead made it exotic and familiar at the same time. Sometimes we used blocks of scrap wood for boats and pretended we were on them. The water flowed all the way to Chapman's Pond, which was the old slip back in the days of sailing ships. The wooden hull of a wreck was still visible there, and when we fished by the Pyramids, we saw dozens of speckled and golden carp swimming back and forth among the fronds waving in the current.

We called the stone structures Pyramids because of their shapes, but whatever purpose they once served for loading and unloading ships was not known by any of us, even though Jerry DiBello's father worked as a supervisor for the docks. My Uncle Harry was an electrician who worked on the massive Hewlett that tended the lakeboats when they came in. He used his influence to help me get my first berth as a deckhand on the *J. Burton Ayers* leaving Ashtabula Harbor. I was nineteen by then. I had been in a car accident at a drive-in with my girlfriend; we were nearly broadsided by a car full of teenage boys coming toward us. My girlfriend, whom I married that summer when I got off the boats in South Chicago after Labor Day, was unhurt. We were stopped, a left turn half-completed when we were hit by the car coming at us going about sixty. I can still see that right front fender crinkle into an instant sculpture before my eyes as the swerving car just kissed the front of my car. I was worried about how to tell my parents about the accident.

I got the call to go sailing the next day, a Sunday morning. It was like fate stepping in to absolve me of a decision.

I already had my ordinary seaman's ticket and I was waiting for word of a boat. I did not take any warm clothes with me and by the time we were going through the locks at Sault St. Marie at five in the morning, it was only thirty-three degrees, and I was freezing on deck in a flannel shirt and a summer jacket. I took the first mate's raingear from a hook in the windage room. When they swung me over the side in the Bo 'sun's chair, I was able to handle the cables without my limbs shaking from the cold.

In my youth we built forts from lumber and tools we took from our garages, we fished for discarded carp and sheepshead that the Negro fishermen used to toss into Turtle Pond on their way home. (The big changes in civil society were a few years away, like the civil rights marches and the Tet Offensive. JFK was our president because most of us were Catholic, being Irish or Italian.) Jerry used to kill birds with his slingshot; he hit them with the taconite pellets he had picked up on the railroad tracks. Sometime we'd hang a dead carp from a tree branch and punch holes through it and cry out with glee when the guts would extrude from the holes, puffing out like tiny dandelions.

There was a boy we all feared running into in Bumstown (our name for the two hundred acres of wilderness and wetlands owned by the Norfolk & Southern). His name was phonetically pleasing, yet like Yahweh's, you did not utter it much for fear of conjuring him up. He was as feral as the animals we encountered in our forays. I was fishing by the slip one day when he and a friend approached me as I stood on the shoreline with my bamboo pole and my hook stuck in the lily pads. My dog was always with me, chasing rabbits and breaking the necks of any muskrats he discovered. I was much smaller and I was afraid of this bully anyway. I remember telling him my dog wouldn't bite, and I was hoping with all my might he took that to mean the opposite. Jerry told me that this bully used to pick on older boys, ones in high school even, and challenge them to fight. Jerry would contort himself like a discus hurler and then spring up with a whoop throwing a right hook at an imaginary opponent. Even Jerry, who was the bravest among us and had the smartest mouth, would decline into a respectful silence if any sighting of this white-blond kid occurred in our neighborhood. It was widely believed by all of us he would hang from tree limbs on Walnut, our main street, and land on the roofs of passing cars, terrorizing whole families driving to church. We were greatly relieved when we learned that his aunt in the Harbor had had enough of him and sent him back home to Europe.

We spent many summer days "over the hill," our common phrase to our parents who wanted to know where we were but were never worried about our day-long absences. We'd come back grimy with the dirt of our escapades emblazoned on our bodies and clothes. Our faces red and sweat-streaked, our arms bearing streaks from twig lashings and the dots of insect bites. We carried the smells of our adventures into our houses at dusk, along with the odors of ragweed and mint. In winter we'd go tobogganing by the waterworks hill. One winter a boy from a large family died when he hit a tree on his sled.

Sometimes we would seek out bums lying under Sunday newspapers beneath the willow tree in a place we called the Vines, so named because we swung on them like Tarzan. There were so many broken bottles and rusted cans that the occasional slip from the vines often led to deep gashes. In the old days there had been boarding houses for arriving sailors, and we would find older bottles of curious shapes, with the names of obscure medicines on them, mixed among the newer wine and whiskey bottles left behind by tramps. We used to torment these harmless, grizzled old men by hurling crab apples and running for our lives. One of them in particular drew us like pack animals; we nicknamed him Tubby because he was short and round like a Ben Franklin stove. He drank cheap Thunderbird, and when we spotted one of his empty bottles, we'd twist it by the neck and say, "Looks like old Tubby's been here." He would make loud noises and shamble after us but he was barely able to walk, let alone run. He favored us with epithets like "rubberneckers" and "sons of bitches," so slurred that it all sounded the same. It was, however, music to our young ears and set us wild with emotion. I saw my uncle help him up from the curb where he was sitting, happily drunk, just across the street from the house where he was allowed to stay.

I often went over the hill, alone except for Tony, and hiked along the familiar sandy paths. I never realized that Lake Erie was also under my feet. I liked watching my black-and-white terrier pick up an animal's scent. He leapt above the straw grass to look around, his tongue lolling, and then raced through the brush, following the scent of whatever animal it was. It was hard to get him to come back to me because of the frenzy of his chases. I was sad when he broke into a rabbit burrow and killed the babies. I held their tiny bodies in my hand and felt the matted fur, a single drop of ruby blood showing where his tooth had punctured flesh.

If Jerry wasn't home, I'd go down his backyard hill to Bumstown. Jerry's father cultivated his sloping backyard every day in summer and never wore a shirt; he was as lean as a whippet and his skin was walnut brown by the end of August. He had put in cement steps down the center of the yard and planted fruit trees, raspberries, and a willow at the bottom of his property. Standing at the top of his hill, he whistled for Jerry to come home to supper, and we could hear it all the way to the end of the rocky outcrop, well past the Pyramids where we dove into the water.

We called that part of Bumstown the Peninsula because it narrowed to a slender rocky outcropping like a finger into the middle of the slip. The few trees here were mostly stunted and crooked from the blasts of northern winds roaring down from the Arctic across Canada during winter. Some poisonous plants grew among the big slabs of quarried rock that once served as a breakwall, and because I had a bad case of poison ivy just before school began one fall, I was always wary on my solo travels. That time happened to be the first day of the new school year; despite the fact that my face was a swollen, grotesque pumpkin and my arms scabrous from helpless itching, I convinced my mother I had to go to school. By the middle of the morning, I was in agony, a sere-like ooze wept from the open sores of my face, and all that long afternoon I had to endure the horrified looks of my classmates sneaking looks at the freak I had become.

Just beyond this shallow inlet where the water remained bath-water-warm in summer, I used to fish for perch and sunfish and watch the clouds forming over Lake Erie. It was never the same color twice, but certain colors stuck with me: a dirty, oily green meant stormy weather coming, usually a chilly rain; blue meant good weather, high waves; turquoise meant a flat calm; but milky white or pewter meant big trouble if it extended to the horizon. A big thunderstorm with high winds that picked up the sand and blasted it in dusty sheets against your legs; your skin would be stung raw from your knees to your ankles. Anyone fishing at the end of the mile-long breakwall, between the buoys and the ship channel where the schools of yellow perch were rumored to be active, would come back drenched and backlit by the lightning over the lake.

My dreams were not yet erotic, but I was fighting with my mother about getting my normal butch haircut. I wanted to wear my hair long—nothing like the Beatles' shags, because our fathers would never have allowed anything like that. My friend Stevie read his older sister's teen magazines and said the Beatles would be coming to New York. In those days we were aware of nuclear annihilation from the civil defense ads that used to run on Saturday mornings with the cartoons. I remember the ones with stick figures most. The missiles arcing over the North Pole looked like the ones we used to draw, except that ours often featured swastikas on the fins. In those days we attended church and sat in the same desk in school all year long; being promoted to the next grade had the slowness of a glacier to it. The sun in September warmed me uncomfortably; I always ended up with a spot near the windows because seating was always done in alphabetical order.

When we were eighth graders, we played Red Rover in good weather. In winter we played King-of-the-Hill on the massive snow piles at the edges of the playground, and all the boys in the younger classes attacked us. We flipped baseball cards and played marbles, mostly "steelies," right up to the first snowfall. We cordially despised the nuns and felt they hated us. Certain nuns were dreaded because of their fierce reputations; many of them hit with little provocation in those days. We never told our parents out of fear we'd be punished there too.

My uncle, who lived across the street from our house, was a mean drunk but a kind and generous man and a good father otherwise. When he came back from the tugs, he would spoil my three cousins with loose money from his pockets to buy candy at Thomson's Emporium. After the hangovers, he would drive them to McDonald's for hamburgers and fries. McDonald's being new, displayed its golden arches, and we'd pile eagerly into his station wagon. I always waited in anticipation for one of my cousins to ask if I could go too, and my uncle's answer was always the same: "If he wishes."
One Saturday morning my mother told me to take the box of Epsom salts across the street to my uncle. My cousins weren't there to let me in, so I knocked and walked inside past the porch. I heard the television set. My uncle was the first of my relatives to get a color TV. He was lying on the couch on his side watching the screen. I handed him the box and he mumbled thanks. I saw his face. The side of his cheek was lumpy and one of his eyes was shadowed in a large purple bruise. I felt his embarrassment and immediately turned to walk out. My mother told me that he and Pekko, the diminutive, tattooed tugboat captain of his crew, had gone to the Iroquois Club on Bridge Street and my uncle had gotten into a fight with some TV wrestler from Cleveland when Piecho said something insulting to the wrestler, who was an Indian with jet-black braids.

In the fall after that summer, a smaller boy replaced me on the seventh- and eighth-grade tackle football team as the wide receiver and I was bitter with envy. His name was Danny and he was very agile. He used to hang one-armed from a giant sumac tree that was reached only by jumping from a broken window of the abandoned sweater factory on Hulbert across from my other cousins' house. I stood in the window frame watching him act like a monkey scratching his armpit and making grunting noises. I hoped he would fall and get seriously hurt so I could have my position back. I was thirteen then and stealing girlie magazines from the pharmacy. I hid them in a hollowed tree near the sweater factory. The women inside were all "famous" burlesque dancers, middle-aged, many flabby, and all wore pasties over their nipples with spangled costumes. My compulsion to steal was almost uncontrollable. Finally, out of remorse and fearing I could no longer withhold this from my confessions, I saved up my money and put several dollar bills into an envelope and wrote the word *Restitution* on it. I slipped it into the mailslot of the pharmacy's front door after it closed. The guilt was replaced by the pride I felt in using a word like *restitution*. It seemed to fit the changes that were happening to me at that time.

Tony died when I was away at college; my father died when I was twenty-five and in graduate school in another state. I traveled back to my university on Thanksgiving Day and was the only passenger on one of those puddle-jumpers flying between small cities. The pilot said something sarcastic to the lone stewardess about tending to "those two hundred passengers back there" and banked left so hard coming out of the St. Louis airport that I was reminded of the Scrambler ride at the county fair.

I never had a DUI but I should have had many. I didn't finish my doctorate and so was never able to get a full-time teaching job. My marriage ended a few years later. I haven't seen my children in several years and the older one stopped writing me. He lives in Virginia now. My wife remarried and takes my phone calls once a year. We get along all right and sometimes we even have a laugh about the kids when they were growing up. I have one aunt left alive in an Alzheimer's clinic and my favorite uncle died of a massive stroke last summer. He had been in poor health for many years. At the last moment, I decided not to go to the funeral.

I pick up part-time teaching jobs even though I have to drive long distances and cross state lines. I also do some private tutoring, and I'll pick up an odd job in the slack periods, like delivering pizzas or the *Plain Dealer*. In the age of internet, not many people read the dailies, so it's mainly nighttime pizza runs. That suits me better. I prefer the night. I attended an AA meeting seventeen years ago, but it didn't help me stop drinking. I don't like the clubbiness of organizations, for one thing, and I realized I don't want many friends. Facebook and reality shows nauseate me.

I still see Mickey in town once in a while and we have a laugh about the good old days roaming wild and free around Bumstown. I remind him of the cigarette box full of "loosies"—single cigarettes he acquired through theft at various shops in the Harbor. That was my first time smoking. I can see him with that box, chattering away despite his missing front teeth. I tell him he was called the Smiling Cobra for a while because of it, but he doesn't remember that. Mickey's a politically active citizen nowadays. He lost his job at the plastics plant after twenty-two years, but he kept his boilerman's license and has a job. Jerry works on the docks like his father. I heard he has a handicapped daughter.

When I was a boy hanging onto the bars at the flush while my legs and trunk split the rushing waters into manageable streams, I was happy in a kind of mindless way. I never stopped to think that the sludge we trod through and tossed at one another's heads was really bacteria-rich shit that enabled all those vivid colors to bloom at the flush. The silver tanks behind the headworks were aeration cells, surrounded by a cyclone fence topped with barbed-wire, where the bacteria worked continuously to break down the malodorous fecal matter after it had passed through the grit chambers and the bar screens. The big screw pumps were turbine-powered, very noisy when they started up, and we were not permitted by the few men who worked at the plant to get a good look inside. From the hill behind the waterworks where we sledded in the winter, you could see through the glass windows on the roof to the tops of those massive blue-painted Archimedes screws that lifted the sewage and sent the foul effluent of the city's toilets to the hoppers with their big filtering screens. In those days gasoline, pesticides, and toxic chemicals from the factories where some of our fathers worked ran directly into infamous Field's Brook, and it is still widely believed that much of the cancer in in our town derives from that practice. I have time to read nowadays, those books I never found time for in graduate school. I'm not happy or unhappy and I can see the end from here. My boyhood wasn't enchanted and I don't think the world treated me differently from anyone else.

Those memories of that time are brightly colored like the fungi at the flush lagoon. Certain sounds or smells will bring them back to me wherever I am. Some memories are vague, unfinished, like the one of that older boy coming toward me in the near-dark when I was alone by Chapman's Pond. He sported the familiar greasy ducktail haircut and white t-shirt, and carried a pack of Winstons rolled in his sleeve like the hoods, as we called them then. I hid myself under a bush and stayed very quiet, made myself invisible, the way cats or young birds will do when a threat comes near. One of my earliest memories isn't about Bumstown but about watching two older boys hang a kitten from the top of a fire escape of the school I would attend when I turned five and had to go to kindergarten. I sometimes wake up and want to scream at them to stop but I didn't do anything then and I can't now.

Our memories.

What are they? Filaments of thought-energy, synaptic blips from a muscle that feels no pain yet easily processes point-one quadrillion bytes of information per second?

No, they're our souls.

Philosophy of the Detroit Body Collector

"Vietnam. I seen plenty of 'em—no damned heads, no legs, they arms all fucked up and shit. Black people kill themselves, white people die of old age, Chinese people don't die. Most people die on the toilet, naked. I get thirteen dollars for every one of 'em I picks up."

Notes on Stories:

"Desideratum of the Adjunct Professor" and "Bright Sky, Blue Waters of Rio" were first published online in *Storyglossia*, 2007, with the former story short-listed for its annual fiction prize. "Twins" was adapted from "My Twin Brother," published in *Flash Fiction Offensive*, 2007. "The Frotteur in the Dark" was first published by *10,000 Tons of Black Ink* online and published as one of its Six Best Stories for 2009 in the print magazine (Chicago: Literary Writers Network, 2010: 27-33). "When Are You Ever Coming Home?" was retitled and first published in *Plots with Guns* in 2010. "Last Match in New Orleans" was first published in *Yellow Mama* in 2010 and is reprinted here with the kind permission of publisher/editor Cindy Rosmus. "Alice and Bob at Play in the Zero Field" was first published in *Fiction Fix* (U. of North Florida), 2010. The title story, "Out of Breath," was first published in the *Midwest Literary Review*, 2011, and republished in *Great Lakes Review*, Issue 2, Spring 2013. 1-25.

Terry White has published two hardboiled detective fiction novels under the name Robert White: Haftmann's Rules (Grand Mal, 2011) and Saraband for a Runaway (2013). His noir, crime, and mainstream stories have appeared in several webzines. His feature-length film script, East Palestine, has been nominated for an award in the action category at this year's TrindieFest in Trinidad, Colorado. He is an almost lifelong resident of Ashtabula, Ohio, is married, has three children, and two grandchildren in Austin, Texas.